Time Won't Erase

by

Stacey Wilk

Big Sky Country, Book 1

Time Won't Erase

Contact Information: info@thewildrosepress.com

Cover Art by *Diana Carlile*

The Wild Rose Press, Inc.
PO Box 708
Adams Basin, NY 14410-0708
Visit us at www.thewildrosepress.com

Publishing History
First Champagne Rose Edition, 2020
Trade Paperback ISBN 978-1-5092-3264-2
Digital ISBN 978-1-5092-3265-9

Big Sky Country, Book 1
Published in the United States of America

He wouldn't allow her to stay out at the motel all by herself. She'd be safe on his ranch and down the hall from his brother with plenty of firearms and ammo.

"I can't go there." She pushed away from him.

Her body heat dissipated, and he missed it instantly. "Mom will be glad to have you there."

"Your mother doesn't want me there. And Jett. He hates me."

"That isn't true."

"I hurt you. It's only natural for them to side with you."

"Calista, can you put the past aside for one damn night? You were hurt in a robbery and should be at the hospital. If you won't go home, then come home with me so someone can keep an eye on you." He wanted to blur the line that separated his life into two parts. The first part was the one with Ajay, Ava, and Calista in it, and it was filled with sound and textures. The second part was the one without, and it was silent and hollow. Even though he had Izzi during that second part, and she filled in so many spaces for him, he wanted something he could never have.

"I couldn't bear having your mother fuss all over me."

"You're being ridiculous. She loves to fuss." He hoped humor would light the way to reason.

"It hurts too much when she's nice to me. Her kindness only spotlights what's missing in my life."

"Your mother." Her mother had walked out on her family not long after Ava died. That was probably his fault too.

"No. Not my mother. You."

Dedication

This book is dedicated to Janice and Anne.
I went looking for family and found friends.

Chapter One

A gun had changed her life forever. How could a phone call have as much power today?

Calista Hartman stared at the phone. She didn't know how he had her number. They hadn't spoken in years. Her mouth opened to respond, but she slammed it shut, wavering between wanting to say she missed him and wanting to tell him to go to hell. She couldn't talk to him. He must know that.

"Calista, are you there?" The timbre in Gage Ryker's voice rumbled over the line and sent her stomach into a tailspin.

She would have recognized the cadence of his voice anywhere. It had certainly haunted her dreams enough. "I'm sorry. I'm here. What did you say?" What had he said? She couldn't remember. Something about her father.

He let out a deep breath. "I'm sorry to bother you. I arrested your father for public drunkenness."

No "How are you?" Or "It's been so long." No easy segue. Right down to business. Well, that was better. It wasn't as if they were friends. He made sure that could never happen. Or maybe it was her.

She hung her head. Her father was drinking again. She really didn't have time for this because she was due at the yoga studio to teach a class in thirty minutes. She grabbed her mat and her vegan leather tote and headed for the front door of her apartment. "Is he okay? Did he hurt anyone?"

"He's fine now, and no one was hurt. He was singing outside Kennedy's Pub at one in the morning. Someone called me to complain. He paid his bail, slept it off, and went home. But this wasn't the first time he's been that drunk. I thought maybe if he got arrested, he'd get some help. I don't think he has. You might want to come home."

"I don't know if I can get there. I have a lot going on." She had nothing that couldn't be rearranged. No one would miss her if she left Billings. That was how she wanted it. Don't get attached. Safer that way.

Her father wouldn't want her underfoot, and he wouldn't want any advice on staying sober. They'd been around that block a number of times over the years, and it always ended badly.

"You should also know the B and B isn't booking guests." Gage's voice dragged her back to the present moment.

"How can that be?" The B and B was always booked. The Fourth of July was coming. They sold out every year. "You must be wrong."

"My mother told me. I wouldn't have called if he didn't need you. I…well, never mind that. I wanted you to hear about his arrest from me."

She fought the urge to ask him what he was going to say. She wanted to hear it, and she didn't. Time did not heal all wounds. Whoever came up with that saying was an idiot. She wasn't over what happened between them—or him, for that matter.

She pushed out into the hallway and closed the door to her apartment. Habit had her locking it. The

2

hallway with its peeling paint and worn-out floor smelled like sweat and fried food. She stared at her neighbor's door. If she strained to hear, someone cried on the other side. Berta. The breath caught in her throat when she thought about her brokenhearted neighbor.

She couldn't live in this apartment building any longer. She would always see Berta's grandson covered in blood. She couldn't live in this city another minute either, with all its crime and hate. She needed to start over, or was it run away? She had fled Backwater all those years ago to keep her sanity. She wasn't sure it had helped.

"Calista, will you come home?"

Home. Where was that? It wasn't Backwater where Gage kept order, and it wasn't here in Billings in a bad neighborhood where young men died for no good reason. The way her sister had.

"I have a funeral to attend at the end of the week. I'll come after that. Don't tell my father you called me."

"I wasn't planning on it."

She hesitated, questions burning her lips.

"Take care," he said.

She opened her mouth to say "thank you" or "how are you" or "I think I still love you," but he ended the call before the words had a chance to slip free.

****

The Montana sun turned the inside of her 2003 Honda Pilot into an oven. Calista prayed her old vehicle would make the two-hour ride to Backwater because if it didn't, she'd be hitching the rest of the way. The air conditioner worked overtime, and still the sweat pooled between her breasts.

As every mile brought her closer to her hometown,

3

the knots in her stomach grew until they sat low in her throat. Backwater represented all the bad things in her past.

She heaved a sigh and signaled her departure, finally, from the highway. Too late to turn around now. The Pilot would never make it back, and she didn't have a whole lot to return to anyway.

Main Street hadn't changed in the three years she stayed away. The fronts of the buildings appeared as if children had dressed them for a mismatched day. Some were brownstone, while others were stucco. A couple of the buildings resembled old houses. Their heights varied, but most buildings had sun-faded awnings in different colors. Baskets of bright flowers hung from the hardware store and tea shop. People meandered along the sidewalk, peeking in the windows of the flower shop, bookstore, and boutique.

Backwater's summer season was in full swing. Tourists came to get away from their hectic lives and reconnect with nature. They could hike, fly-fish, horseback ride, or simply sit by the lake and enjoy the view. The big Fourth of July celebration was only a month away and so was the anniversary of her sister's murder. Tourists today didn't know that story.

Calista turned right at the end of Main Street where the evergreens reached the big sky, and a cold chill ran over her heated skin. The sheriff's department squatted on the corner with its red-brick façade and small parking lot. She wanted to avoid the sheriff this trip, but her father's behavior made that nearly impossible. Gage was part of the reason she hadn't been home, even for the holidays, in three years and a big part of why she moved two hours away years ago. The only way she could take a cleansing breath was to stay away from Gage Ryker. Except she had allowed his phone call to bring her home.

She turned onto the long drive for the B and B and wound her way along the two-acre front yard dotted with Douglas firs and pines. She lowered the window and allowed the fresh air to swirl in and dry the sweat on her skin. But it did nothing to relax her shoulders. She would have to summon some real discipline to find peace here.

The Hartman B and B sprawled out in front of her with barn-red clapboards faded and chipped from too many months fighting harsh weather. The sides of the building stretched right and left, as if the old girl wanted to give someone a giant hug. The poor thing needed one. The screen door rocked open and closed on its hinges. The chairs that usually invited guests to sit and read a book no longer appeared on the porch. The split-rail fence missed a few logs, as if they were lost teeth. Leaning on that thing could be dangerous.

The grass was patchy in places. Even the American flag hanging by the garage doors limped on the pole. What had happened? She suspected she knew, but that was no excuse. Heat burned her veins, and it had nothing to do with the hot sun.

She parked by the garage and shoved her way out of the car. Her father better explain what he'd been doing to their beloved home.

"Dad?" She held open the front door and waited for a response. "Dad, are you home?" She should have looked inside the garage to see if his car had been there.

Her father was absent from the front room with its paneled walls and fireplace. The leather recliners covered in layers of dust waited for someone to wipe them clean. The dining room and open kitchen were also void of human interaction.

If she looked close enough, the signs of old age cracked and peeled inside the house too. The whole place could use a facelift. The kitchen faucet dripped to its own melody. She tried to tighten the handle, but the water continued its ugly, out-of-tune song. Some of the kitchen cabinet doors hung slanted. The wood floors were worn in places from years of footsteps ambling across them.

She forced open the slider stuck in its track and stepped onto the deck. The Glacier Mountains gave a million-dollar view from the second-story landing. This was her favorite place in the house and one she came to often when she was younger and they weren't booked with guests.

She had loved living in a bed-and-breakfast growing up. When her sister died and her family fell apart, what was once beautiful and rich with color had shriveled up and turned brown. She couldn't stay in the absence of that vibrancy. Her father had barely noticed she'd left.

She shielded her eyes from the dipping sun's brilliant rays against the lake. And there was Dad.

He sat on the bench down on the dock. His feet were planted on the ground, and what appeared to be his hands clasped in his lap. His thinking pose. She headed down to him.

She should have changed her clothes before getting to town. The pencil skirt and matching black jacket made it hard to breathe. Out on the lake, shorts and T-shirts were all she needed, but she had wanted to leave right after the funeral. If she had stopped for more comfortable clothes, she was afraid she would not have made the ride back home. Her high-heeled sandals clicked against the wooden steps and along the long dock.

"Hey, Dad." She waited.

His clouded gaze behind wireless glasses met hers. He stared for several breaths before the light replaced the dimness in his brown eyes. His face burst into a smile that won everyone over. A smile that used to come much easier. Men far younger than Dad would be jealous of his full head of white hair. He usually kept it swept back, but today a few wisps fell against his forehead. He wore his classically handsome look well.

"Lissa, what are you doing here?"

She flinched at the use of the nickname only Ava had used, but she righted herself and went into her father's outstretched arms. His familiar earthy scent filled her up. His giant hug warmed her, and for a second it was like old times. But that feeling never lasted long.

"I thought I would come and spend some time on the lake. I needed a vacation."

"This is a surprise. You haven't been home in, what? Five years?"

"Three."

He waved a hand in the air. "Doesn't matter. I'm glad to see you. I've missed you." He hugged her again.

She eased out of his hold. "Yeah, me too." Her voice lacked conviction, but she doubted her father would notice.

"How's work?"

"It's fine." No point in discussing Gage's call yet.

They'd get to it soon enough.

He plopped down on the bench. "What's with the clothes? Did you finally have a job interview for decent employment?"

"I like what I do. Stop asking me about job interviews. I was at a funeral." She would wait to tell him she quit the bar. He might see it as a sign she would stay here permanently, and that would never happen.

"I'm sorry." The distant look returned to his eyes.

The subject of death was off limits. She took a long breath and fingered the mala beads around her wrist.

"My friend Fox died, Dad. He was young." She waited for his eyes to clear and for him to tell her everything would be all right the way a father was supposed to.

He kept his gaze on the water. She bit back the disappointment and took the spot next to him on the bench.

"Fox was seventeen. He was shot. Like Ava."

"I can't have the Ava conversation right now, okay?"

He never wanted to talk about Ava. The timing was always wrong when she brought it up. She wanted to tell him Fox's death was like losing Ava all over again, but she remained silent to keep the peace. Since Ava was gunned down, Calista had become the only one who could juggle the tough emotions. Her mother had even packed her bags and left the two of them behind.

"How long are you here for?"

She kicked off the strappy sandals cutting into her ankles. "Through the Fourth." Hopefully, that was enough time to get him on the straight and narrow and maybe fix this place up some. She never liked being home around the Fourth anyway.

She hadn't expected the B and B to be in such disarray, but she did need some time away from the city. She was tired of the grit and dirt. Tired of the gunshots outside her apartment building. Tired of watching over her shoulder when she went to her car at night. And tired of young people dying senselessly.

"It will be nice to have you around. This place isn't the same without you, but you don't have to stay that long. My registration is a little light right now. You could come back for Labor Day weekend. I have plenty of reservations then. I could use the help."

"Gage called me." Saying his name cut lines on her tongue. "What happened?"

"I don't want to talk about it."

Of course, he didn't. "Are you going back to meetings?"

He turned to face her. "What really brought you home? Are you and Gage getting back together? Please don't tell me it's that."

"No, Dad. Gage and I will never get back together. I came home because you got arrested, and now that I'm here, I see the B and B looks terrible. What is going on? Have you been in touch with your sponsor?"

"There is no need to call Pete. I have everything under control. Sheriff Ryker overreacted is all, and he should never have called you and worried you."

"I'm glad he called me." That was a truth on many levels. "How long have you been drinking again?"

"It was one time."

"Gage said it was more than once. He arrested you so you'd stop. Dad, it's been sixteen years since Ava died. When are you going to stop falling apart? Or are you sick?"

Was that what all this was about? Did her father have some terminal disease he didn't want to tell her about? She couldn't lose him too. She would have no one left.

He waved her words away. "Healthy as a horse. I had a slipup. It won't happen again. You can tell Gage arresting me worked. No more drinking. Are you ready for dinner? It's just me tonight, but I can whip something up." He stood and ended the conversation. He smoothed his wrinkled clothes.

She stood too. "I want you to promise me you'll go to a meeting while I'm here."

"I promise." But the distant stare returned to his eyes. He took her elbow as they made their way to the small owner's cottage where her family had once lived.

"Why won't you stay in the main house?" She held the door open for him.

With five bedrooms and a king and queen connecting en suite taking up the second floor, the main house had plenty of room for him. He could have been renting out the smaller cottage for more money than one room. But he wouldn't hear of it. His family lived in the cottage on the water. Even if his family had basically been nonexistent for years.

"I think I'm going to stay up in the main house." She braced herself for his reaction.

"Why would you do that?" He rummaged around in the kitchen, not bothering to turn in her direction while he spoke.

"Because it's empty, for one." And she didn't want to sleep next to Ava's shrine.

"And for two?" He pressed his lips together in a thin line.

"How long have you been having trouble booking the rooms?" She fisted her hands on her hips. There was no two. She didn't come home because of Ava. She didn't sleep in the lake house because of Ava. Everything was always about Ava.

"Stay in the cottage tonight with me, okay?" He filled a pot with water.

"Don't avoid my question. How far behind are the bills?" They might be in jeopardy of losing their home. She needed to know what she was up against.

"Why do we have to have this conversation every time you step foot in my house?"

"Because you keep drinking."

He slammed his fist on the counter. "Enough, Calista."

She jumped but forced herself not to flee. "I'm just wondering when you want your life back."

"I lost my life the day Ava died."

She fought the tears threatening to spill. She would not cry in front of him. "I lost something that night too. When will you see that?"

He turned his back and busied himself with the burner that wouldn't light. "Losing a child is very different. You never get over it."

"She isn't coming home, Dad. But I'm standing right here." The ache of loss and frustration lowered her voice.

She turned on her heel and went out the door, closing it quietly behind her.

This would be a long four weeks. But she would stay and help him out. And maybe if she were lucky, she'd fill the void in her heart opened by Ava's death, spread wider by losing Gage, and blown apart by the senseless loss of a seventeen-year-old kid she loved.

Except she had never been lucky.

Chapter Two

The bell over the door to Howard's Hardware greeted Calista as she stepped inside. Like most things on Main Street, Howard's was exactly the same. The long metal shelves were filled with everything all the large chain hardware stores carried. The fluorescent lights flickered overhead, always unsure if they wanted to keep burning but were too stubborn to go out.

And of course, there was Howard. He was a permanent fixture behind the counter, wearing the blue smock with his name embroidered over the pocket. He was older, like the store, with his hair now the color of snow and three chins where there had been one, but his smile was as sure as it was when she was a teenager.

"Well, if it isn't Miss Calista Hartman front and center in my store. Call the press. I have a celebrity from the big city here." He laughed a full, hearty sound that managed to welcome home everyone who entered.

"Hi, Howard. Thanks, but I'm hardly a celebrity. I just live somewhere else now."

"Anyone who leaves and makes it in a crowded, dirty city is a celebrity in my book. Came back for the fresh air?"

"And the big Fourth celebration. Didn't want to miss another year." She hoped that sounded believable.

"What can I help you find?" He tapped the counter with his meaty fingers.

She pulled a list out of her purse and handed it over.

He grabbed a pair of readers from under the counter and plopped them on his nose. "Whoa. That's a lot of projects. Are you hiring someone to help?"

"I thought I'd do it myself. I wanted to get my hands dirty." Maybe the work would help what was ailing her. She wanted to redecorate Ava's room this time too. She hadn't figured out how to break it to her dad. They hadn't spoken since she walked out of the cottage the day before.

"You'll have plenty of projects to get dirty with." Howard waved her list in the air.

The bell above the door stopped her from responding. She clamped her mouth shut and turned toward the sound. A sigh of relief escaped her lips. Not Gage.

A lanky young man with sepia-colored skin and inky hair bounced toward them as if he might be a Labrador retriever puppy. His smile was wide, and his long hair floated on the wind he created in his wake.

"Hello, Justin." Howard waved.

"Hi, Mr. Hornsby. How's it hanging?"

"Hanging low, son."

Justin laughed and revealed slightly crooked top front teeth. His smile floated up into his dark brown eyes. His jeans hung loose on his legs. Two people could fit inside those pants with him.

"Justin, I would like you to meet Calista Hartman. Her dad owns the Hartman B and B over on the lake. Calista, Justin lives in the next town over and likes to come by to ask me silly questions."

Justin stuck out his hand. "Nice to meet you."

She was taken with him and slid her hand into his firm grip. The tattoo on his arm snaked its way under the sleeve of his Grizzlies football T-shirt and peeked out on his neck.

"Mr. Hornsby, any openings in the store?" Justin leaned against the counter.

"Afraid not, young man. But I have your application on file in case something changes. Calista, I'll gather up some of the things on your list. Just plain white paint for the walls?"

"I think white will freshen everything up a bit. I can accent with color if I want to make any real changes. Thanks, Howard." She turned to Justin. "Do you go to UM?"

He glanced down at his shirt, then back at her. "First year. I want to be an architect."

"Are you looking for summer work?"

"Yeah. I'm trying to save money. I can do just about anything. I'm pretty good with my hands. I took a lot of shop classes in high school." He held up his hands and wiggled his long fingers.

"Do you have any references?"

Howard returned with three cans of white paint, most of the things on her list, and placed them on the counter. "I'll vouch for him. He helped me paint my fence over at my house. Showed up every day on time. Worked hard. Paints pretty well. Not as good as I do, of course." Howard spilled his warm laugh all over them.

Justin smiled again. "Thanks, Mr. Hornsby."

"Are you looking for some help at the B and B?" Howard kept his gaze on the register, as if his comment were no more important than the weather.

She hadn't planned on hiring anyone this morning

when she left the house. She wasn't sure if she wanted to dip into her savings to pay someone, and her father would fight every change she tried to make. Bringing someone into their arguments seemed pointless. But Justin reminded her of Fox, a young man with a future.

Fox had wanted a job too. He'd wanted out of the gang life that turned him upside down. He had considered becoming a social worker if the local community college would accept him. They hadn't for the fall semester, but he wanted to try again. He'd wanted to make his grandmother proud of him.

Maybe there was a mother back home rooting for Justin, and he wanted to show her he was a good man who could support himself. Or maybe there was a grandmother like her neighbor Berta who had prayed for her grandson night after night only to have her prayers go unanswered.

"Justin, I have some projects at the B and B that could use a little male strength. I can't pay much, but I will feed you breakfast and lunch every day. It's dirty work, but if you're willing, I'll hire you."

His eyes grew to the size of those paint cans, then narrowed to slits. "Really? Just like that? Why?"

She recognized the suspicion. Why would some stranger want to help him? "I can't do it all by myself. My dad is there, but he won't help. And he'll probably get in the way and try to take the paintbrush right out of your hands. It won't be pleasant. He's stubborn. But if you think it's too tough for you, I understand." She rummaged through her purse for her wallet and handed over a credit card to Howard.

Justin's gaze bounced from side to side. She kept her mouth shut and was thankful Howard did the same.

16

"What kind of projects?" Justin said.

"Painting." She pointed at the cans. "Lots of painting. Some minor plumbing work. Fixing anything that doesn't hang right or open right. A few other odds and ends. Maybe some landscaping."

"For how long?"

"I need the B and B looking good for the Fourth. After that, I'm heading home." Hopefully, her father could carry out the rest of the summer on his own. And if Justin proved to be an asset, she could keep him on and pay him from her personal checking account.

She'd have to do some advertising for the B and B too. She could focus on bringing in the guests if she had help repairing the place. She was pretty sure her father would make himself scarce.

Howard handed her the receipt. "Do you need any help getting your belongings in the car?"

"I'm fine, thanks. It was nice to meet you, Justin." She grabbed the items Howard had bagged and one paint can. "I'll be back for the rest."

She popped the Honda's hatch. Voices drifted over from across the street as she stored her new purchases in the back of the car. Her spine straightened, and she tried to ignore the effervescence of excitement and confusion in her belly.

One voice held the telltale low timbre she would never be free from. That voice had whispered endearments and promises in her ear while strong arms held her close. She could close her eyes and conjure Gage Ryker as easily as glancing across the street to him standing there.

The love she knew with him warred with the hurt. The dull, endless ache in her chest spread into her stomach. He had let her down. What he'd done was unforgivable. Ava was dead because his brother killed her, and Gage had done nothing about it. She and Gage could never be together. She wished her heart would get on the same fucking page as her head. She took a breath and rubbed her mala beads between her fingers.

Howard's glass door opened, and Justin bounced out holding the last two cans. His presence derailed her thoughts, and she was grateful.

"Here you go, Miss Hartman." He placed the cans in the back of the SUV.

"Call me Calista."

He wiped his hands on his legs. "Okay. You didn't mention how much your job paid."

She hadn't thought about it. She probably should have checked the going rate before opening her mouth. "How's fifteen an hour?" Even if that was a little low, she would pay cash. That would equate to more. She had money saved for a rainy day. It looked as if the skies had opened up and deposited Justin to assist her.

"I guess that's cool."

"So we have a deal?"

"Yeah, sure." His voice stayed neutral, but his crooked smile gave him away.

"Why don't you come and see the place this afternoon?"

He scratched the back of his neck. "Um, I have some stuff to do first. Is four o'clock okay?"

"Perfect. See you then." She stuck out her hand.

He shook it. "Thanks."

"No, thank you. You're going to help me a lot." She would do herself a favor and not get attached to this young man. Everyone she loved left her, and Justin couldn't replace Fox, just as Fox couldn't replace Ava.

He turned to go, and she made her way around to the driver's door. A magnetic pull forced her gaze to drift toward the café.

Gage stood there with his hands clasped at his waist. His cold stare froze her in place. Her heart wanted to run over to him, but she fought her heart with her head and told it to stay put. She gave him the slightest of nods and climbed into the SUV.

She drove away without checking to see if he noticed. It didn't matter. He'd arrested her father when he could have probably issued a warning and given her dad a break, but Gage would never ignore the rules. And he would always be the brother of the man who killed her sister. She owed Ava her loyalty.

She had nothing else to offer.

Chapter Three

Gage craved a cold beer, a hot meal he didn't have to cook, and one night to himself. The beer was the only thing he could guarantee. His teenage daughter always required his attention, whether she appreciated it or not, and his deputy was bound to call him before the night was through.

He dragged himself up the front steps of his small cottage. All the lights were out. Had Izzi gone to bed already? He was late coming home tonight because Mrs. Steadman over on Pinewood called about some neighborhood boys making a lot of noise. When he arrived, the boys, if there even were any, had long gone. He suspected Mrs. Steadman had only imagined the noises outside. She was lonely since her husband died, and called the department weekly requesting he come by.

In a small town, everyone thought the sheriff was in charge of fixing all their problems. He twisted the unlocked doorknob and stumbled over shoes right inside the door. "Shit." How many times had he told Izzi to move her sneakers?

He took a second to allow his eyes to adjust to the dark room. Two pairs of shoes? Rustling and whispers scurried to his right. He drew his gun. His heart broke into a canter. Were they being robbed this time? He flipped the light switch. "Freeze."

The living room was bathed in light. He blinked against the stark brightness or against the vision in front of him.

"Dad," his daughter yelled. She shoved her arm into her shirt and tugged the hem down her bare stomach.

A tall young man tripped over the coffee table filled with beer cans. Was this guy yanking up his zipper?

His heart went from a canter to a furious gallop. He wanted to break this kid's neck for putting his hands on his baby girl.

"Isabelle Ryker, what the hell is going on here?" With shaking hands, he shoved his gun back in its holster.

"Nothing." She pushed her hair away from her face. Her lips were red and swollen. Her chest heaved.

He stifled a groan. There was a hell of a lot more than *nothing* going on. "Who is this?"

"Dad, this is—"

"Never mind, I don't give a shit what his name is. Where did you get the beer?" He glanced back to the table. Four beer cans.

Red blotches bloomed on her face. "From the fridge."

"Our refrigerator?" He must have heard her wrong. She knew the rules. The liquor was his and his alone until she was of age.

"Sir, let me explain—"

"Young man, shut up while you still can." Had he seen this kid somewhere before? He looked familiar. "Do you two go to school together?"

The boy looked from Izzi to him. "Yeah, we both

21

go to UM."

"Did you tell him you went to college?" She was going to give him a heart attack.

"Dad, let me explain."

"Isabelle, yes or no."

She worked her teeth over her bottom lip. "Yes." She turned to the kid. "I go to Backwater High."

The color drained from the boy's face. "You told me you went to Montana."

Gage didn't care if the kid had been snowed by Izzi. That didn't excuse the heavy petting he'd interrupted in his own damn home.

He couldn't believe what was playing out in front of him. "Son, she's fifteen. If you're any older than that, you'd better get the hell out of my house before I arrest you for statutory rape."

"Daddy, stop it. We weren't doing anything wrong. I like him." She put a hand on the boy's arm, but the kid moved away.

"You told me you were eighteen. I'm sorry, sir. I didn't know. I'd better go." The kid tried to sidestep the table.

Gage held up a hand and stopped him in his delinquent tracks. "How old are you?"

"I'll be nineteen this summer."

"Are you drunk? And don't think about lying to me." He ground his teeth. He would have to give this kid a ride home and explain to his parents their son and his daughter were engaged in underage drinking. He could arrest them both and maybe should just to prove a point.

"No, sir. I only had one and a half."

"Get out." He pointed to the door.

The kid grabbed his shoes and ran out the door.

"You're grounded forever." He turned away from her.

"Dad, it's no big deal."

"No big deal? You're a child. That kid could go to jail for what you were doing. And what the hell are you doing allowing some boy to put his hands all over you? Didn't I teach you better than that? And the drinking. You're underage. That's illegal and against my rules. Why would you take my beer? How did you even meet him?"

"I met him at a party." She hung her head. Her dark hair fell over her face.

"Whose party?"

"Rebecca's sister goes to UM. We went with her."

He pinched the bridge of his nose. Izzi's friend Rebecca always rubbed him the wrong way. He couldn't put his finger on why, but he had a sense that young lady was trouble, and he didn't want Izzi hanging with her. He was right.

As Izzi continued to grow up and get closer to the age Ajay was when he died, Gage wanted to protect her more and more. If he'd been paying better attention back then, maybe Ajay would still be alive.

"You went to a college party after I told you not to, and you drank three beers."

"It was two and a half. I'm sorry." A tear ran down her cheek.

"Grounded. Three weeks. Go to your room." His head hurt.

She slunk away from him without another word. A throbbing began behind his eyes. He gathered the cans and tossed them in the recycling bucket under the sink.

He changed out of his uniform, locked up his gun, and popped open the fridge. He grabbed the last Cold Smoke Scotch Ale, cracked the seal, and pressed the cold can to his forehead.

Being a single parent had never been more difficult. He had no idea how to handle his daughter. How his mother raised five boys by herself was beyond him.

He moved around the small kitchen and pulled a can of soup from the cabinet. He dumped it into a pot and lit the burner. Not much of a dinner, but he wasn't as hungry as he thought he was.

The pain in his head went up four notches when he pictured Calista standing outside Howard's Hardware. She had come home at his request but was probably mad about her father's recent arrest. Andy had it coming, though. His drinking was becoming a problem.

Of course, the death glare from Calista's amber eyes might have had more to do with him than her father. She would never forgive him for what Ajay did. When she looked at him, she saw his little brother, the man who killed her sister. After sixteen years, it might be nice if she tried. He wasn't holding any grudges. Well, not many.

A knock came from the front door. That kid had better not be back. He turned off the soup.

"Gage, are you home?" His mother walked into his house as if it was hers. In a way, it was.

"In here." He poured the soup into a bowl.

Karen Ryker stepped into his kitchen wearing the smile she reserved for her children and grandchild and carrying a large white binder in her arms. Her black-rimmed rectangular glasses sat in their expected place on her nose.

"Please tell me you didn't come over to talk about the barbeque for the Fourth." After what he saw in his living room, he only wanted to nurse his beer, slurp his soup, and forget he had a teenage daughter who wanted to have sex.

"I need some of your input for the barbeque and the fireworks. Give your mom a hug."

She waved him over, and he indulged her. He leaned his frame down to her petite one, and she wrapped her arms around his waist.

"I don't care that you're a foot taller than I am and a grown man. I still love hugging my boys."

"We noticed."

She swatted his arm. "Wiseguy."

"Why don't you ask Jett and Lock what they think about the barbeque? They're the ranchers. Or did you fire them again?" He pulled out a chair at the kitchen table for her and took the seat opposite.

"I have never fired my children from the ranch."

He raised an eyebrow in question.

"That was one time. And you all deserved it." She opened her binder.

"We were kids." He dumped the spoon in the soup.

She sat back with a distant look in her eyes. "We had some good times back then, didn't we? You know, before Dad and Ajay were gone. For the briefest of moments, I thought I had it all." She waved her hands in front of her eyes. "Oh, look at me. I'm sorry. Sometimes this time of year sneaks up on me and steals my breath. Now where were we?"

He gripped her hand and gave a squeeze. She smiled but pulled her hand away and patted his arm.

25

"Mom—"

She put her hand up. "Gage Michael, I'm fine. Really, but thank you. Is that your dinner?"

"Want some?" He held up the spoon.

"Let me make you something. You and Izzi can't eat like that." She stood, but this time he put a hand up.

"Mom, I'm fine. Just like you."

"Don't sass your mother." She gave him a small smile. "Okay, fine. Have your soup." She pulled a page from her binder. "Now Jett wants to change the menu. I printed out some ideas. What do you think?"

He took the paper from her. She wanted the conversation about the past over, and he would oblige. She was the toughest woman he'd ever met, and she had expected her boys to be just as tough. If she needed something, she would ask. Maybe.

She rattled on about the Fourth of July celebration on the ranch. The town and their guests expected a celebration every Fourth. It didn't matter their family experienced the worst tragedy on the nation's birthday. The Ryker Ranch had to perform, but he missed his kid brother. The guilt never loosened its grip on his chest.

"Jett wants everything the same as last year. He won't budge. I thought you might be able to persuade him to try a few new things. He listens to you," Mom said.

Jett wasn't going to listen to anyone. "I'll talk to him." His first younger brother was a lot like him in some ways. Jett believed in order and rules that needed to be followed. They had inherited that characteristic from their father and his Kootenai work ethic. Even if Dad was only part Native American, his staunch work philosophy was what killed him.

"Where's Izzi?" His mother took his soup bowl and washed it.

"She's in her room. Grounded." He sipped his beer.

"What could that sweet girl possibly have done? Go easy on her." Mom might be tough, but her rules could be bent with nothing more than a hug. All her children knew how to play her when one of them wanted something. No one had been better at that than Ajay.

"Please don't undermine my authority with her. I caught her making out with a boy and drinking beer."

His mother waved her hand in the air. "Oh my. Well, I'll leave it to you to figure out."

She wiped down the counters, straightened the mail, and moved Izzi's shoes away from the door. "Silver Bell didn't want to come in from the pasture again today. Jett said to leave her and he'd bring her in when she was ready."

"Is she sick?" He needed to get over there and spend some time with his horse. He'd been neglecting her because he'd been so busy since Memorial Day weekend.

"She's old, Gage. You're going to need to face that." His mother wiped her hands on a dish towel.

"She's okay, Mom. Jett would have said if she wasn't."

"I'm saying that Silver Bell may be winding down. I want you to be prepared."

He couldn't lose her. She had been Ajay's horse. "I'll stop by the barn tomorrow."

"Fair enough. I'm going to head back to the main house." She hugged him.

"Do you want me to drive you back? It's late now."

He had picked the farthest guest cottage from the main house to live in when he came home with a toddler and needed his mother's help to raise her. He wanted to keep some of his dignity, and at least the half mile between his cottage and the main house allowed him a morsel.

"I think I know my way." She winked.

"I should take you."

"You worry too much." She held her binder to her chest with her arms crossed like a shield and adjusted her glasses with one hand.

"It's my job to worry." He reached for his keys.

"It's your job to serve and protect. Everyone else. Good night, my love." She closed the door without another word.

He dropped onto the leather recliner and grabbed the remote. Usually around ten or eleven, he would take a quick ride through town to make sure everything looked tucked in for the night, but tonight his muscles ached, and his head still throbbed. Maybe his mother was right. He did worry too much.

His eyelids grew heavy. He was ready to surrender to sleep, but the shrill sound of his cell jarred him awake. Without looking at the screen, he answered. "Sheriff Ryker."

"Sir, we have a report of a two-one-one," his deputy sheriff said, using the old number codes.

"Is anyone hurt?" The second robbery in as many weeks. A chill ran over his skin. He jumped from the recliner.

"No, sir. The subject was in and out fast."

He stopped. Not much could be done at this hour if no one had been apprehended. "Take a report of what's missing. And make note of anything the victims can tell you. And how many times do I have to tell you to use plain language instead of the number codes?"

"Sorry, sir."

Gage shook his head. His hands were tied when it came to hiring Barry Pearce. No one else had wanted the job, and he couldn't run the department all by himself. They had Phyllis who answered phones and smart-mouthed anyone who got in her way, but other than her, it was him and Barry.

"Any neighbors hanging around?"

"No, sir. No neighbors nearby."

A house without neighbors in proximity probably meant the robbery had occurred at one of the farms on the outskirts of town. "Don't miss anything. I'll check on them in the morning." He'd review the report and canvas the area again then.

"But I think you should come out here. The victim is pretty upset."

"Is it Mr. Logger?" The Logger farm bordered the next town over. Kids usually just pegged his house with dried peas. They made a racket against the old man's metal siding. He would come running with his gun, and the kids would run into the fields laughing.

"No, sir. The robbery was at the Hartman bed-and-breakfast."

A cold hand of dread ran down his back. "Has Andy been drinking? Is he out of control?"

"I wish it were that simple. It's Calista. She won't stop crying, and she won't let me call an ambulance. Took my phone and threw it across the room. I think she's in shock. Probably never been robbed before. Will you come?"

"I'll be right there."

Chapter Four

Gage turned onto the long drive leading to the Hartman B and B. His truck bounced over the uneven asphalt. Barry's cruiser sat up ahead with the overhead lights still spinning red and blue ribbons across the front of the house.

Every window was lit up from the inside. He parked off to the side and crossed the grass in two strides.

He reached inside the cruiser and turned off the lights. A glance around told him everything appeared as usual. He went to the front door but didn't bother to knock. He was there in an official capacity. She would have to let him in even if she didn't want to. Which was likely.

"Deputy Pearce, where are you?" he hollered into the house. The front rooms were empty.

"In here, sir."

He hadn't been inside the Hartman in sixteen years, but he headed for the kitchen as if he'd been there only yesterday. The back door hung open, and the glass pane closest to the doorknob was broken. Splintered glass littered the floor. A chair was on its side. The faucet dripped water. Several cabinet doors hung crooked. Was the burglar after plates and glasses?

Barry stood to the side, taking photos with his phone. Andy huddled in the corner, cradling a whiskey glass. Great. His hair stuck up in different directions, as if he might have been sleeping when all this happened. The plaid pajama pants were also a giveaway.

"Andy, are you okay?"

"What do you think? We were robbed. They took the televisions in every guest room. The stereo equipment. And who knows what else."

"I know this is difficult. As long as no one was hurt, that's what matters. Insurance will replace the things you lost."

Andy downed a large gulp of whatever he was drinking.

"It's ginger ale." Andy snarled at him. "Do you want to smell it?"

"It's none of my business. Just make sure to tell Barry everything you know. Do you have guests now? Did anyone else see or hear anything?"

"No guests. Just Lissa. She wanted to stay up here instead of in the lake house. I told her to stay with me in her old room. What if that bastard had hurt her?"

"Did you see a man?" He wanted to break in half the person who did this. If he were smart, he'd let Barry run with this investigation and he'd stay out of it altogether. But he couldn't stand the idea of someone hurting her. Or Andy for that matter.

"Lissa yelled for me. I came outside and saw what looked like three tall figures running. They jumped in a car and sped off." He nursed his drink.

Gage hoped it really was ginger ale. "What kind of car was it?"

"I couldn't tell in the dark."

"Where is Calista?"

"Out on the back deck."

"I wouldn't go out there, sir. She's liable to throw you over the rail." Barry shook his head and pulled out a notebook.

"I'll be right back." He took a deep breath, trying to prepare for seeing her up close, and stepped onto the deck.

Her back was to him. She'd lost weight, but her curves still tempted him. His fingers wanted to run across her skin because his memory had always been his enemy. He clasped his hands to keep from touching her. Her hair hung in waves below her shoulders. He had once asked her to keep her hair long for him. It would be foolish to think she had continued to honor his request.

He cleared his throat, and she turned around. Her eyes grew wide, but she turned back toward the lake. "I didn't expect the sheriff to come out for this. I gave my report to the deputy."

"Were you hurt in the incident?" He focused on using the voice he reserved for questioning eyewitnesses so his emotions didn't get the best of him. He needed to stay professional, especially with her.

"No, thank you for asking. Why are you here?"

"Deputy Pearce said the scene was unsecured."

"In other words, I'd lost my shit, right?" She leaned on her elbows.

He took a tentative step toward her and braced himself in case she pounced. "Are you okay? It's frightening when something like this happens."

She pointed her gaze on him. "You think so? Have you ever been robbed, Sheriff? Because I have. Tonight makes twice. I know exactly how scary it is to be held at gunpoint and forced to hand over your belongings."

The need to snap someone's neck burned through him like a wildfire. He wanted to kill the person who'd pointed a gun at her. Even though his knee-jerk reaction was to protect her in a way that was completely different than his job as sheriff, he no longer had the right. "Did someone have a gun tonight?"

"Just me. I heard the glass break and grabbed my dad's twenty-two rifle. I shouted I had a gun and they had better get running. There was some scurrying. I didn't come out of my room right away. They were quick. They stole all the televisions and some other stuff. They found the cash in the cookie jar. It all happened in minutes, as if they'd known where everything was."

They could have been casing the place, but the B and B was so far off the road it was hard to keep a good eye on the comings and goings. That would mean in order for the unsubs to know where things were, they would have had to walk across the property to peer inside the windows. Or they had been here before.

"I'm sorry that happened to you. We'll do everything we can to catch the people who did this."

"Yeah, right. Cops are always sorry."

"What does that mean?"

"Nothing. Forget it. I'll apologize to Barry. I overreacted." She continued to give him her back.

"That's not necessary. No one is judging your actions tonight."

He wanted to ask her what her life had been like since she left. Had she found the happiness she wanted? Was she able to get through a day without thinking about her sister? Because he couldn't go a day without thinking about Ajay. But the memory of her hand slapping his face stopped him from asking.

He forced his mind to stay on the investigation. He didn't want to think about her or the way his skin was on fire while he stood beside her. He had a job to do. Nothing else mattered at the moment.

"Do you have to be here? Can't Barry handle this? I promise not to throw his phone again." She fumbled with the bracelets on her wrist.

"It's my responsibility. Have there been any recent deliveries?" Without guests at the B and B, he wouldn't have to question anyone who was from out of town.

She dropped her stare. "I don't know what my father's been doing with the business, but I doubt a delivery has arrived in a while since we don't have any guests. That probably makes you feel good, doesn't it?"

He flinched. "Why would you think something like that? Why do you hate me so much?" Maybe they needed to deal with her anger once and for all. He didn't want to watch everything he said around her.

"I don't hate you." She turned back to the lake. "I shouldn't have said that. I'm sorry. I'm just upset about tonight."

He could understand that, yet he wasn't sure he believed her entirely. She was upset about what happened here with every right, but he was still the same man she couldn't bear to be around.

In the morning, she might regret some of her verbal attacks, but he doubted it. He stood beside her, forcing her to look up at him. Her eyes smoldered, most likely from anger and fear. Her lips were pressed into a thin, colorless line, and her shoulders hunched. She did not want him anywhere near her. He couldn't move away. She had always been a magnet for him.

"Was there something valuable in the kitchen cabinets?"

She narrowed her eyes. "I'm not sure what you're talking about."

"It appears someone vandalized the kitchen cabinets. Do you know if there was something inside them worth stealing?" He willed his legs to move and leaned against the rail to create some space between them. His lungs expanded and sucked in the lake air.

Red blotches bloomed up her neck, but she never let her gaze waver from his. "The cabinets are in need of repair."

He wanted to kick himself. He should have guessed. "What about contractors? Have you hired anyone to work on the kitchen?"

"No. Wait. Yes. I hired a young man to help out with some of the projects around here. But he wouldn't do this." She rubbed her arms.

"Who did you hire?" He wanted to give her his zip-up, but she would never accept an offer from him.

"His name is Justin. I don't know his last name. Howard vouched for him."

"You hired a kid without a last name?" Which would mean she hadn't asked for references besides Howard. He didn't know any kid named Justin, and he knew everyone in Backwater. "How old is this kid?"

"He said eighteen. I think. He lives in the next town over. Needed a job, and I need the help. But it wasn't him."

"Did he start working?"

"He just came by to see the house. He starts tomorrow."

"What time will he be here? I want to question

him." And he would not allow Deputy Sheriff Pearce to do it. He didn't want any mistakes. A stranger in his town and at the B and B the day it got robbed made the back of his neck prickle.

"Gage, why would a kid who needs a job rob it the day he's hired? No one is that stupid."

She would be surprised how stupid people could be, especially a young kid who thought he knew it all and had it all figured out. Like Ajay.

She pulled closed the threadbare sweater she wore over her pajamas. The breeze off the lake was cool this time of night. The adrenaline was probably wearing off too. He didn't want her to shiver.

He forgot reason and shrugged out of his zip-up. "Take this."

She shook her head and stepped away from him. "Is there anything else you need, Sheriff? I'd like to clean up the broken glass and put up a piece of wood on the door until the morning. It's been a long day."

"Do you want me to call my mother and tell her you and your dad need a room for the night?"

"No." She shook her head. "I mean, we'll be fine. I don't want to bother her. She's done enough for my father."

"Like what?" He didn't know about anything in particular. Andy usually avoided his family at all costs.

"She bailed him out of the jail you put him in."

"No, she didn't."

"Apparently, she doesn't tell you everything. After you left the station that night, he called her. Barry handed him the phone."

He pushed the growl in his throat back down and wiped a hand over his face. Barry might have kept the cell door open too. His deputy sheriff could be easily persuaded to push procedure aside. He would have to speak with Barry about his lapse in judgment.

"From the twitch in your jaw, I guess you didn't know about that. He paid her back, so don't worry." A smile whisked across her lips.

She must enjoy watching the fury on his face.

"I did not know she bailed him out." He would have a talk with his mother tomorrow. "At least stay in the lake house with your dad. Lock all the doors. I doubt anyone will come back, but don't take any chances. If you hear anything at all, call for help. We'll come right back."

"It doesn't matter if someone does. The damage is done. No one will want to stay with us now. I shouldn't even bother to fix the place up." She heaved a weary grunt.

"It's going to be okay."

"Really? When? Do you have an answer to that question? Because I don't. My dad is never going to be all right. This place is a mess. And I…"

"You what?" He wanted to erase the crease between her brows. He'd known how to do that once. He'd been the person she leaned into when her world tipped until Ajay pulled that gun. He wished she would try to trust him again.

"Never mind. I'm just tired. Can you go now?"

The words, laced with impatience, were like a shove out the door. "I'll come by tomorrow to speak with your new employee. Make sure you call the insurance company first thing. You can have those items replaced in time for the Fourth."

"There is no insurance. Why do I keep talking to

you?" She threw her arms in the air.

"Your father didn't keep the insurance on the place?" He ignored the last question because he didn't want her answer.

"Nope. That's why I went nuts earlier. We're screwed, and I don't know how to fix it. And I'm still talking." She faced the lake again.

He took a step toward her, hoping to make things right for her. Even if she no longer had feelings for him, she didn't have to do this alone.

She put her hand up. "Gage, could you please go? This is hard enough without having you here."

He wanted to stay. He could keep watch all night so she could get some needed sleep. In the morning, he could help her find a way out of this mess. "Sure. Good night, then."

He left her standing there all alone and forced himself not to take another look at her when he went inside, or he'd run back. "Barry, are you about done here? Let's allow the Hartmans to get some sleep."

"All set, boss." Barry tapped his notebook.

"Andy, call right away if you hear anything suspicious. I'll be by tomorrow to check on things." He shook the man's hand.

"Thank you. Both of you." Andy showed them to the door.

Gage turned his truck around and headed back to the road and through town. He wasn't going to get much sleep tonight. A drive around to make sure everything looked as it should wouldn't take long and would give him some peace of mind.

Because standing inches from Calista Hartman with pain etched on her face when he could do nothing to help her did anything but give him peace.

He should have done a better job of getting over her. He thought time would take care of that for him.

He thought wrong.

Chapter Five

Calista trudged into the kitchen. She hadn't slept a wink after Gage left, and she had hammered a piece of plywood on the broken window. Her thoughts raced from the fear of the burglars coming back to Gage standing beside her looking so damn good it hurt to breathe.

His broad shoulders filled out that sweatshirt he offered her. It would have smelled like him, and she couldn't handle that, which was why she backed away. His hair was still black, even now, and days' worth of scruff had covered his strong, tawny jaw.

She needed her damn heart to get on the same page as her head. So what that they'd had a good thing once? All good things must come to an end. They would never have made it. Every time she looked at him, she saw Ajay.

She dumped the ground coffee into the filter and stared out the window. If Ajay hadn't pulled that trigger, Ava would be here now, married with a bunch of children running around the B and B. Maybe her parents would still be together and they'd be a real family.

Ajay and Ava had become friends because she and Gage dated. Quiet Ava had been the moth to Ajay's flame. They were the same age with similar interests. Ajay had the Ryker good looks and a bold personality with a great sense of humor.

Calista returned the coffeepot to the machine with a little too much force. The coffee sloshed up the sides and onto her hand.

"Damn." She ran cold water over her hand already-turning red.

She tried not to picture Gage when he laughed. His top lip curled up when he really got going and he could let that shield down. The lines around his eyes would deepen as he smiled. Last night she hadn't missed the way they were etched on his grown-up face.

The hot coffee burned her mouth too. "Stay focused."

Her new job was to start the repairs and find the money to replace the stolen items. How could her father have stopped the payments on the insurance? What if this place went up in flames?

Advertising for new guests would have to wait until she knew how much it would cost to replace the valuables. Without new guests, she couldn't afford to fix everything that was broken and in need of repair. She would have to prioritize the list and hope she didn't completely fail. The coffee burned her mouth again. She should have stayed in Billings instead of coming home. She hadn't been here a full week, and her father had her tangled in his messes again.

She wasn't being fair. The robbery wasn't his fault. Everything else was. The chime from the front door sang out. She wiped the errant tear from her face and went to greet whoever was at the door. A guest would be too much to ask for.

"Hi." Justin stood by the front desk tucked near the staircase. His smile reminded her to place one on her own face. He wore the expected oversized jeans and Grizzlies shirt. But this time a shiner outlined his eye.

"What happened to you?" She stepped forward and reached for his face, but he ducked.

"It's nothing." He pulled at his hair, but it couldn't cover what she'd already seen.

"Are you sure?" The skin around his eye was swollen and had turned a dark purple. Scratches and a hint of a bruise near his mouth suggested he might have been hit there too.

"My brother and I were fucking around. Sorry about the language." He stared at his feet.

"What's he look like?"

"He's fine."

"I get it that guys throw a few punches to deal with a difference of opinion, but this looks more serious than that." She couldn't explain her gut reaction, but she liked Justin and didn't want anyone hurting him. Maybe it was the crooked smile or that he reminded her a little of Gage at that age.

"You wouldn't understand."

"Try me. I have breakfast." She headed into the kitchen. Telling a tough story over food was always easier than just standing there.

"I'm not hungry. I already ate." But he followed her anyway.

"I did promise you I'd feed you as part of your payment. I hope you'll take me up on that. I have cinnamon rolls this morning. Would you like one with some coffee?"

"Um, okay. I mean, I guess so. Thanks." He slid onto the stool at the counter.

"Great. Now tell me what you and your brother

were fighting about." She wanted to fix everything—even things between her and Gage—but that was impossible. She placed a cinnamon roll on a plate and slid it over to him. She poured two cups of coffee. She needed another one too.

Justin tore the bun into pieces, then licked his fingers. He kept his gaze on his hands. "Do you promise you won't think this is stupid?"

"No way."

"He thinks I'm disrespecting our family because I want to leave the reservation permanently. You know, make a life in Backwater."

"What did you say to that?" She wrapped her hands around the mug and watched him over the rim. Leaving the reservation was a tough thing for Justin's people. Families expected everyone to stay together, but the younger generation often wanted something different.

"I told him to go fuck off, and he hit me." His lip curled into that crooked smile.

"I'm sorry."

"It is what it is. What projects am I working on today?"

And just like that, the subject was closed. She recognized that set jaw and cold-as-steel look in his eyes. Gage was very good at doing the same thing.

"I want to start in the front room. Paint the walls. I think the ceiling is okay. You'll have to cover the furniture and the floors. I can't afford to redecorate just yet. All the painting supplies are in the garage."

Even though the sound of the chime was something she should be used to, when it dinged again, she jumped. She took a deep breath. It was normal to be out of sorts today. They'd experienced a trauma last night.

"I'll get the door."

No one was expected this early, but that didn't mean anything. In Backwater, news traveled like a boat on the rapids. Anyone could be here with a casserole because the B and B was robbed last night. She took a deep breath to steady her frayed nerves.

The deep breath caught in her throat. Gage stood inside her front room in his sheriff's uniform. The brown shirt fit snug against his broad shoulders and tapered down into his beige trousers. She didn't allow her gaze to linger anywhere below his belt. Her neck was probably bright red and giving her away. The last thing she needed was him catching her stare. His hair was still wet from a morning shower, and his clean-shaven face taunted her fingertips. She wished she had run a brush through her hair and bothered to get out of her pajamas.

He clasped his hands at his waist. "Good morning."

"Good morning." She struggled to keep a level of calm in her voice. "What can I help you with?"

"I came by to walk your property for any possible clues. Also, I'm afraid Deputy Pearce forgot to dust for fingerprints. I'd like to do that too. I have the kit in my cruiser."

"I've been all through the kitchen. Isn't it a little late to look for fingerprints now?"

"Maybe. I'd like to try with your permission." He stood ramrod straight. Which meant he wasn't going to take no for an answer.

"How long is that going to take?"

"I'll be as quick as possible. Have you or your father thought of anything else that might be helpful?"

"If I remember anything else, I'll come by the

department. If you'll excuse me, I have work to do." Having him standing in her house looking professional in his uniform, and menacing with a gun strapped to his waist, made the tension ease from her shoulders. He had been the only person ever capable of giving her that gift, but the minute Ava died, all the things Gage could offer were no longer important. She needed him to go so she wouldn't forget her needs didn't count.

"Is your new employee here yet? I'd like to question him too."

"Can that wait?" Until she was somewhere else or at the very least wearing a bra.

"The quicker you allow me to do my job, the faster I'll be gone. That's what you want, isn't it?"

"You read my mind." She regretted allowing the words to form outside her head, but they hovered in the air like pollution that would never be cleaned up.

He marched past her and strode into the kitchen.

She followed on his heels, wanting to grab him and shove him out the door, but his damn long legs cleared the space faster than she could. "Sheriff Ryker, now isn't a good time."

He stopped in his tracks. She slammed into his solid body. He glared at her over his shoulder, then turned his attention back inside the kitchen.

"You?" Gage growled.

She weaved around Gage. Justin jumped and tripped over the chair, knocking it down. He backed up until he was pressed against the door with its new wooden patch over the broken window.

"This is Justin, my new employee." She righted the chair and glanced between the two men. The uneasiness spiraled between them.

"We've met."

"She told me she was eighteen." Justin held his hands up in front of his face.

"I'm not following. When did you two meet?"

Gage ignored her question and stepped forward, towering over Justin. He had the benefit of age to broaden his shoulders and years of hard work on his side to Justin's boyish, still-growing stature.

Justin squirmed against the door, as if he wanted to put more space between him and Gage. "Please, sir, let me explain."

"Stop talking."

"How about I get you a cup of coffee? You seem like you need one." She didn't wait for Gage's response but grabbed a mug and poured coffee, leaving room at the top for milk. At least that's how he used to take it.

He pushed the mug away, and his frown deepened. The glare in his eyes would freeze anyone in their spot. "After you left my residence, where did you go between the hours of nine p.m. and twelve a.m.?"

His residence? "Wait a second. Do you really know Justin?"

Gage turned his furious stare on her. "I found this young man in my home behaving in an inappropriate manner with my daughter." He turned back to Justin. "Now answer my damn question. Where were you last night?"

She closed her eyes and took a deep breath. There were no coincidences. Her fingers sought her mala beads. Justin knew Gage's daughter in the biblical way. This would never end well for Justin. She had to try and protect him from Gage's fury.

"I was home."

"Can anyone corroborate that?" Gage made notes on his phone.

"I was by myself. My brother was out most of the night with our cousin. We live with him. For now."

"Who'd you get into a fight with?" Gage pointed at Justin's eye.

"It's no big deal."

"Looks like someone clocked you good. Was it another young lady's father, or did you fall?"

"Can I ask why you're asking me these questions?" Justin stopped fidgeting and stood to his full height, which almost put him eye level with Gage.

"There was a robbery here last night. Do you know anything about that?"

"Is that why there's wood on the door? I'm sorry, Calista. I hope you weren't hurt." He peered around Gage to see her.

"I'm fine. Gage, all these questions aren't necessary. Justin didn't do anything." The tension in the room thickened like morning fog on the lake. She was going to need to burn some sage to clear the air after both men left.

"Calista, let me do my job." Gage never took his gaze off Justin.

"Anyone want more coffee?" She held up the carafe, hoping to bring levity into the mix. They ignored her.

"You didn't answer my question. Do you know anything about the robbery?"

"Why would I know anything about a robbery here?"

"Because you look like trouble."

"You think that because I'm Indian and I have a

48

rez accent." Justin tried to puff up his thin chest.

Gage narrowed his eyes. "I don't care about your heritage or your accent. I think you're trouble because you had your hand up my daughter's shirt, you dumb shit."

"Gage, maybe name-calling is too far." She hoped her voice held a strong warning. She really didn't want to dose him with hot coffee to make him shut up.

"All you white people think we're stupid and don't belong in your world because we're poor. I might be poor, but I don't steal."

Gage pointed a finger at Justin. "You don't know the first thing about me, young man. I suggest you show some respect, or I will throw you in jail for sexual misconduct with a minor."

"Gage, please. You're being unreasonable. For the tenth time, Justin did not rob my home." She needed to derail him. He was picking up too much steam.

"Okay, Justin, tell me this. How is it Miss Hartman hires you to work for her and that very night her house is burglarized? Doesn't that seem strange to you?"

"I don't know anything about it. I left here around four and went to your house and then home. Are we through? I have work to do." Justin pushed away from the door.

"Not until I say we are." Gage blocked his path.

"I think he answered all your questions." She broke her own rule and gripped Gage's arm. The strength of his muscles sent shivers over her skin.

"Don't go far. I may have more questions." Gage eased out of her grip and leveled a cold stare on him.

"You got it, chief." Justin saluted.

"It's Sheriff Ryker, son."

"Yeah. Okay. Calista, I'll be in the garage, if you don't have a problem with that?"

"That's fine. Thanks." She waited for him to leave, then turned on Gage with rage flowing through her. "What is wrong with you?" She could not summon an ounce of her yoga practice.

"What are you talking about?" He reached for the mug, but she stopped him. Her hand gripped his wrist, and the current between them ran up her arm to her heart. Touching him twice in five minutes was liable to kill her.

"You come in here and practically accuse him of robbing the place. How could you do that?" She walked away from him. No touching.

"I did not accuse him of anything."

"Why didn't you tell him your father is from the Kootenai tribe? You let him believe you dislike him because he's Indian."

"No, I'm pretty sure he knows I don't like him because he had my daughter half-naked. Besides, my heritage is none of his damn business. Can I have that coffee?"

"No."

He reached for the coffee pot anyway, but she got in his way.

"Calista, he knows something about last night. He's probably one of the three guys your father saw running away from here. It's too much of a coincidence."

"You're being ridiculous. What makes you think he's a criminal? You don't know him."

Fox hadn't been a criminal. He had been a good kid who wanted to make something of himself. He'd wanted out of the neighborhood and to do his grandmother proud.

Gage put his hands up. "I can tell you're upset—"

"Do not patronize me. My feelings are real."

"I've been doing my job a long time. My hunch says Justin is involved. My hunches are rarely wrong. He knows something. If you're smart, you won't keep him around. Let him find employment in another town. Your father has enough problems without this kid causing trouble."

"Have you become a police officer who accuses everyone before they have all the facts? Are you any good at this job of yours, or are you just a dad who's mad he caught his daughter rounding second base?" She didn't really know him anymore. Her mission had been to stay away from him. He could have burned out over the years. She certainly had.

She couldn't even believe Gage had a child. He had wasted no time falling into bed with another woman, but what did she expect? She had slapped his face when he was covered in blood and searching for her to help him. Only she couldn't help him.

"She's fifteen. Why am I explaining this to you? I've seen plenty of good kids do something stupid thinking they'll never get caught."

"I don't know a whole lot about Justin, but I do know he didn't commit this robbery."

He crossed his arms over his chest. "Is that what you've been doing this whole time you were away?"

"I'm not following. What do you think I've been doing?" Besides working two jobs to make ends meet and forming an attachment to her neighbor because she had no one in her life.

"Saving the world. Have you been trying to save the world so Ava wouldn't have died in vain?"

"I don't know what you're talking about." She dropped her gaze to the coffee. His piercing glare made heat travel from her chest to her scalp.

"Let me tell you something—you can't change the past. There isn't anything you can do now that will change how that night turned out. Believe me, I've already tried."

She would not side with him. They could not erase the fact Ajay pulled the trigger and fired the bullet that took her sister. They were not victims in this together. She fought a sob. The truth was, they were in this together. Both of their families had suffered. But if he had been paying attention, if he had not pushed Ajay away when he needed Gage most, their lives would be so much different today.

"When are you going to forgive me for being Ajay's brother?" He leaned in close enough she could smell his spicy scent.

"Every time I look at you, I see him."

He pounded his fist on the counter and walked out of the room. He slammed the front door, making it rattled in its frame.

She dropped down in a chair and held her head in her hands.

"I'm sorry," she said to no one.

Chapter Six

Gage slid open the door to the barn and inhaled. The smells of feed, grain, horse blankets, ammonia, and minty medicated mouthwash mingled together and assaulted his nose. Up in the loft, the place held the sweet smell of hay, but down here, no matter how clean Jett kept the barn, the distinct barn smell lingered.

As the oldest of five boys, Gage should have wanted to be the one to run the ranch. He had become "the man of the house" at twelve when his dad died of a heart attack out in the acreage. He had helped his mother as much as he could, and when college called, he went and used it as his excuse to find another career.

His mother had understood. She never judged him. She had set him and Kace free. Jett and Lock had taken to the ranch the way their parents had. Ajay had been rebellious, but their mom had faith he'd settle down and stick around. He loved the horses. Especially Silver Bell. His horse.

Gage went down to Silver Bell's stall. She snorted as he approached. "Hey, old girl." He rubbed her white coat and ran his fingers over her soft, silky mane.

His parents had bought each boy a horse when they were born. His horse had been gone for some years now as were Jett's, Kace's, and Lock's. Silver Bell still moved around even at thirty-three. It was as if she knew what happened to her owner and was determined to stay alive in his place.

Her coat lightened over the years, going from gray to all white, but she was still beautiful and other than memories, the last thing Gage had of his brother. And not all those reminders were good.

"How are you feeling today?"

She nudged his hand, and he pulled out the carrots in his pocket. "I can't fool you. I'm sorry I haven't been out to visit. I've been busy with work." He had been so busy he didn't even go for a run anymore, but he could have made time. "Jett and Izzi are taking good care of you. Want to go for a walk?"

He opened the stall door, grabbed the lead, and led her out. He'd walk her to the pasture for some exercise before he went to work. He wouldn't ride her today. Jett had taken her out for light exercise yesterday, and her muscles would need a day or two to recover. She might not appreciate his large frame on her back.

The sun warmed his skin, but a soft breeze pushed through the trees. The picture-perfect day did nothing to ease the knots in his neck. "She's back, Bell."

He had a ritual of spending time with the horse every morning before work. He had stayed away more and more, making one excuse after another. He had promised Ajay he would take care of her. It was one promise that shouldn't have been hard to keep, but recently it was. Maybe because he was getting older and so was Silver Bell.

He had believed that with time he and Ajay would have had long talks out on the ranch, but there hadn't been enough time. He talked to the horse instead.

"She's been home before this, so why does this time make me want to punch something? Maybe it was the robbery. I can't have robberies happening in my town weeks before the Fourth. They can't happen ever, but especially now."

He led Silver Bell to a nearby tree.

"This is a good place to spend some time." He sent Jett a text telling him he took Bell out and left her in the shade.

"I wanted to protect her the night the robbery happened. Like before. She would not want me to do that. The look on her face said it all."

He and Calista had dated on and off through college, but when he came home and joined the police academy, they became serious. They talked about marriage and a family. She only had her sister and her parents. She wanted a big family like his, and he was more than ready to give her exactly that. Even out there under the tree with Silver Bell, he could recall Calista's sweet scent and the way she smiled up at him when they'd made love.

Then the tragedy happened. The image of Ajay pointing that gun was seared behind his eyelids. Gage had been a rookie cop and had frozen in place. Time had slowed and sped up the way it did in a nightmare. The sound of thunder had rumbled through the air, but it hadn't been the weather. Ajay fired the gun. He stumbled back from the recoil. Ava's face filled with horror first, then knowledge next. More guns fired. Dark red blood spread out from the center of Ajay's shirt. He clutched his chest and fell.

Gage's phone buzzed. A text from Jett.

—*Andy Hartman is here to see you. Can you come to the main house, or should I tell him you're not around?*—

It was early for a visitor. Or had the man spent the night and Jett just caught him on the way out?

—*You sure he's not here to see Mom?*—

—*Shut up.*—

He laughed. Andy Hartman had no romantic interest in their mother. He saw the Rykers as the enemy just as much as Calista saw him that way. —*I'll be right there. Silver Bell is staying outside.*—

"See you soon. I promise not to stay away so long this time. Enjoy the grass." He patted the horse and trotted back to the house.

Andy waited for him on the front porch. His white hair fell in strands above his eyes, which were red behind his glasses. His nose spread across his face from too much drinking. He usually wore a white button-down shirt. Gage thought white dress shirts were the only thing Andy owned, but today a gray pullover sat in its place.

"Everything okay?" He stood on the long step beside Andy.

"Do you know who the kid is that Calista hired?"

Better than he wanted to admit. "I met him yesterday at your place. Why?"

"I don't like him, and I don't want him working there. Can you convince her? Because she won't listen to me."

"Me? She isn't going to listen to me, Andy. My mother would have better luck with that. But why don't you like him?"

"Those tattoos, for one. I know my place needs a little TLC, but not what she's suggesting. She doesn't understand. We had plenty of guests last month."

A couple who wanted their money back because

the room smelled like fried food and the place didn't resemble the photos on the website. They had made so much noise Andy called for him and Barry to come over and escort his guests out.

"A little paint won't hurt." He wanted to help her. Pleading her case in a small way would be the only opportunity he would get.

"I don't want that kid in my house. Have you found out anything on the robbery?"

"Barry is asking the neighbors, but I doubt they heard or saw anything. You're too secluded."

"That's nonsense. Someone must've seen something. I want someone arrested for this. I have a reputation to uphold. You need to do your job."

A bitter taste filled his mouth. "We're working on it and the last robbery. Why don't you head home and help Calista today? Your time would be better spent with a hammer and a few nails than standing on my family's front porch."

"I'm not lifting a finger until she fires that boy. We don't need a handyman." Andy ambled off the porch and slid into his car.

"What was that all about?" Jett pushed through the front door as Andy drove away. He wore his baseball cap backward, and his flannel shirt was open over a white T-shirt.

"Nothing important."

"He didn't come, then, to apologize to Mom for always playing the guilt card with her."

"Do you think he might have a crush on her?" He had seen stranger things, and Andy had called her to lend him money.

"He'd better not even dream about it. I'll take him

on a little hunting trip he might not return from if he tries to date Mom."

"You realize you're speaking to the sheriff of the town. I can have you arrested for planning a crime."

"You're my stupid big brother before you're the sheriff. You don't have the balls to arrest me."

"Is there a point to all your anger? I have to get to work."

"I feel like picking a fight with someone, and Andy seems like a good enough choice."

"You're going to fight someone old enough to be your father? What's really going on?"

Jett removed his cap and scratched at the top of his head. "I had to turn away two families who wanted to book the week of the Fourth. We're already booked solid. I'm not complaining, but I can't afford to let business go like that. I tried to get them to schedule another time this summer, but they only wanted that week. Their memory of us will be how they couldn't get what they wanted. They won't be back."

"They might think if the place is booked up, they should try earlier next year. We must be doing something right."

"It doesn't always work that way."

"How about you send them to the Hartman and let them use our services at a discount?" The money would help Andy and Calista. He would have done something to help her, and she wouldn't be able to shove him away.

"You know, you're not so stupid after all." Jett laughed and shoved his cap back on his head. "I'll go give them a call." He turned but stopped. "You know, I was about to throw you out of your cottage so they could stay for the week."

"What? I pay rent, asshole."

"Keep your pants on. I would never do that to Izzi. Listen, my horse trainer quit too. I hate to ask you this, but can you take a few people out on the horses this weekend?"

"I'm working this weekend."

"It's just for a few hours. The town can take care of itself, and you have Pearce. I need you. Lock is taking some of the guests hiking into the mountain."

"Did you ask Kace?"

"He has a race in Wyoming. I tried to find a backup, but there isn't anyone on this short notice. And I can trust you. I can't trust just anyone with the horses or the guests."

"Mom can't do it?"

"She's trying to retire, Gage. She deserves that. She's worked hard all these years. It's one damn afternoon. The ranch isn't that bad."

"I never said it was."

"But you'd rather be anywhere but here. I can't figure you out."

"I wanted to be something other than a rancher. Figuring me out isn't that hard. Why do you keep bringing my career choice up? Haven't we had this conversation enough times?" Jett had been grilling him forever about leaving the family business for something else.

"I think you didn't want to be like Dad. There's no shame in what we do. I'm proud of us. You should be too."

He didn't want to admit that Jett was right. By the time Gage started high school, he was tired of the ranch. He could never get the smell off him at night. It was in his hair and on his clothes. The kids in class teased him for being a farmer, even though his family wasn't really. He didn't want to spend his life working so hard he'd end up dead in a field for hours before someone found him.

It was bad enough he had to come home with his tail between his legs, needing his mother to help him raise Izzi. If he ended up working on the ranch too, what would he have to show for his life? He would have gone nowhere and accomplished nothing. At least as the sheriff, he could keep order. "I'll think about it."

"I'll take that as a yes. Thanks, man. I appreciate it. The tour goes out at eight a.m. An hour out and an hour back. You know the route."

"Can I take Silver Bell?"

"I don't think she should work that hard. The trail is too rough for her. Take Kit Kat."

"Kit Kat hates me."

"She hates everyone." Jett laughed. "I need to check on the breakfast. I'll catch you later. And thanks."

"Yeah." He was going to regret this.

****

Gage jogged back to his cottage from the main house, still thinking about taking the guests on a ride. It was the last thing he wanted to do because he had a town to run and crimes to solve, but he wouldn't tell his brother no. When one of his brothers needed something, he made sure they had it. He'd learned his lesson the hard way. He didn't make the same mistakes twice, which was why after his failed marriage he never wanted another long-term commitment.

Unfortunately, the woman in his dreams had returned and screwed with his practical side. He changed into his uniform and found Izzi packing up for school.

"Izzi, I'm leaving for work. Do you want me to drive you to school?" He shoved his phone and his keys in his pockets.

"Dad, you promised I could ride my bike the last two weeks." Her thumbs tapped away at her phone.

"Please look at me when you speak. I don't think riding that far is a great idea."

"Dad, you said." She took her gaze off the phone and twisted her voice into a whine.

When she pouted to get her way, it cemented how young she still was. How could she be the same person he found untangling herself from a boy? He could tell her the bike-riding privileges were revoked due to recent behavior, but that would make her hate him. He didn't want that. At least not today. He let out a long breath. "Be careful."

"Thank you, Daddy." She flung herself into his arms, kissed his cheek, and pushed away before he could grab on and savor the moment. Her strawberry scent lingered around him like a reminder of her as a preschooler when he had all the answers to her questions.

"Come straight home after school," he said to her retreating back.

She heaved her backpack over her shoulder and closed the door. Shutting him out. He wanted time to stand still for just a minute or tick backward to a simpler place. Since neither of those things was going to happen, he headed for work and convinced himself he could control a thing or two.

He made one stop before pulling into the parking lot of the sheriff's department. He had skipped breakfast because of his visit with Silver Bell, and bought a dozen donuts for the office. He was a walking cliché, but he had a sweet tooth.

"Sheriff Ryker, how many times do I have to tell you not to bring fried dough into my office? My hips can't take it." Phyllis Jump glared at him with wide brown eyes from behind her uncluttered metal desk that shared the space with his deputy, who wasn't anywhere to be seen.

Phyllis had worked here long before he became the sheriff. She'd probably started when the paneling went up on the walls to cover the peeling plaster. She knew every detail and secret floating around Backwater and could run this office with her eyes closed. Plus, she scared him a little.

Her red glasses were plopped on top of her head. Her long gray hair, streaked with brown from her early years, was pulled back from her lined face. She was tall and thin but not frail. Mrs. Jump could hit a bullseye at three hundred feet with her shotgun. When he took the job, he hadn't wanted to replace her for fear she would hunt him down.

He opened the box and held it under her nose. The smell of sugar filled the air around them. "I bought the pink one with sprinkles for you."

She blushed and waved him away with her paperwork. "Oh, pooh. You're trying to clog my arteries so I have to retire."

"Sorry, Phyllis. You can't retire until I do."

She placed the pink donut on a napkin. Then she

came around the desk and took the box from him. "I'll be dead by then, young man. I remember the moment you came into this world yelling your head off."

"You're going to outlive us all." His mother had told the story a million times, how Phyllis was her ride to the hospital after her water broke and his father was out in the fields.

"Are you implying I'm a vampire?" She locked the box in the three-drawer filing cabinet and pocketed the key.

He cocked an eyebrow at her. "Give me the key."

"Absolutely not. You'll eat the whole dozen by the end of the day. Every time you pass the box, you'll grab one. You can have one tomorrow."

"I already have a mother. She doesn't look like you. She's a lot shorter for one, and she doesn't have a long, pointy nose, green skin, and a black hat sewn to her head."

"Sheriff Ryker, I believe I'm being harassed. I'm going to be forced to issue a report. You've insulted me twice in two minutes." She threw her head back, slapped her leg, and burst out laughing at her own joke.

He couldn't help but laugh too. "If you thought someone was harassing you, you'd box them on the ears."

"Bet your ass I would." She grabbed a notepad and pulled her glasses down from her head. "Now, I've received three calls already this morning about the robbery over at the Hartman. Does Barry have any leads I don't know about?"

"No." It pained him to admit that.

"I feared that much. What do you want me to tell these people? Logger is threatening to camp out on our doorstep until we arrest someone. I don't want that farmer leaving dirt all over my recently swept steps."

"No one wants to steal his dried peas. What's he worried about?"

"He isn't happy unless he's complaining."

"Tell whoever asks we're working on finding the suspect. They would rather I take out a full-page ad with the criminal in handcuffs, but that's not real life."

"I could take out an ad of Logger in his long johns," Phyllis said.

He resisted the urge to laugh at the truth in that statement. "Don't make my job harder than it is. I'll go talk to the neighbors near the Hartman, but I doubt anyone saw anything." He wanted another shot at that punk sucking face with Izzi. He'd take a ride by the B and B later this afternoon for another try. "Any other calls?"

She flipped the page of her notebook. "The mayor called. He wants to go over security for the parade, the concert, and the pie social."

"Tell him it's the same as last year." He and Barry would keep a watchful eye. A few of the firefighters with some police training usually volunteered during the town's three-day celebration for the Fourth. The budget didn't allow for him to hire more officers.

"With the robbery being the second in a month, he wants more. He'll be here at one to meet with you. I told him I didn't control you. I couldn't promise him you'd be here. I tried to give you a way out."

"You are an angel. Now please let me have one of my donuts." He'd leave the office by lunchtime and stop at the Hartman. Hopefully, Calista's new hire would be there. And he had to admit he didn't mind the idea of seeing her again.

"So now I'm an angel. Make up your mind, Sheriff. Angel or the wicked witch." She pointed a finger at him.

"Wicked witch. If you don't hand over that key." He held out his palm.

"I'll need to get a better hat. One more thing."

"What's that?" He was going to have to buy more donuts.

"Margo said someone is pinching all her tomatoes at the market. She wants a surveillance camera installed, and since the market is outside on public property, she thinks the sheriff's department should be responsible for doing it."

"She does, does she?" When he returned to Backwater to raise Izzi with his mother's help, giving up real police work didn't seem like such a sacrifice. Now he wondered if he'd been wrong about that.

"I told her you'd get right on it."

"Definitely the wicked witch." The people of his town relied on him, and he did like the way his chest filled with pride when he thought about that. He needed to find the scumbags committing robbery so his residents didn't lose faith in him.

Phyllis leaned a hip against the metal desk. "Seriously, Gage, who do you think robbed the B and B? Why would someone do that? Backwater is a safe little town. Nobody here wants to hurt anyone else."

"I suspect the criminal doesn't live in Backwater. They found their way to us. We'll stop them before it happens again." Though he wasn't entirely sure how without more evidence.

Phyllis was right about Backwater. The worst

crime he'd seen was someone racing the yellow light on Main Street, and that person had been a tourist. In fact, most trouble came from the tourists. He'd need to ask around at the café and the bookstore too. A motel out on the highway booked up during the Fourth. The motel was close enough for tourists to come and go during the festivities. He could check there too.

"You don't think Andy has a gambling debt or something, do you?" She flipped her glasses back to the top of her head. "You know, someone who wanted to make good on what he owed?"

"I hope not, and that doesn't explain the other robbery." It wouldn't be much of a stretch, since Andy's drinking seemed to be picking up, but he didn't believe it. Andy was a lost soul in need of some tender loving care. He would nose around in that area just to make sure. Maybe his mother knew something.

The phone jangled its ring into the office. Phyllis slid off the desk. "Backwater Sheriff's Department. Phyllis speaking."

He went into his private office and shut the door. If the call was for him, she could patch it through. If it wasn't, she'd handle it.

He stared out the window toward the street. People went by on bicycles. A few cars hurried to their destinations. He couldn't see Main Street from this window, but there would be people strolling up and down the cobblestone walk in front of the stores.

Which one of them could have robbed the B and B? Was it the old guy with long white hair and a beard? Or was it the man walking with him? Could it be the couple on the bicycle built for two? Everyone was a suspect as far as he was concerned, but his gut churned when he thought of Justin.

He would need to learn more about Justin whatever his last name was. What he already knew, he didn't like.

The intercom on his phone buzzed. "Gage, Izzi is here. Before you—" Phyllis's voice filled the room.

"I'll be right out." He didn't wait for her to finish. Izzi should be at school by now.

He flung open the office door. "Isabelle Ryker, you'd better have a good reason for not being at school."

His daughter's knees were scraped, and blood trickled down her shins. The ponytail she had pulled her hair into earlier that morning hung limply by her ear. The mascara she wore—and he hated—left streaks under her water-filled eyes. She gnawed on her bottom lip, but he didn't miss the tremble in her chin.

"What happened?" He leaped forward. "Phyllis, get—"

"Already have it. Come sit down, sweetie." Phyllis led Izzi to a chair and helped her into it. She tucked stray hairs behind Izzi's ear, then handed her a cloth. "Can you wipe up your legs?"

Izzi nodded and took the cloth.

He squatted down to look her in the eye. He really didn't want her riding her bicycle from the ranch to school. He should have trusted his gut this morning. The school was several miles away from where they lived. But she wanted the independence. He had told her a flat-out no the first time she asked, but his mother took him aside and set him straight. "Did you fall?"

She nodded again and pressed the cloth to her mouth. "It was so stupid. Someone was calling my name. I turned to look over my shoulder. When I glanced back, a car swerved too close to me. I had to turn the bike too quickly to get out of the way. I hit the curb and went flying over the handlebars."

Kace had helped Izzi find the bike. He also read him the riot act on being too tough on her. For his second youngest brother, bike riding was nothing compared to the cars he raced. Sometimes Kace just didn't understand his fears. And other fears Kace understood too much.

"Do you know what kind of car it was?" He would hunt down this reckless driver.

"Like something Uncle Kace might drive."

A sports car. Low to the ground with an engine that growled. "How about the color?"

"Black or dark gray. Or maybe blue. The sun was in my eyes too."

Phyllis handed her a cup of water. "Who called your name, sweetie?"

Izzi took a few sips. He pushed up off his haunches and paced the room. He wanted to tear his hair out of his head or out of the head of the person who'd done this.

"I think it was Justin."

Gage stopped. His hands fisted. "Are you sure?"

"No. It kind of looked like him, but everything happened so fast. I could be wrong. It wasn't his fault anyway. It was the car. It was so close I could feel the heat coming off it."

"It was just an accident." Phyllis squeezed Izzi's shoulder. "I can put a report together just to have something on file. Let's get some bandages on your knees."

"I don't want to go to school." Izzi's gaze met his.

He pinched the bridge of his nose. What was the right thing to do in this moment? "Why not?"

"Look at me. I'm dirty. And my bike is mangled."

"Did you leave your bike? What road were you on?" He could call Kace and ask him to grab it.

"I walked it here from Ponderosa Pine. It's outside. Can Uncle Kace fix it?"

"We'll see how bad it is. If you're not hurt, I think you should go to school."

"I knew you'd say that." She bunched the cloth in her hands. "Why can't I take a mental health day? I almost got run over."

"But you didn't, and that's what matters. I can drive you home to change if you want."

Phyllis eyed him from behind Izzi. He knew what she was thinking with that eyebrow cocked. His mother would probably say the same thing. But Izzi could not duck out of life just because something went wrong. She had to face the tough stuff. She wasn't going to end up like Ajay, running from responsibility.

Izzi stood and threw the cloth down. "I don't want you to drive me. I'll walk." She turned to Phyllis. "Thank you for helping me."

"You're welcome, sweetie. Before you go, do you want a donut? Your dad brought some in this morning." Phyllis scrambled for the key to open the filing cabinet. She presented the box to Izzi.

Izzi eyed him, as if to dare him to tell her no. She chose the chocolate glaze. "Thanks. I didn't eat breakfast."

Phyllis hugged her and smoothed her hair. "Are you sure you're okay?"

Izzi nodded. "I have to get to school."

"You'll need a note." He reached for a piece of paper.

"No, I won't. When Mrs. Schneider sees my knees, she won't question me." Izzi limped out the door without another look back.

He flopped into the chair by Phyllis's desk and wiped a hand over his face. "She's going to be the death of me."

She took her seat behind her desk and dropped her glasses on her nose. "If you want my opinion—"

"I don't."

She shrugged and tapped at her keyboard. "A young lady is not a deputy in a sheriff's department."

He pushed out of the chair. "What are you getting at?"

"Nothing at all. Just making an observation."

"Phyllis, please don't bust my nuts. I've had enough of that for one day." He pushed outside into the warm morning.

Izzi's bike lay on the ground by the steps, with the front tire bent in half. She had somehow snaked the lock around the twisted handlebars and the railing. He didn't have a key to the lock. He'd have to cut the chain. He heaved a sigh and pulled out his phone.

"Ryker's Garage." Kace's voice came through on the third ring.

"It's me."

"I saw that on the screen."

"Why didn't you just say hello, then?"

" 'Cause I never get tired of hearing my own name. What's up?"

"Izzi fell off her bike. It's pretty banged up."

"Is she all right? You need me to come to the hospital?"

His brothers would do anything for him. And he would do the same. All he had to do was ask, and one or all of them would be there. "No hospital. She's a little bruised but okay. She went to school and locked her bike on the steps of the department. Any chance you can come and cut the chain and then fix it for her?"

Kace's laugh hurt his head.

"I'm not laughing that she fell. I'm laughing because there's a pretty good chance she locked that bike up and left without giving you the key because you pissed her off."

"Funny."

"Shit, she's so much like you at that age it scares me. You made her go to school, didn't you?"

"Kace, just answer the question. Can you come? I can't leave her bike here." And he wanted to fix it for her so she wouldn't be so mad at him.

"All right. All right. I'll be there in five." Kace ended the call.

He waited on the steps until his brother pulled his red pickup into the lot. Kace jumped out, adjusting his greasy baseball cap. He reached into the back of the truck and grabbed the chain cutters.

"This is going to cost you." Kace's smile showed all his bright, white teeth.

"It already has. Just tell me how much to get it looking like new."

Kace snapped the chain in two with a grunt. "I'm not going to charge you, prick. Though I could use a few hours of help in the garage. I'm short-staffed again."

"Let me know when. I'll be there." He often pitched in at the garage when Kace needed an extra pair of hands. Just as he'd told Jett he would take that tour out, even though he'd rather not.

He had promised his father while standing over his gravesite that he would watch out for all his brothers. Since he let Ajay down, he would never let another brother need something from him—even when he'd rather be doing something else.

Kace laughed again. "Man, you're gullible. I don't need your help. I just wanted to see what you'd say."

He punched Kace on the arm.

"How about you work my pit crew with me sometime? I'd like to have my big brother standing by." Kace wiped his hands on his pants, which were as greasy as his hat.

"Sure. But you know I'll help out at the garage if you need me."

"I know you will. Take this and walk to the truck with me." Kace handed him the cutters and carried the bike to his truck. "Are you holding up okay?" He lifted the bike into the pickup's bed.

"Why wouldn't I be?" He placed the cutters beside the bike with a clang.

Kace arched an eyebrow. A Ryker-man twitch. "It's June. Backwater is getting busier with crazy tourists. The Fourth is coming. We've had two robberies, and one involved you know who."

"I'm fine." As long as he stayed focused on work and keeping Izzi safe, he'd be fine. The Fourth would come and go. The summer would end before he knew it because he'd be too busy to notice the time, and then the quiet days of fall would be around him. He couldn't wait.

"I say this to you every year. What happened wasn't your fault. Ava Hartman was in the wrong place at the wrong time. Ajay was the fuckup. Stop dragging this shit around." Kace squared his shoulders and met his gaze with his dark, stern one.

He would drag around the guilt of letting Ajay down until he was in the ground. His baby brother had come to him and asked for help, but he'd pushed him away. He had grown tired of Ajay's mistakes. He wanted him to straighten up, and he had thought a little tough love was the answer until Ajay looked up at him from the ground with blood running out of his mouth. He had begged Gage to save him.

"What are you going to do about Calista?" Kace's words shocked him out of the past.

"She's back in town for a few weeks. I can handle it." He hoped he sounded believable, but his voice rang hollow.

"She came into Kennedy's while I was having a drink."

"That's not surprising. They used to be best friends." He checked his phone, as if he couldn't care less about Calista's whereabouts. He assumed she and Kennedy were still close. Kennedy had been giving him the cold shoulder for years.

"I overheard Calista offering to work a shift or two."

He might be staying out of Kennedy's Pub while Calista was in town. If she stayed permanently, he would have to find a new place to have a drink on a Friday night.

"Were you there alone sitting at the bar and flirting

with the pretty owner?" He'd been meaning to bring this up to Kace. He couldn't let the chance pass by even though what his brother did in his spare time should be none of his fucking business.

"I'm not flirting. And I wasn't there alone. Jett came with me."

"You dragged Jett, more like it. I heard you fixed her flat the other day."

"She needed help. I would do that for anyone." Kace swung his keys on his finger.

His turn to cock a brow. "You're walking a fine line. I don't want you to get hurt. She isn't ready to start dating."

"Shut up, big brother. Kennedy doesn't want anything to do with me. She's made that perfectly clear."

"Like when you tried to kiss her?"

"That was an accident. She tripped over the barstool and landed in my lap. Her face fell against mine." Kace's top lip curled up.

"You lost track of how many drinks you had and swept her off her feet."

"Stop worrying. I don't want anything to do with her like that. We're just friends. You should stay away from Calista Hartman, though. She's no good for you."

"I think we were just talking about you."

"Now we're talking about you staying away from the woman who has done nothing good for you. You lost someone that night too. She never took that into account."

Kace had been the one to drag Calista away when she clawed at his face. He never forgave her. Kace believed she hadn't cared that Ajay was shot too. That wasn't fair. She wasn't heartless. She just cared more that she lost her sister senselessly.

"Other than the investigation, I'm not going near her." Even though he couldn't stop thinking about her standing on that deck the other night. Or yesterday morning when he found her still ruffled from sleep. She eased into his thoughts the way the quiet mountains eased his worries or a long run eased his stress.

"Let Barry run with the investigation. You don't need to get involved with a simple robbery. You've got more important things to do than that."

"Yeah? Like what? Finding out who pinched Margo's tomatoes?" He kicked the dirt.

"That's Ross Nettle. He wants to ask her out." Kace hitched a leg into his truck and kicked over the engine.

"Seriously?"

"That old geezer shows up at the farmers' market every Saturday and paces back and forth near her table, hoping for a chance to talk to her. She pays him no attention. He squeezes tomatoes when she isn't looking. He wants to get caught."

He shoved the truck door shut for his brother. "How do you know this?"

"The old men at the diner on Sunday mornings. Not one of them can hear. They all yell."

"You're as bad as Mom. You know that?"

Kace flashed his bright smile. "Nah. I don't meddle. I just listen. I'll bring the bike around tonight. Maybe eight or nine. Is that too late?"

"I appreciate it. Thanks."

Phyllis opened a window and stuck her head out. "Sheriff Ryker, your services are needed. It looks like someone knocked over Millie's azaleas. She has dirt all over her front walk. She wants to press charges. I told her you'd be there in five minutes."

Kace burst out laughing.

"You watch yourself, Kace Ryker. Show some respect to your elders." Phyllis pointed a finger at him. She slammed shut the window.

"She hates me."

"You need to sweet-talk her more. I'd better get to work." He patted Kace on the shoulder and backed away from the truck. "I'll see you tonight."

"Don't go near Calista Hartman." Kace narrowed his eyes and spun his tires on his way out of the parking lot.

He should listen to his brother, and he would if a crime wasn't involved. It was his responsibility to investigate. Barry couldn't handle the whole thing by himself. He'd bet money on the culprit being Justin. He just needed the proof.

If that punk had anything to do with Izzi getting hurt, he'd lock that kid up for good. He'd make up a charge if he had to.

He unlocked his cruiser and slid inside. He'd stay away from Calista as soon as his job was done. Then she'd be gone, and he could go on pretending he didn't still think about her late at night.

But first, a stop about some azaleas.

Chapter Seven

"Thanks, Kennedy. I appreciate you giving me the extra work." Calista pushed open the front door of the B and B and left the warm afternoon outside. Her shoulder kept the phone against her ear while she juggled the bags full of fresh vegetables. The money in her bank account seemed to disappear into the air like sun-kissed fog. She wouldn't be able to buy groceries next month if she didn't find some kind of employment.

"You're the one helping me. The nights are getting busier thanks to summer. My favorite time of year. Besides, I miss having you around." Kennedy's voice drifted through the phone.

The front room smelled of fresh paint. She had neglected her friendship with Kennedy over the years. She often canceled on plans to meet between their two towns because Kennedy was too much of a reminder of what she lost. But Kennedy would never allow her to completely end the friendship. "I miss you too. I'll see you later."

"Later." Kennedy ended the call.

She slid her phone into the back pocket of her jeans. Justin rolled white paint over the walls as if he'd been doing it for decades. The windows had been covered with plastic to protect them from splatter. He had hardly dripped any of the paint on the floor tarps. Only some of the white paint drizzled on his arms. He was a natural.

"You've done a great job, Justin."

"That's what I keep telling him." Izzi sat perched on the arm of the sofa pushed to the center of the room with the other furniture draped in drop cloths. Bandages covered both her knees.

"Ya think so? That's cool," Justin said.

She had been surprised when Justin walked in with Izzi about an hour ago. Her first thought had been that Gage would be close behind, and she had tamped down the excitement the idea brought. But it didn't take long to figure out these two were trying to steal a moment in time the way young people did. Not all that long ago, she'd been a young woman with a very adult-size crush on the handsome Gage Ryker.

She recognized the look in Izzi's eyes and the way she leaned in with a blush on her cheeks every time Justin spoke. He either didn't notice or was very good at playing it cool.

Justin flashed his crooked smile and moved the paint tray. "I can start the dining room tomorrow if you want."

"That would be great. Izzi, do you want to help me pull a snack together? I've got some veggies and hummus." She hitched a thumb over her shoulder toward the kitchen.

"Um. Okay." Izzi hopped off the sofa arm and followed her.

Calista pulled celery and carrots from the bags. She washed her hands and grabbed the cutting board. "Do you want to cut?"

Izzi also took a turn at the sink before slicing the vegetables into various sizes. Calista shoved chickpeas into the blender.

"What are those beads on your wrist?" Izzi pointed with the utensil.

She glanced down, almost forgetting the bracelets she wore every day. "Mala beads. They're for meditation and relaxation."

"They're nice. Where did you get them?"

"I made them. We could make some together if you're interested."

The words had popped out without thought, and now she couldn't take them back. She shouldn't spend time with Gage's daughter. Her heart couldn't handle the pain when she went back to Billings and left Izzi behind. But the desire to know the one person who meant so much to him crept into her brain and slithered around, wanting to take hold. Sometimes she wondered what their child would have been like, but she never stayed on that thought long. It only accomplished carving another hole in her already-broken heart.

"I'd like that." Izzi kept her gaze on the food.

She slid the bracelet with brown wood beads off her wrist and handed it over. The small gesture didn't have to mean anything, and yet it meant too much. "Here. Take this one until we make you a set."

"I can't take that. It's yours."

She kept her arm extended, even though Izzi had given her a way out. She doubted Izzi knew about Calista's past with her father. There would have been no reason to share it. Still, Izzi hesitated. "Go ahead. It's fine."

Izzi's smile lit up her face, and she slid on the bracelet. "Wow. Thank you. That's very nice."

"My pleasure. So are you and Justin dating?" She

continued to allow the need to get to know Izzi better swarm around and stir up feelings that should lie dormant.

This girl could have been hers. Would she and the daughter she never had have stood together in this very kitchen and shared secrets? She had never been close with her own mother. Her mother's emotional needs had always come ahead of her children's. When she finally left after Ava's death, Calista hadn't been all that surprised.

"My dad won't allow me to see Justin. He picked me up after school today. I didn't want to take the bus home. My bike needs to be fixed. My uncle thought he'd have it done by now, but something came up with his race car." Izzi switched from cutting the celery to cutting the carrots.

"Kace still races?" He was always the daredevil. She squeezed lemon juice into the blender.

"As often as he can. Is this okay?" Izzi pointed to the pile of carrots too small to dip into anything.

"Perfect. Did you grow up in Backwater?" Where was the woman Gage made a child with? She had never asked questions about him when she visited her father. She kept her times home too short for catching up.

"Yup. My whole life. We live on the ranch with my Gammy and Uncle Jett. But you probably know that."

She didn't. "Your dad and I didn't keep in touch."

"Oh. Well, we moved back when I was two. I think. Something like that. Right when my parents divorced."

He must have married soon after they broke up. She scooped the hummus out of the blender and into a bowl. She had so many questions, but none she could ask this young lady. "I'm sorry your parents are divorced. Does your mom live nearby?"

"She lives in New Mexico. Anyway, I'm another Ryker raised in Backwater. My dad wants me to go to college and then come back to town like everyone else in the family did, but I don't know what I want to do yet. I like Backwater, but there's a whole world to see."

The mother was in another state. How could that woman want to be away from her beautiful daughter? If she had a child like Izzi, especially Gage's child, she would die before being more than a minute away from her. "You should go see the world and then decide if Backwater is right for you."

"That's what Gammy says. I don't think my dad is on board. I don't have to decide now. I'm only fifteen." She shrugged. "Do you have a tray or something to put these on?"

She pulled two bowls from the broken cabinet and handed them over. "Let's see if Justin is ready to take a break."

Justin wiped paint from the rollers with a rag. "Yes. Food. I'm starving."

Izzi handed him the bowl. His crooked smile burst wide. Izzi ducked her head and tucked her hair behind her ear. Gage wasn't going to like this. He had been furious the other morning when he spoke to Justin. She really didn't want to be the adult who spoiled all the fun, but she probably shouldn't give these two a place to meet. She would have to pull Justin aside later and make the suggestion he not visit with Izzi too often.

"I should be going. It's getting late. Thanks for letting me hang out, Calista." Izzi shook her wrist.

She checked her phone. "How are you getting home? Is your grandmother coming to pick you up?"

"I thought I'd walk home."

"All the way from here? Does your dad know where you are?" If Gage found out she allowed Izzi to walk from the B and B to the ranch, he'd arrest her and throw away the key. And he'd be right to do it.

"Um, no. Technically I'm grounded." A blush crept up her cheeks.

"I told her to let me drop her home. I don't want her dad really hating on me." Justin scooped hummus with a carrot and shoved it in his mouth.

"I'll handle my dad. As long as I'm home before he is, he won't even know."

"This might not be my place, but I don't think you should lie to your dad. He was always a rule follower. I'll drive you home." She searched for her keys.

Justin chomped on a carrot. "If you can wait five minutes, I'll take you."

The front door opened. She caught her breath. Gage filled out the doorway with his broad shoulders and six feet, four inches. His brown eyes were hooded, and end-of-the-day scruff dotted his jaw. Heat ran over her skin. She pulled a hand through her hair and wished he didn't always look so damn good.

"Hello, Sheriff Ryker." Her voice rescued her heart.

"Hi, Dad." Izzi's face bloomed red.

"Isabelle, you are grounded. What are you doing here?" Gage held up his phone for Izzi to see.

"I hate that app. Why do you need to track everywhere I go? I was about to leave anyway." She grabbed her backpack and phone.

"You are supposed to go home straight from school. I don't want you anywhere else, and I sure as hell don't want you hanging out with him." Gage pointed at Justin.

"They weren't doing anything wrong. He's been working, and I've been here the whole time." A little white lie wouldn't hurt anything. She had only been gone thirty minutes to get groceries.

"He is too old for her, Calista. It's against the law, for Christ's sake."

"Gage, come on. They're kids." She wanted to break that stubborn streak of his. He always wanted his way. Even if their tragedy hadn't happened, they would never have been able to make a life together. He could never bend, and she was too much like the wind.

"Wait for me out in the car. I have some official business here, and then I'll take you home. Uncle Jett needs help putting Silver Bell to bed." He handed Izzi his keys.

"Thank you for having me, Calista. Bye, Justin." Izzi tucked her hair behind her ear.

"See ya." Justin nodded with a carrot poised.

"You're welcome any time, Izzi. I'll text you about the bracelets."

She scooted out the door, but not without a final glare for her father. Calista tried not to smile. Izzi Ryker was a lot like her father. He deserved that. He was being too tough on her.

"How can I help you?" She might as well get this official business over with. She didn't want Gage standing in her living room any longer than he needed to be.

"What bracelets are you talking about?" He

glanced from her to the door, then back again.

"Izzi and I are going to make mala bead bracelets." She held up her arm.

"Is that some kind of voodoo thing?"

Justin laughed, and Gage shot him a look. "They're cool, Sheriff Ryker. For yoga and stuff, right, Calista?"

"You know them?" She hoped her face didn't show the surprise that reverberated in her words.

"Sure. Steve Jazzy T wears them. He's that workout instructor on in the middle of the night. He wants you to buy his videos and shit. I mean, stuff. Sorry."

"Whatever they are, I don't know if I want her to have them. You should check with me first before making plans with her."

"The bracelets are harmless. It's just wood. I'm not corrupting her or anything. If it makes you feel better, we can do it at your house where you can keep a watchful eye." Now that he told her no, she wanted nothing more than to spend time with Izzi.

He cleared his throat. "I'll think about the bracelets. Have you made a list of the missing items?"

"I forgot." The day had slipped away from her. Justin had arrived early. She and her dad argued about Justin's presence in his house before the painting began. Before she knew it, Izzi sat on her couch listening to everything Justin said.

Gage heaved out a long breath. "Calista, I can't complete my report without that list."

"Can I email it to you later?" The missing items didn't matter. She couldn't afford to replace them without the insurance. Nothing would give her greater pleasure than to have this whole ordeal behind her so she could get on with her life. A life that didn't make much sense anymore, but it was still hers.

"I need it before tomorrow. I want to compare it to the things stolen from the last robbery."

"I'm heading out for the night. See you tomorrow." Justin saluted.

"Don't move." Gage pointed at him.

"Sheriff Ryker, may I have a word with you in the kitchen?" She forced a lightness she didn't feel into her voice.

"Does that mean I get to leave?" Justin flashed his crooked smile.

She was certain smoke came out of Gage's ears. She almost felt sorry for him wanting to control every situation and not being able to. "Can you hang out a few more minutes? I'm sure the sheriff has some questions he'd like to ask both of us."

"I'll stay for you." Justin plopped down on the drop cloth over the couch.

She turned on her heel and marched away, hoping Gage followed. She passed through the kitchen and out onto the deck. The pounding of his boots echoed behind her.

"Before you say a word about that kid in your living room, I meant what I said about Izzi. Don't make plans with her unless you check with me." He closed the door.

"She's old enough to make plans of her own. What's the big deal?"

"The big deal is I don't want you to be friends with my daughter. And why would you want to? You've made it perfectly clear how you feel about me." He crossed his arms over his powerful chest.

That wasn't the truth. She had battled her feelings for him for years. She'd lost her best friend and her parents all in a matter of seconds. She couldn't be with Gage anymore, but it didn't mean she didn't want to. She had chosen to show the anger that surfaced in order to keep herself safe from thoughts about the loss in her life. Thoughts that she had all the time.

"I'll stay away from your daughter." The words tasted as if they were made of dust. She would never take anything out on Izzi, but he thought she would. She had wanted him to stop loving her, and he had. She should be grateful.

"Thank you. Now why did you drag me out here?"

"Because I didn't want Justin to hear us. Why do you have to be so obstinate all the time? Do you realize teenagers will give you a lot more information if you don't talk to them as if you are their prison guard?" She tilted up her chin. She wanted to stand on a step stool and take away his height advantage.

"Why is my daughter hanging out at your place talking with that punk?" He inched closer.

She backed up into the deck railing. "He's not a punk. He's a kid. He's well behaved and has manners. He's never disrespectful of Izzi or me. Not every kid is bad."

"Because you've seen it?" He smirked.

Her hands collided with his hard chest, and she shoved him. Afraid her fingers would remember their way across his body, she yanked her hands back. His mouth fell open, but she hurried to speak before he could say anything.

"I think Justin is trying to change his circumstances. Kids like him want a better life off the reservation all the time. You need to lighten up on him and Izzi. Otherwise, you'll send her right into his arms and his bed."

"Whoa." He put his hands up in defense. "That's my little girl you're talking about."

"She's not that little, Gage. She's a young lady, and she's beautiful, smart, and funny." So much like her father it took Calista's breath away.

"I don't want her seeing him. That's my final word. I don't need any more parenting advice from you."

The words pummeled her. He was right. She had no place telling him what to do with his child. She had no place in his life, and that's how she had wanted it. Why did the separation hurt so much more now? "Still as stubborn as ever." She shook her head and laughed. "You won't be able to stop them. They'll find a way to be together."

He cleared the space between them in two steps. She had to look up to meet his smoldering gaze. Heat rolled off him and through her thin shirt.

"You don't know what you're talking about. I know my daughter better than anyone. She will listen to me, and she will not waste her life on a guy like him."

"Like what? Like your grandfather who bought a ranch and turned it into something special?"

He stepped back, but the set jaw remained. "That kid is nothing like my grandfather. They're not the same just because they come from the same reservation. Don't you dare compare them."

"You're upset because you caught them doing some heavy petting. You're being a dad before a sheriff. You have nothing to go on that points to Justin as the criminal. Not to mention you will smother your daughter if you won't allow her to make some of her own decisions. The world doesn't have to live by your rules."

"My rules keep her and everyone in this town safe. As long as she's under my roof, it's my rules. And as long as you're in my town, you'll do yourself a favor and follow my rules too."

"Or what?"

"I can arrest you." He crossed his arms over his chest again.

"Is that a threat, Sheriff Ryker? Because I don't believe the law protects harassing sheriffs."

"Go ahead and report me." He narrowed his eyes and curled his lip.

He was enjoying this. She would not give him that satisfaction. "I may just do that. You can't abuse your power."

"Deputy Sheriff Pearce is on call this evening. Do you want his number?" He reached into his pants pocket and pulled out his phone.

She turned her back to him. "Get out of my house, Sheriff. Your business here is done."

She closed her eyes and held her breath. She wanted him to come back across the deck and put his strong hands on her shoulders. She had wanted that for a long time, but she sealed her fate when she slapped him in front of everyone sixteen years ago.

She hadn't been thinking straight in that moment. Ajay had pulled a gun and pointed it right in Ava's direction. Ava had screamed at him to put it down. Ajay said something about her moving, but she walked toward him. The gun fired. Ava's hair fell over her face as she looked down. Calista couldn't see if she'd been hit, but Ava's legs gave way, and she slumped to the ground as if she were a graceful dancer.

Calista searched for Gage. She couldn't find him. No one was going to Ava. Someone was screaming. She found out later the screaming came from her. When everything was over, and the bodies had been taken away, Gage dragged himself over to her, covered in blood. Tears were in his eyes.

"I'm sorry," he said.

Sorry for what, she wanted to know. Sorry that he hadn't tried to save Ava first? He'd run to Ajay instead. He opened his mouth to respond, and she slapped it shut. Her palm hitting his face and the cracking sound it made still haunted her at night.

Now Gage closed the door without another word and left her on the deck.

Untouched and alone.

Chapter Eight

Gage cursed under his breath while he stood in Calista's kitchen. That woman could get under his skin like no one else. How dare she tell him how to be a parent? What did she know about raising kids? His job was to keep Izzi safe. It was the most important thing he would ever do, and he wouldn't fuck that up. No way.

He glanced out the door at her, still giving him her back. He wanted to walk over and pull her in his arms. He needed to get his shit together. The feel of her hands on his chest when she pushed him away still burned on his skin. That tilt of her chin when she didn't want him to have the upper hand only provoked all his blood to his groin. Still. Her fearlessness and determination were the first things that had attracted him to her. She didn't take anyone's crap. Especially not his.

Calista was the past. Where she belonged. His present situation required him to interview the punk in her living room and drive his daughter home with a reminder to stay away from Justin whatever the fuck his last name was.

He found Justin in the same spot they'd left him. At least the kid was trainable. He took a spot near the door so Justin couldn't make a run for it without going past him and so he could glance outside. Izzi sat slumped in the cruiser. Her face was planted in her phone.

Justin stood. He cocked his hip so one shoulder fell lower than the other, as if he were relaxed and talking to a law enforcement officer was nothing more than a stroll in the park.

"What's your last name?"

"Crow." Justin's eyes gave him away. His gaze bounced around and landed on his, then found something more interesting to look at.

"Where do you live?"

"I live with my brother and my two cousins." His Adam's apple bobbed, and he scratched at the underside of his arm.

"Where?"

"My cousin has an apartment in Little Lake. We're crashing there for now."

The kid was couch surfing. Many Natives did it because they couldn't afford housing of their own. Families would never allow their relatives to go without a roof over their heads, so they offered what little they had. His grandfather had told him many stories about life on the reservation when his granddad was a child.

"How come you don't live on campus?"

"Can't afford it." Justin raised his chin and met Gage's gaze.

"Where are your parents?"

"Why do you want to know?"

Because he wanted to know if anyone was paying attention to this kid so Justin would stop paying attention to Izzi. "Why don't you live with them?"

"That's none of your business, sir. I haven't done anything wrong here. I'm done answering your questions. If you're going to charge me with something, then do it, but if not, I have to go. Could you please move?" Justin pointed at the door.

He didn't budge. "Wait a second. I'm going to dig further on you, and if I find a hint that you're connected to these two burglaries in any way, I swear I'll nail you. So if you have anything to tell me that might prevent that from happening, I suggest you do it now."

Justin said nothing.

"Stay away from my daughter." He slammed the door on his way out.

****

Gage pulled into the gravel parking lot of Kennedy's Pub and turned off the truck's engine. The lot was full with the evening crowd. After he'd brought Izzi home, he stood in a cold shower to numb Calista's burning touch on his chest and called Kace to meet him for a drink. He needed the drink to get the day off his mind because the shower had done shit to ease what ached him.

Kace's black, shiny Mustang sat horizontally across two spots. Kace didn't like anyone parking next to him and wasn't afraid to say it. Gage pushed out into the warm night filled with the smell of lake water. People packed Kennedy's back deck to get a view of the lake. She should charge extra for that view.

Kennedy's was the best place to come for a drink or a burger. The scent of grilled beef met him right inside the door, and his stomach rumbled. He hadn't eaten anything since lunch. Not even one damn donut.

The oval wooden bar took up the left side of the room. Every stool was full. Tables and booths were cluttered with people on the right. Two pool tables saw plenty of action across their felt. The back of the pub was ready for whoever the musical act of the night was.

He scanned the room a second time for his brother. He should have known. Kace sat at the far end of the bar in deep conversation with a pretty lady on his left. He had discarded the greasy baseball cap. Gage was glad to see that. But Kace's eyes never left Kennedy Stark while she ran from one end of the bar to the other, pouring drinks from the tap or shaking them up in silver shakers.

He stopped short. Calista moved behind the bar with ease and grace, as if she'd been there for years. The sight of her scraped away at his gut. Her long, brown hair was pulled back. Her black, sleeveless top outlined her breasts and flat middle. It also showed off her sculpted shoulders and the tattoos on each. Her shoulders had been one of his favorite parts before the tattoos. They looked pretty good with the ink too.

Calista and Kennedy exchanged words. Calista's face broke into a smile, and she bumped hips with her friend. The look of joy on her face ran the heat in his body south. He used to make her smile like that.

He weaved through the crowd, offering a few hellos and waves. He kept his gaze straight. Pain built behind his eyes. A crowded bar had been a bad choice. Too many beers might only make him mad. If he got mad, he would regret a decision or two. He needed the quiet to stop the crashing thoughts of Calista.

The stoic peace of the mountain above him, a star-filled sky, and the whisper in the wind would heal what was hurting him. He should have pitched a tent on their acreage or grabbed a sleeping bag and joined Silver Bell in the barn. He could turn around and sneak out before Kace caught him. He'd send a text from the truck. Kace would understand.

"Gage, over here." Kace stood and waved him over.

Too late, then.

"Hey." He sidled up to Kace.

"Gage, I'd like you to meet Lori. She's visiting our beautiful little town from Billings with some friends. Lori, this is my oldest brother and our esteemed sheriff, Gage Ryker." Kace waved a hand in the air with the flair of a Broadway actor. He flashed Lori the smile that had a slew of ladies following Kace Ryker around as if he were the Pied Piper.

"It's nice to meet you." Lori leaned over Kace to shake his hand.

He didn't miss the hooded glance pretty Lori gave Kace.

"I follow Kace on the circuit. I never dreamed I'd ever meet him." She leaned back but left a lingering hand on Kace's shoulder.

Kace held a modicum of celebrity from racing cars. He drove in smaller races that didn't get the notoriety of the bigger ones, but he was good on the track— attractive and full of personality. He could probably have any woman he wanted. He just didn't seem to want to stick with any.

"Then it must be your lucky night." He turned to Kace. "Look, man, I think I'd better get out of here. I'm no good for company tonight."

Kace leaned in and whispered, "Don't leave me with her."

"Not your type?" He smirked.

"She wants me to go back to her hotel with her. That's not happening. If you stick around, she'll get the hint. Please, man. I need to be rescued."

"You're buying." He slid onto the barstool that opened up.

Kace slapped him on the back. "You are the best. Thanks. Lori, I have one hell of a big brother."

"Is he available?" She gave Gage the once-over.

Christ. Kace would owe him more than a beer if his groupie started draping herself all over him.

"Him?" Kace laughed. "I wouldn't waste my time. He hasn't dated in sixteen years. In fact, all the Ryker men are bad news. Not one of us is marriage material."

She narrowed her gaze. "Maybe you haven't met the right woman."

He leaned over Kace. "He's met all the women. Tried on most of them too."

Lori wrinkled her nose. "I better go check on my friends." She took her drink and slid away.

"Thank you." Kace waved Kennedy over. She gave him the one-minute sign and mixed a Jack Daniels and ginger ale for a lady at the other end of the bar.

"She's got to bust my nuts every chance she gets." Kace shook his head.

"Tonight it's me."

Kennedy came over and placed a napkin in front of him. "What can I get your brother, Kace?"

"Hey, Kennedy. How about a Sucaba?" He answered for Kace.

"I'm out. I've got Last Stout. That's good enough for you."

If she could, Kennedy made a point of giving him the cold shoulder. She had sided with her best friend sixteen years ago when he and Calista broke up, and she made sure he knew it. They had found a way to coexist in their small town, and out in public when he was in uniform, she showed him the respect his badge earned. But in her place of business, she turned on the ice and froze him out. Some women kept very good score of the past. He also assumed he was the reason Kennedy rebuked Kace's advances. She didn't want to get involved with Kace and have to put up with him on a regular basis.

She put the bottle down and walked away without another word. He raised the bottle to Kace. "Here's to women, and why the hell do we get tangled up with them?"

Kace raised his glass. "Because nothing is sexier than a smart, confident, beautiful woman looking up at you when you hold her close."

His brother was right about that, but the only woman he ever really wanted doing that was Calista. He hadn't had time for long-term relationships after he got divorced. He had to spend all his available time raising Izzi. Still, nights got lonely from time to time. And the summer season afforded him plenty of women who wouldn't make roots in Backwater. He had taken advantage of a few summer flings, but there was security in knowing the season would end and so would the relationship.

Every year Calista came to visit he'd been able to avoid her. As long as she didn't come up to him, he could keep going on with his business. This time had been different, and just standing close enough to get a whiff of her sexy, female scent blew up all the walls he'd kept in place. She stayed at the opposite end of the bar helping customers, and he was glad about that. At least that's what he kept telling himself.

Kace nudged his arm, knocking him out of his thoughts. "Stop staring."

His gaze dropped back to the beer. "I'm not staring."

"You keep telling yourself that."

Kennedy called out to Calista, and she turned in his direction, giving him a view of her face and the lip gloss across her full lips. She never wore a lot of makeup, and he loved the natural side of her. She would hike right into the mountains with him or take a ride with the horses. She used to pitch a tent as fast as he could.

She could also wear a black dress covered in lace that showed off her legs and made him as hot as those nights lying in his barn.

"When I told my new friend Lori that you weren't worth getting involved with, the part I didn't say was because you were in love with someone else."

"I'm not still in love with her. We're ancient history."

Kace turned on the stool, putting his back to the bar. Three guys grabbed the instruments set up to play. One guy sat behind the drums. The lead guitarist tuned the strings.

"Here's what I know. You take care of everyone. Me, Jett and Lock, Mom, of course Izzi, Silver Bell, and this whole damn town. What you don't do is give yourself the time to enjoy your life. You're not getting any younger. You might want to walk right over to that woman and tell her how you feel because you sure as hell aren't listening to my advice to stay away from her."

"Stop lecturing me."

"I'm just saying you deserve some happiness too, and if she's it…" His words trailed off.

"Kace, man, please shut up."

"You don't have to keep punishing yourself. You did the time. The time you committed yourself to. No one else did that. Not even Mom."

He put the beer bottle on the bar a little too hard. "That's enough." Now wasn't the place or the time.

He'd come here to forget about Ajay for a few hours and to forget about Calista. Now she was smiling at other men while handing them drinks, and Kace had picked at the wound he never wanted to touch.

Kace held up his hands. "Whatever you want, but I'm not sorry I said it."

The band kicked up their first rock song. The singer's gritty voice growled along with the guitar. The volume of the crowd rose to be heard over the music. At least Kace would shut up for now.

Kace had hit too close to the truth, and he hated that his brother could read him so well. He had worked hard to keep his feelings for Calista tucked away and out of sight. He might not always do a good job of it. His ex-wife had known there was a ghost in the bed with them. She had blamed him for getting her pregnant and ruining her plans. She'd left him and Izzi on a cold night while he held his sleeping daughter in his arms.

He downed the rest of the beer. A few people danced and nodded their heads to the music. The band had switched to a faster-paced song.

"I'll be back." Kace went to the dance floor. He tapped on Phyllis's shoulder and put his arms out. She gladly took his hands and danced with him.

Calista took the stool a few feet away. She peeled

the label off her beer and tore it into pieces. He eased off the stool and moved in her direction before he could talk himself out of it with some excuse of checking on the town.

"What did that label do to you?"

Her head snapped up. A smile spread across her face, but she dropped it when she realized where the voice came from. "Is there some law on the books that says I can't tear up my label, Sheriff Ryker? Am I breaking one of your precious rules?"

She was still mad at him for what he'd said earlier about not wanting any advice from her. He hadn't appreciated her comparison of his grandfather and Justin either.

"I'm sorry about what I said at your house today. You can break any law you want. I'd still have to arrest you for it, but it's your choice to follow the rules or not."

Her lips twitched in a small smile. He'd take that as a score and sat next to her.

"I didn't invite you to take the seat next to me."

"Sure you did. You just don't know it." He hoped her small smile would spread a little wider, but she only glared at him.

He didn't move. Maybe it was the song the band played now. Something quieter with lyrics that spoke of things that were still the same. Or maybe it was what Kace had said to him. He wanted her to smile for him the way she used to.

"You're not going to go away, are you?" Her voice dragged him back to the crowded bar and away from thoughts of her smile.

"It's a public place. Can I buy you another beer?"

"Is this man bothering you, Calista?" Kennedy appeared in front of them. She wiped the bar and scooped up the torn pieces of paper. She shot him a glare from the corner of her eye.

"Kennedy, I'm the damn sheriff of the town. Do you really think I'd harass someone?"

"You're not the sheriff here when you're sitting next to her." She shoved her finger in his face.

Calista put her hand up. "I've got this. Go pour some drinks before you do something you regret."

"I'll go, but only because you said so. Not because of him." She turned on her heel.

He yearned for some peace and ran a hand over his face. Coming here had been a bad idea. "She's a good friend to you."

"She's a little overprotective. That's something you should be able to relate to." She curled her lip.

Now she smiled at him.

"We broke up a long time ago. She needs to get over it. You have." He pushed off the stool.

She blinked. "I had no choice."

His blood turned to ice water. "You had plenty of choices."

"You don't understand how I feel. I had to move on."

He leaned in to be heard over the music. "The bar isn't the place for this conversation. I don't need the whole town to hear us."

Tears filled her eyes. She opened her mouth but shut it.

He should walk away and go home, but the anguish on her face and the longing in his chest pulled him closer to her. "I never hurt you or lied to you. I only ever loved you, and you didn't want us anymore. You could have trusted me."

"I know you were in pain and angry too, but your brother—"

"My brother what, Calista? My brother killed your sister. I know. I know every day, but I'm not Ajay."

He was tired of fighting this fight. The past was the past. He wished he could undo it. He'd lost plenty of sleep over the helplessness that tied him up.

The band segued into a slower song. He held out his hand and took a chance. What he could never say with words he had tried to tell her through his actions. "Would you dance with me?"

"Did you just ask me to dance with you?" She shook her head.

He hesitated. "Dance with me. Please."

"I have to get back to work."

"Can you trust me for two minutes? Besides, Kennedy isn't going to fire you." He only wanted a few minutes to show her he had not gotten over her. If she saw that, she might listen to him about his feelings for her.

She stared at his hand as if the answer was in his palm. He was about to give up and go home, but she placed her soft, small hand into his calloused one. The heat from her touch ran up his arm and straight to his chest.

He laced his fingers through hers and led her onto the dance floor before she could change her mind and run away.

He didn't look anywhere except straight ahead, not wanting to make eye contact with Kace or Phyllis. If he did that, he might falter. He weaved Calista through the crowd that had formed and found a small open space in the corner of the dance floor.

He pulled her closer and placed his hand on her waist. She worked her bottom lip under her teeth but laid her hand on his shoulder. He wanted to tuck her against his chest the way he used to but kept a few inches of space between them.

He held her gaze to make sure he wasn't dreaming. In that moment, there was nowhere else he wanted to be.

"Why did you want to dance with me?"

"I don't know. Maybe so you'd stop glaring at me."

"Gage, this…this feels wrong." She tried to pull away.

"No, it doesn't. Nothing has felt this right in a long time." He turned her on the dance floor to keep her with him.

He meant what he said. His world made sense with her in it. Because of her, he could remember who he was before Ajay died. He wanted to be that man again—young, fearless, driven, and free.

"Thank you." She stared up at him with wide eyes.

"For what?"

"For somehow knowing I needed this and forcing me off that stool." Her grip against his shoulder tightened.

"I can still read you pretty well." He spun her around again. He knew all her tell signs. He had studied her when they dated, wondering the whole time why she wanted him, and just when he thought he had that part figured out, they were over.

"You thought a dance with you would cheer me

up." She smiled at him. Finally.

"You've been through a lot since you came back. I know having me around doesn't always help that."

"Being with you confuses me."

Her honesty cut him. "I wish that weren't true."

"Me too."

Chapter Nine

Calista could not hear the band playing over the roar of her heart in her ears. She hoped she appeared calmer than the way her insides shook. When Gage asked her to dance, the world tipped on its side. She should have said no, run from the place, but her emotions poured out of her mouth with a resounding yes. *Yes. Hold me. Yes. Dance with me. Yes. Still have feelings for me.*

She could not read more into this moment than it was. He asked her to dance because he'd taken pity on her. She probably did have a sour look on her face while she took her frustrations out on that beer bottle. And she hadn't been all that nice to him when he sat down next to her.

She glanced up to find him looking at her. The intensity in his brown-eyed stare sent shivers over her skin. She wanted to run her fingers through his thick, full, wavy hair. Instead, she gripped his broad shoulder tighter as he moved her around their little space on the dance floor.

His earthy, masculine scent drifted toward her and rendered her hotter than she already was. She could blame the crowded dance floor for the extra heat, or she could be honest and say that no man had ever made her light up like a brush fire the way Gage Ryker did.

When she was with him, her shoulders straightened

a little more. Gage was the fabric of this town. He'd garnered respect taking care of his family's ranch until he graduated from college and went to the police academy. Which only gave him more admiration from the people of Backwater. He was handsome and funny and protective of his loved ones. He could have had any woman, and he had wanted her. Until she dumped him.

The band started up an old Phil Collins song. She expected Gage to step away from her, but he tugged her closer to him, only not so close that they touched. She tried to ignore the disappointment taking up residence in her belly. She wanted to feel his hard chest against her. She'd have to settle for the touch of his strong hand on hers.

"How are the renovations coming?" His words tore her away from her errant thoughts.

"Okay." Terrible.

Her father would not allow her to take Ava's bedroom apart. They had fought about it after Gage had left earlier. Dad had even poured out two cans of paint before she could stop him. She didn't want to tell Gage that. He might encourage her to fire Justin. She believed in her heart that Justin needed this job as much as she needed to give him the job to help her heal from losing Fox. Or because she needed to mend her heart some way, and nothing had worked before now.

"Do you have enough help?"

"I'll manage. I might need a contractor for the plumbing issues. And I found rot on the deck and the dock."

He turned her on the dance floor. She tripped over his feet and fell against him. He pressed his hand on the small of her back to keep her in place. Her heart lodged in her throat. She would do something stupid if she stayed pressed against him. Her body was remembering what it was like to be beneath him.

"I can make some calls for you if that would help. I know a few guys looking for work."

How was he staying so calm through all this touching? He made it look so easy, as if he didn't miss her at all.

"No, thank you. I'm sure you're busy enough with your own job." Plus, she had Justin, which he seemed to have conveniently forgotten.

He shrugged. "Do you want to get some air?"

"Air?" What did he mean by that? Did he mean go outside? With him? Alone?

He laughed a thick, juicy laugh. "Let's go for a walk." He didn't wait for an answer. He gripped her hand and led her back through the crowd. He shoved the glass door open.

The sticky warm air wrapped around her like a wet towel. "Where are we going? Kennedy is expecting me to help her." She needed to stop him, but her treacherous feet disobeyed the orders her mind yelled.

"Let's walk down to the lake. We won't be long."

She skidded to a stop. "I think that's a bad idea. I mean, the last time we went down there...the lake...people will see us from the bar. Do you really want to walk with me? I mean, I don't mind the idea of a walk, but it's late and it's us and it's...oh, I'm rambling." Heat flushed her already hot face.

He released her hand. She wanted to grab ahold of him to steady her racing nerves, but she kept her hands at her sides, empty and longing for his touch.

"It's just a walk, not a marriage proposal."

A small laugh escaped her lips. "I'm being ridiculous. Let's go. For five minutes. Then I have to get back to work." She was playing with fire and couldn't seem to stop herself.

The second-story bar gave access to a staircase and the path to the lake, but they went out the front. From the parking lot they followed a cobblestone path and a short set of stone steps.

The crowd had moved out onto the deck. No one paid attention to two people walking on the boards toward the dock. She had allowed her nerves to get the better of her, but being with Gage always kept her on the edge of excitement. Sometimes she missed that breathlessness only he could cause. She was tired of the sadness always fighting for a place in her existence. He had been the part of her life before there had been so much hurt and loss. Was it wrong to have just a little of that even for a few minutes tonight?

The sound of laughter and clinking glasses mixed with the deep thump of a bass drum became the soundtrack for their walk. She wanted to take a chance and touch him again, but she didn't. The touch would burn, and she would remember how good that burn was.

He smiled down at her. "This isn't so bad, right?"

"Right." Her voice caught in her throat. "Thanks for this. I needed the peace and serenity of the lake."

What would it be like to just grab him and kiss him? She wanted to feel his soft lips against hers. He might want her too. The dance had to mean something.

"Are you enjoying your visit to town? Besides the robbery, I mean." He sat down on the edge of the dock. His long legs dangled over the side.

She sat beside him and stole a glance at his jean-clad muscular thighs. She tried not to picture the scar that ran down the side of his left leg from the time he fell off Silver Bell. That scar was as sexy as his smile. "Things are different this time. I'm making changes to the B and B, and my dad doesn't like it."

"You're just trying to help him."

"He doesn't see it that way. He thinks I'm making him forget about Ava. I just want him to have guests again so I can go back to my home in the city and know he's okay without me." She didn't think she could go back to that apartment. She could tend bar anywhere. Maybe it was time to drive out to the West Coast and start over in Oregon or something.

"When are you leaving?" He traced his thumb over the top of her hand.

His touch drove her mad. She couldn't sit here with him as if nothing had ever happened between them. Her thoughts of wanting him and wanting to avoid him waged war in her head. She pulled her hand away. "It's hard to be here with you like this. It reminds me of what we had, and we don't have that anymore."

"I never wanted things to end between us."

"We couldn't stay together." She turned her gaze away, afraid the look in his eyes would have her leaving all sense behind. Her feelings for him were a betrayal to Ava.

"We might have been able to help each other back then. No one else understood what I was going through. Even my brothers didn't completely understand how I felt. You knew me like no one else did."

"I had my own hurt and anger to deal with. I couldn't help you. I should get back." She pushed up to stand. They were coming dangerously close to the ugly wound of their past.

He stood too. "Don't go. Please let me say this. I should have been able to stop Ajay from getting involved with those guys. If I had, they would both be here now. That shoot-out was my fault."

"Why, Gage? Why didn't you listen to him? Why didn't you help him when he asked you?" Tears choked her. She sucked in deep breaths to keep from breaking down. He had had the power to make it all right. He had always been her protector, and when she needed him the most, he hadn't come through.

Tears filled his eyes too. "If I could go back." He stopped. That was all he would give her. He was never good at sharing his emotions. He hadn't been raised that way.

She didn't know what to say or how to go on. Her heart had been broken in so many pieces for so long she didn't even know how to put it back together. Her fingers sought out the bracelets on her wrist. The lake rippled beneath them like a black satin sheet moving over two lovers. She needed to get her mind away from those kinds of thoughts.

"I can walk you back to the bar." His voice held a note of defeat.

"Wait." She was about to do something she might regret, but she had to end the tug-of-war between her head and her heart.

He looked up at the sky, then back at her. "Let's not pretend we're friends or even okay with each other."

"Gage, you don't understand." How did she make him see her confusion?

"Here's what I know. If the bullet had only been an inch in the other direction… Ava was gone by the time I got to her. My feet moved, but the distance between me and her only grew longer. It seemed like forever before I was on the ground beside her. When I couldn't feel her pulse, I knew in that second I'd made the biggest mistake of my life. I let everyone down in a way I could never make right. I can't forgive myself. How can I ask you to forgive me?"

"I don't remember you going to her." Her mind clicked through the reflections as if they were photographs in a filing cabinet. She begged her memory to give her a small inkling of that moment, but she came up empty.

"Well, I did."

"I remember the gunshots shattering the sounds of people having fun. I remember you racing to Ajay. I went to Ava. She wasn't breathing. I held her head in my lap and smoothed her hair away from her face. Ava had always hated when her hair tickled her nose."

He stared off toward the lake. "I scrambled over the ground to stay out of the line of fire. I reached for her. I wanted to move her behind the spinning wheel game where she'd be safe, but she was already gone. Maybe if I had moved faster…I don't know. Maybe nothing would have mattered."

"Gage, I…" She had been wrong this whole time. She'd believed he ran to Ajay first and left Ava alone lying on the ground. She had selfishly wanted him to save Ava, which would have meant he had saved their relationship. Fear, anger, and hurt had trembled inside her like an earthquake that night. It still did.

When the gunshots had broken open, she had

ducked and covered her ears. She thought Ava was at the cotton candy machine, but she had been right there. During the seconds it took to open her eyes and realize what was playing out in front of her, Ava was on the ground and Gage was with Ajay.

She hadn't closed her eyes for seconds.

It had been minutes.

Shame on her.

"We can't change the past, and that means we can't be together. You're right about that. You've always been right. Whatever feelings I have for you are tangled up in who we were. I'll keep my distance." He turned to go.

"Gage, wait."

"What?" He turned back and threw a hand up.

Instead of talking, maybe she could show him she hadn't understood until this moment. There had been too much talking. She stepped closer and placed a hand behind his head to pull him close. She pressed her lips against his and prayed he wouldn't pull away and embarrass her. His lips were soft, and his kiss unsure at first. But then he clung to her with an urgency. His arms wrapped around her back and crushed her against him. A kiss wasn't a complete betrayal to Ava. Ava would understand a kiss.

She held on to him for dear life as her tongue found delectable passion. She brought her hands back to his neck and pulled him closer. White-hot light of pleasure exploded behind her eyes while she traced his teeth and his lips with her tongue. Without more from him, she might become delirious with desire. She let out a small moan.

He tangled his fingers in her hair and tugged her

head back. The gesture made the heat run between her legs like lava. Her hands sought the lines and angles of his chest through the fabric of his shirt. If they didn't slow down, she might tear his clothes off right there on the dock.

She had hidden her emotions so far down and for so long her life played on automatic. Fox's death had been the final nail. She couldn't remember the last time her insides came alive. Every nerve was on overdrive, and she loved it. She wanted more of life again.

He broke the kiss and pulled away. She stumbled in the space between them. Her heart pounded in time to her heavy breathing.

"What's happening here?" He arched a brow.

"I think we're kissing."

"Why now?"

"Do we have to talk about it?" She didn't want to talk. She wanted to feel him against her. Preferably without clothes on. That thought got caught in her breath. Sex was more than a kiss, but in his arms the person she was before the tragedy seemed real again.

"Is that a pity kiss?" Anger brimmed in his glare.

"What? Of course not." She did want to take the pain off his face, if only for a few minutes, but she would never pity him.

The heat between them cooled with the breeze from the lake. Her skin tingled with goose bumps, and she rubbed her hands up and down her arms.

"Don't kiss me again unless you mean it." He marched away without another word. He didn't turn back to see if she followed or if she was okay.

Which she would never be again.

Chapter Ten

Gage paced his small cottage. The image of Calista staring up at him with swollen lips from their kissing played over and over in his mind. One minute she pushed him away, and the next she blew his mind with that kiss. For a brief moment, he believed she had forgiven him and wanted him back. It was a dream come true. But the joke was on him. No dream. Just a nightmare. And a hard-on he couldn't get rid of.

He ran a hand over his face and scratched at his day-old beard. He should have stayed the hell home tonight. He picked up the phone to call her but stopped himself. What was he going to say? Her words had been clear even if the kiss sent a mixed message. She would never forgive him for being Ajay's brother. The end. He needed to get the fuck over her and move on once and for all.

He had called Barry and told him to drive by the B and B to make sure she got home okay after she finished working at the pub. He checked the time. Barry hadn't called yet to report what he'd witnessed. Calista should be home by now. He tapped at his phone but tossed it back down before he could finish the text to her.

She was a grown woman who didn't need him. He would keep his distance other than to investigate the robbery at the B and B and nail Justin Crow to the wall.

The desire to punch something ran down his arms and into his fists.

He padded into the kitchen and opened the fridge. He yanked out a can of beer and held it to his head. He looked at the phone again. It was too late to call Kace or Jett. They both had to be up early. He sent a text to Lock. Even though Lock worked the ranch with Jett, he never needed more than four hours of sleep.

—*You up?*— He waited for his brother's response.

Nothing.

Lock was either out cold or in bed with someone. After Ajay died, Lock became the baby of the family at twenty. He had the wild streak too but had more sense than Ajay did. It was probably his love of horses. He cared more for them than anyone or anything else. In addition to the horses, Lock loved his family, which included their mother and his three brothers and even Izzi. But never an outsider. No woman had ever turned his head other than for a few hours. Lock was the unattainable bachelor. Gage believed Lock wouldn't get involved with anyone because of Ajay, but Lock never spoke about Ajay. That was how he dealt with it. He respected that since words were never his strong suit either.

No time for too many emotions when a ranch needed to be run. The animals and the guests came first. When Dad died, Mom kept right on going. She barely missed a beat. She said she didn't have the luxury of spending too much time with her pain. She gave it its due, but then she moved on. She had five boys to raise and a ranch to run. Because of the seven years between him and Ajay, Ajay had been only five when Dad died. Ajay had barely remembered their father. Gage hoped

Dad was waiting for Ajay with open arms when he crossed to the other side since he had never opened his arms to his brother. He was too busy taking his new role as man of the house seriously.

His phone vibrated against the counter. Lock must be around after all. He grabbed it, ready to ask his brother to come over and share a beer with him. He stopped short. The call wasn't from Lock.

"Sheriff Ryker."

"Sheriff, it's Deputy Sheriff Pearce."

"I know, Barry. What's up?" A call at this hour would never be good. He hurried into his room to put on his jeans.

"There's been another robbery. At Kennedy's Pub."

****

Gage pulled into the parking lot much as he had earlier in the evening. This time the lot was empty except for Barry's cruiser with its blue and red lights flashing and the Backwater EMS ambulance. *Shit.* He jumped from his truck and hurried inside.

The lights were dim. Nyx Blackwood performed her job as lead volunteer on the EMS squad and leaned over Calista as she pressed a bandage to her head.

The dark circles under her eyes could have been bruises, and her cheeks were sunken like pits. Was it only a few hours ago she'd looked up at him with a rose blush across her face? Now she was hurt and vulnerable. His stomach dove south. A blanket hung over her small shoulders. Barry stood to the side, scribbling in his notebook. His uniform shirt hung half-tucked in and the buttons misaligned.

Gage took a step toward her, but Luke Patterson

115

pushed the gurney in the way. Kennedy was laid on the stretcher with oxygen tucked under her nose. Marco Torino held a bag of clear fluid over her head.

"What are her injuries?"

"Unconscious. Possible concussion. Abrasions. Contusions." Luke hurried out the door, not waiting for his reply.

"Barry, what the hell happened?" he shouted to his deputy.

Barry looked up with eyes the size of tractor tires. "Calista called in a break-in. She was in the back room and came out to investigate. They thumped her on the head."

"You'll be okay, Calista. You don't need stitches. That skin glue will hold." Nyx stood and pulled off her latex gloves. She wiped her hair away from her face with the back of her hand.

"Are you okay?" He didn't care about what had happened between them earlier. He wanted Calista to be safe.

She waved her hand in the air. "I'm fine. It's just a bump. They took all the money in the register. Kennedy hadn't counted it out yet. It's her I'm worried about. Two men came in, and one hit her in the head with a golf club. I ran back inside the office and called for help, but the other guy shoved his way in. We fought, but he managed to push me into the cement wall." Her fingers tapped around the bandage on her head.

He really wanted to punch something or someone now. He would find the person who did this and crucify them.

"You might have a concussion." Nyx boxed up her supplies. "Do you want a ride to the hospital?"

"Only to see Kennedy. I want the bastards caught." Tears filled her red-rimmed eyes. "Gage, don't let this keep happening. Twice in one week. What's going on in this town? Kennedy's hurt. Someone could die."

He wanted to fold her into his arms and make her feel better, but he stood his ground. This was an investigation, and he needed to do his job. "Did you give your statement to the deputy?"

"She did, boss." Barry tapped the notebook. "I'm going to dust for fingerprints now. Maybe something will match up to the other two robberies."

That would be a small break. It would be better if the prints were in the system, but so far they had nothing. Which was exactly what he thought they would have. Robberies rarely got solved.

"Did the subjects have any distinguishing marks? Any accents?" he said.

"I don't remember any accents. I didn't see the guy's face because of the mask. He was tall and strong. He shoved me from behind, and I clocked my forehead against the wall. The room spun. I think he said something like 'unlucky you're here tonight' or 'unlucky night,' maybe. I'm sorry I can't remember."

If it was the first, then maybe the person knew her. That could be a lead. "Please tell me Kennedy ran the surveillance camera."

Kennedy had fought him when he came in three years ago and suggested she put in the surveillance equipment. She'd said she knew all her customers and the tourists weren't in town to steal liquor. Told him he was being paranoid and Backwater would not become a Big Brother state. He was pretty sure she said no because he suggested it. When he sent Kace in making a similar suggestion and giving her the name of the guy to use, those cameras had gone right in.

"They're on the loop in the back office. I think." She pointed over her shoulder.

"Can I go take a look?"

She nodded.

"Barry, stay out here with her until I come back."

"Got it, boss."

"I'm all done here, Gage. Call me if you need anything." Nyx waved to him from the door.

"Thanks, Nyx."

He closed the office door behind him and took a seat at the cluttered desk. The space was small. Other than the desk and one visitor's chair, the room was filled with boxes of liquor lining the wall.

The computer came to life under his touch. No password to protect it from unwanted eyes. He ran a hand over his face. Why did very smart people think they didn't have to protect themselves just because they lived in a small town?

He found the icon for the camera system on the desktop and pulled up the footage from earlier that night. The bar wasn't lit up well. Only the lights behind the bar were on. Two guys with average builds came in right through the front door. It was probably unlocked, or they picked it. He groaned.

Both men wore black hats and masks. Smart. The one guy carried a backpack that could be found in any store. They hurried around the bar and shoved top-shelf liquor into the bag. The one without the bag walked right up to the cash register and pounded on it until the drawer opened. He scooped out all the cash.

The other idiot tripped over the drum set. The

footage didn't have sound, but that must have made the racket that brought Kennedy out. Her office wasn't far from the band area. The clumsy one pressed up against the wall.

Sure enough, Kennedy stuck her head out and said something. She took a step into the band area, and Calista followed her out. He knew what was coming, and he couldn't breathe. The woman he loved was about to get hurt.

The first guy with the bag hit Kennedy over the head with the golf club. She fell to the ground, and he continued swinging. The angle of the camera and the dim light did nothing to identify distinguishing marks. He slammed his fist on the desk. An ugly rage consumed him.

Calista stumbled back into the office, and the other guy shoved his way in after her. Gage jumped from the chair, knocking it to the floor. A few minutes later, the guy came running out, and both men bolted from the bar.

He hung his head. She could have been killed. How many times had he told Kennedy to lock the damn door after the last customer went out? She never listened to him.

Everyone in town knew her, and she had never been robbed. He wanted that to mean these two fuckheads were tourists or gangsters, but he couldn't say with certainty. As much as he would hate to admit it, someone from town could be behind those masks.

He righted the chair and dropped down. He clicked on the outside camera to see if that had picked up anything. He smashed his fist on the desk again.

He hit a few buttons to make the angle zoom in. He

needed to be sure. Unmistakable. The dragon tattoo.

"Gage?" Calista pushed through the door.

"Stay out there. I don't want you to see this." The footage from the attack replayed, and he didn't want her to relive it. He hit the pause button.

She had pulled her hair back into a long ponytail. He swallowed the desire to take her in his arms and hold her all night. In spite of the bruise on her head, she was so beautiful standing there. Someone had hurt her. He would not survive if he lost her too. As long as she was happy living her life someplace, even if it didn't include him, he could keep moving. But if that changed, he wouldn't be able to breathe.

"I wanted to see if you found anything out from the cameras."

"Did Barry leave?"

"He's still out there. I told him to go, but he said he's not leaving until you give him the green light. His words, by the way."

"Sounds like Barry." He tapped at the computer and brought up the outside footage. "I do want you to see this one part."

She came around to his side of the desk. Her sweet scent drifted over to him. He resisted the urge to pull her on his lap.

"Is that Justin?" She leaned in for a closer look.

"Looks like him. The time stamp says this guy entered the camera's frame five minutes before the two men entered the building."

"He wasn't inside. I would have recognized him. Plus, he would never do this. Must be a coincidence."

In his line of work, there were no coincidences. "He must be the lookout."

"But that doesn't make him the criminal." She shook her fist.

"Calista, come on. He's an accomplice." He pushed out of the chair.

"This video doesn't prove that." Her clenched jaw said that would be her final word on the subject.

"The video proves he was standing outside the pub five minutes before the robbers came in. What are the odds he's not involved? He knows something. I'm going to find him tonight. He's got some explaining to do." He didn't care how much she fought him. He wanted to know what Justin Crow knew.

"Can you wait until morning?"

"Why would I do that? He could be long gone before morning."

"Where is he going to go? He doesn't have a lot of money."

"He does now."

She pushed out a long breath. "He'll be at work tomorrow. He hasn't missed a day."

"Why are you defending him? He's on the camera outside the bar. I don't understand where you're going with this. Why does this kid mean anything to you?"

"I don't know. He just does."

"That's not a reason. It's not even logical. You and Kennedy could have been killed." He wanted to shake sense into her.

"I can't explain it. Please, Gage, for me."

"Jesus, Calista, I don't know."

She gripped his arm. "Wait until tomorrow to talk to him. My place will be more neutral than wherever he lives with his brother. If you show up tonight, you don't know what will happen."

"What's going to happen is he will answer my questions." He couldn't believe he was actually considering waiting.

"Just come by the house in the morning. Ask all your questions. I won't get involved or say a word."

Every time she said his name or looked up at him with wide eyes, he wanted to give her what she asked for, but this was different. "We should roll him now. What if he doesn't show up tomorrow because he knows Kennedy is hurt? I will have wasted valuable time finding the person who did this and who robbed your business too. Is that what you want?"

"I want a kid who needs a chance to have one."

"He's a stranger to you."

"I would help anyone in Justin's position." She crossed her arms over her middle.

"Yeah, but why Justin Crow? He seems to be your personal project. You even helped him spend time with Izzi when that went against my rules."

"I didn't know you forbade it. I'm not a mind reader, even though you seem to think I should be."

She wasn't talking about Izzi and Justin any longer. "If talking about how I feel would've saved Ajay and Ava, I would've done it." He leaned against the desk. The day had worn him out. He wasn't sure how much longer he could keep up this argument with her.

"That's where you're wrong. If you had been able to tell Ajay you loved him, he might not have gone looking for love in the wrong places."

Her words were like a punch in his gut. He couldn't suck in any air. She had accused him of not loving Ajay. She was dead wrong.

"Sheriff?" Barry stuck his head through the

doorway. "Are you about finished here? I dusted and came up with nothing."

"Damn. Take a ride by the hospital and see if Kennedy is conscious. Get her statement."

"Will do." Barry ducked out of the office.

He emailed himself a copy of Kennedy's video. He should ask first, but he wasn't hiding what he was doing, and Kennedy would want to catch whoever did this. She'd be worried about her customers and not one ounce about Justin Crow. That they would have in common.

"You didn't answer my question. Why are you so determined to protect some kid you don't know or owe anything to?" He held her gaze. She wasn't going to leave until she answered him.

She let out another long breath and played with the bracelets on her arm. "Why are you giving me the third degree?"

"Why is Justin so important? There has to be a reason. Does he remind you of someone? Or are you trying to make amends for something?" He couldn't stop the need to know.

"I'm not the one who's guilty of anything."

His heartbeat picked up speed, and his ire sprang to life. "I'm tired of you pointing the finger at me for something I had no control of. I loved my brother. It was my job to take care of him. I did the best I could. I was a kid too." His insides shook with fury.

She flinched, but it didn't stop him.

"There is nothing you can say or do that will make me feel worse than I do. I have to live with the fact I froze in the moment they needed me. That image plays in my head day after day. I lost my brother. When will you get that?" He clenched his fists to keep from knocking everything off Kennedy's desk.

What Kace had said to him earlier about putting Ajay's death behind him rang in his ears. He would only be able to do that when Calista finally forgave him. If she didn't love him any longer, he needed her to forgive him.

"Justin reminds me of my neighbor." She moved away from him and dropped her gaze. She tucked her neck into her shoulders, and her fingers ran over her bracelets. "That's why I want to help him. I don't expect you to understand. You believe in the rules at all costs."

Her words hung in the air, waiting to be grabbed, and even if he could, he didn't know what to do with them. Law and order were the things that made the most sense to him. "If Justin is involved in these robberies, I can't change the rules because you like him."

She leaned against a pile of cardboard boxes labeled with different types of liquor. She rubbed her head near the bandage. "Fox was about Justin's age. Trying to make something of himself. He was a poor kid with a lot of disadvantages. His life was cut short by a stray bullet." Tears filled her eyes, and one spilled down her cheek.

He couldn't remember the last time he saw her cry, if ever. "I'm sorry you lost your friend. Let me drive you home. It's been a bad night for you. You need to get some rest." The fight seeped out of him. She chased her own demons. He had to let her do it alone. They would never be okay together.

"I'm sorry I said you didn't show Ajay love. That

isn't true." She wiped away another tear.

He couldn't stop himself from gathering her in his arms. He wanted the pain and hurt to go away for her, especially after what had happened since she came home. She relaxed against him, and his heart knocked on his ribs.

She tightened her grip around his waist, which eased some of the pain in his chest. "I don't think I can go back to the B and B. I don't want to face my dad after this. Could you drive me to the motel out on the highway?"

"I'll take you to the ranch. We have a room available in the main house. I'll call my mother and tell her you're coming." He wouldn't allow her to stay out at the motel all by herself. She'd be safe on his ranch and down the hall from his brother with plenty of firearms and ammo.

"I can't go there." She pushed away from him.

Her body heat dissipated, and he missed it instantly. "Mom will be glad to have you there."

"Your mother doesn't want me there. And Jett. He hates me."

"That isn't true."

"I hurt you. It's only natural for them to side with you."

"Calista, can you put the past aside for one damn night? You were hurt in a robbery and should be at the hospital. If you won't go home, then come home with me so someone can keep an eye on you." He wanted to blur the line that separated his life into two parts. The first part was the one with Ajay, Ava, and Calista in it, and it was filled with sound and textures. The second part was the one without, and it was silent and hollow.

Even though he had Izzi during that second part, and she filled in so many spaces for him, he wanted something he could never have.

"I couldn't bear having your mother fuss all over me."

"You're being ridiculous. She loves to fuss." He hoped humor would light the way to reason.

"It hurts too much when she's nice to me. Her kindness only spotlights what's missing in my life."

"Your mother." Her mother had walked out on her family not long after Ava died. That was probably his fault too.

"No. Not my mother. You."

Chapter Eleven

Calista tried to keep her gaze out the windshield of Gage's truck and not at the outline of his strong jaw covered with his dark beard, but she failed. His unshaven face and thick, jean-clad thighs sent heat to her core. She fisted her hands in her lap to keep from touching him.

Her head hurt. She had a lump the size of a crater on her forehead, and embarrassment burned her cheeks like a sun-cooked sidewalk. How stupid had she and Kennedy been? They could have been killed. They should have called for help sooner and locked themselves in the office without ever going to check on that noise.

She should have known better. Her stupidity caused her to get hurt and end up sitting next to Gage in his truck. "Can we call the hospital when we get to your place and check on Kennedy?" Her emotions strangled her voice. She had been holding it together until now, but his woodsy scent was undoing her. She didn't want to cry in front of him too.

He hit a button on his steering wheel. A computerized female voice filled the cab of the truck. "Safe Gateway phone."

"Call Deputy Sheriff Pearce." Gage gave her a small smile.

A phone rang.

"Thank you." Her heart tugged the corners of her mouth up.

"Evening, Sheriff."

"How's Kennedy?"

"Sleeping. She told me to get the hell out of her room, and she'd talk to me in the morning. Figured I stand guard all night unless you tell me otherwise."

"Sounds like Kennedy," Gage said. "Go home. She'll be safe where she is. We'll talk to her tomorrow when she isn't as ornery."

"Thanks, Sheriff. Night now."

"Good night, Barry." Gage hit the button again, and the music softly playing on the radio returned to the truck.

He turned onto the driveway to the ranch and drove past the main house.

"Where are you going?" Calista asked.

"You didn't want my mother to cluck and flap her feathers around you. I'm taking you to my house."

"Oh no. That's a bad idea."

"Stop trying to get out of your seat. It's no big deal. You can have my bed, and I'll sleep on the couch. Izzi will be glad to see you in the morning. You can talk about your bracelets or whatever they're called." He pointed at her wrist.

Sleep in Gage's bed? She might die. "I would love to see Izzi, but I can't."

He parked in front of a small log cabin tucked between tall evergreens. The front porch invited her in with its rocking chairs and lantern-style lights. "If you don't want to come in, then you can stay in the truck." He pushed out of his seat.

"You could let me take your truck home." As much

128

as she didn't want to face her father or her house, that was a better option than sleeping in his bed.

He leaned back into the cab. "You have a head injury. And no one drives my truck, lady." He tossed the keys in the air and with a swoop, pocketed them.

He didn't wait for her. She squirmed with indecision. It would be so easy to walk inside his house and climb under his sheets. She could wrap herself in his scent, and for a few hours she could let go. Sleep would cover the hurt from the past, she could forget her father's vacant stare, and the ache in her chest would disappear. But the truth was, sharing a small space with him would only make the hurt worse. She wanted to let go of her hold on the past, but every time she flexed her fingers, fear had her grabbing hold again. Like the times they'd go out to the lake to swim and Gage would dare her to grab the rope and swing until she hung over the lake. She never let go of that rope.

He slipped inside but left the door open. She stared out the window.

He returned with hands on his hips. "Calista, stop being so stubborn and get inside the damn house."

With a deep breath, she slid from the truck. Her heart raced as if she were still hovering over the lake. She wasn't much of a calm and peaceful yoga teacher. At least not when his woodsy scent antagonized her as she passed him.

"It's not much, but it works for us." He pulled his phone out of his pocket and tossed it on the small table by the door. "I'll be right back."

"Where are you going?" Panic strangled her words. He couldn't leave her alone now.

He tapped his waist. "I need to lock up my gun. I'll

just be a second. Make yourself at home." He disappeared down a hallway.

She allowed her legs to lead her around the living room. Her hands shook as she dragged her fingers over the top of the leather couch and recliner that faced the television. Hunting magazines and a textbook littered the coffee table.

The brick fireplace was filled with ashes. On the mantel above were pictures in wooden frames. A little girl in a flowered dress looked over her shoulder and smiled at the camera.

There was a second one of five young men. They all wore white T-shirts and jeans. Each man had the same chiseled jaw, bronze skin, and black hair. Instead of looking at the camera, they looked at each other. A twenty-five-year-old Gage smiled at Jett. Jett had his hand on Gage's shoulder as if to push him away, but the light in his eyes showed a playfulness. Lock crossed his arms over his chest, probably frustrated his brothers wouldn't pose, but a smirk pulled on his lips. Kace wore a baseball hat backward and raised his arms to show off his muscles. Ajay pretended to punch Kace. Her breath caught. There was so much love in that photo.

"That's the last picture we all took together. We took it as a Mother's Day present. It was Ajay's idea." Gage's voice yanked her gaze away from the photo.

"It's very nice." She stepped away from it. She should have remembered that photo shoot, but she didn't. She had done a very good job of forgetting. Especially the part that Ajay was a member of a family that loved him very much despite his mistakes. Losing Ava wasn't fair, but this family had suffered too.

Remembering that made the hole in her heart grow bigger.

He stepped into the kitchen. "Are you hungry?"

"No, thank you. I can sleep on the couch. You don't have to give up your bed." Her feet didn't move. She doubted she'd be able to even sit on the couch, let alone sleep. The room closed in on her. Sweat broke out on her lip, and the air in her lungs leaked out.

"I don't think you're supposed to sleep when you have a concussion." Pots and pans played a noisy tune as he moved around the kitchen.

"That's a myth. I'm fine. It only hurts if I touch it. Please don't make me anything to eat." Because she might vomit it right back up.

"I thought pancakes might make a good snack." He poured milk into a bowl. "Take the bed. You'll be more comfortable."

"I won't sleep in your bed. Stop suggesting it." Her voice rose. His kindness was too much to take. She should never have come here. Heat burned her face. The sweat moved from her lip to the back of her neck.

He put his hands up. Pancake batter dripped from the spoon. "Okay. Okay. Relax."

"Don't tell me to relax, damn it." She couldn't summon her yoga training. Instead of finding a way to ground herself, she allowed her anger to push her around.

"Then don't relax. Do whatever you want." He tossed the spoon and the bowl into the sink. They clattered like tin cans dragged by a car.

"Do you know how hard it is to be around you?" She should stop talking, but her mouth spilled the words the way her father spilled her paint earlier. This mess puddled around them, unable to be cleaned up.

"I have an idea. You don't miss a chance to tell me." He wiped a hand over his face. Exhaustion carved out the lines around his mouth.

"How is this so easy for you?"

"What's that? Being in your company? It's not. In fact, I wish you were anywhere but here in my house."

"I'll go, then. You didn't have to bring me here. I would've gone to the motel. This was your stupid idea."

Why had she trusted him? He didn't want her any more than any other significant person in her life. She would go to the motel. A walk that far would take an hour without the exhaustion weighing on her or the pain in her head, but she'd be damned if she would stay. She was scared, even if she didn't want to tell him that. No amount of deep breathing was going to calm her nerves tonight.

She headed for the door, but he cut her off. "Don't go." He stared down at her with his smoldering glare.

"I can't do this."

"It's just one night." He reached for her.

She punched his chest with one hand. "It's been every night for the last sixteen years. I think I'm strong enough to be in town with you, to pretend our history belongs to someone else, but I'm not. I needed you, and you let me down." Her fists continued to move by their own will.

The robbery tonight had been too much. It had sent her over the edge. She had been juggling her emotions well enough until he called and asked her to come home. In Backwater, she couldn't pretend. The scars of her past were around every corner, waiting for her to trip over like broken branches littering the ground.

He tried to keep her from pummeling him, but his hands missed, and she collided with his chest over and over. "Calista, stop."

The tears burned their way down her face. She choked. "Why did they have to die?"

He gripped her wrists in his hands and pulled her against him. "I'm sorry. I'm so damn sorry."

The anguish in his voice stopped her from crying. His eyes were filled with tears, and she winced. He always held his emotions close. He handled them by finding control in the rules. Unlike his brother Kace, who handled his emotions daring death on a racetrack.

He gathered her in his arms and held her. His heart drummed against his chest. She wrapped her arms around his waist and leaned into him. For a moment, they weren't two people lost in a storm. They were two people who loved each other, who shared so many memories, who could see the sun come over the horizon promising a day filled with possibilities.

She opened her mouth to tell him she loved him still, but the words floated away.

"I want you to trust me again," he said.

"I don't know how to find my way back to you." She owed Ava. Being with Gage was an act of disloyalty.

"It's not back. It's forward."

"I can't find my way forward either." She'd been lost for so long. She had run away after the tragedy. She couldn't commit to anything. Not a career. Not a man. She had been frozen in place. She desperately wanted to go back to that night, to take away the slap on his face, to tell him she loved him instead, to hold him because he had to zip a black bag around his brother.

She wasn't any better than her father and his shrine. He wouldn't change anything in Ava's room because it would mean she was gone. If she moved forward and forgave Gage, even dared to love him openly again, then she would also have to admit Ava would never come back. Tears stung the back of her throat, but she didn't release her grip on his waist.

He kissed the top of her head and untangled himself from her grasp. "You can sleep on the couch. There's a blanket in the chest. Good night."

He slammed a door shut.

On her heart.

Chapter Twelve

Calista tore the comforter off the bed. Dust flew into the stream of sun coming in from the window and tickled her nose. She needed to burn up this unrest. Tearing apart Ava's old room was going to be the way.

She hadn't slept a wink on Gage's couch. The blanket she found to toss over herself smelled like his woodsy scent. Like a lovesick schoolgirl, she had balled it in her fists and held it under her nose most of the night.

His embrace had seared her skin. She wanted his hands all over her, but instead he had pushed her away. That had been her fault. She told him she couldn't move forward. This morning she wanted to for the first time. The look on his face last night when he'd allowed his frustration to show nearly broke her heart.

She craved his touch the way she craved air. She tried to forget how good his muscles felt under her fingers. Or the way he would tangle his legs around hers when they slept. She didn't want to remember the intense look on his face when he tried to figure something out or the ease in his stride when he hiked through the mountains.

Every man she had been with had paled in comparison. It wasn't fair to hold them up to Gage's memory, but she never stopped doing it.

The sheets had been on this bed for sixteen years,

collecting dust the way a hoarder collects garbage. She yanked them off and folded everything before placing them in the cardboard boxes. Packing up the clothes, photos, and awards might be the hardest, but it would have to be done.

"What are you doing?" Her father's voice shattered the silence.

She spun around and tripped over the corner of the bed. A pain shot up her shin. She bit her lip to keep from yelling. "You scared me."

He marched into the room with a newspaper rolled up in his hand. "What is happening in here, Calista?" He pushed his glasses up on his red-veined nose. Creases bent the fabric of his button-down shirt.

"I'm going to redecorate this room." She fisted her hands on her hips.

"You will do no such thing. This is Ava's room." He pulled the sheets from the box.

"Leave those where they are." She took the sheets back and clasped them against her chest. "I'm perfectly aware of whose room this was. And it's time to change that." She wanted to tell him her plan would be to move him into the main house by the end of the summer so she could rent out the lake cottage, but one step at a time.

"You don't even live here any longer. Why do you care so much about Ava's room? In a couple of weeks, you'll go back to the city and that bar you work at." He spit out the words. "You'll leave me here. Ava's room gives me comfort. Why would you deny me that?"

"It's not healthy to keep all this stuff. It won't bring her back." She picked up a photograph of her and Ava at Ava's high school graduation only a few weeks before her death. She had pulled her sister in for a hug and knocked her cap off her head. Ava had reached up to steady it just as the picture was taken. Their smiles spread wide. Two sisters who could not possibly know what lay in store for them.

Her father grabbed the frame from her hands and put it back in its spot on Ava's dresser. "Leave that alone." His hands shook.

"Are you drinking again?"

"Why do you think I'm always drinking? You need to show me some respect. I don't answer to my child."

Anger tore at her insides. She wanted to scream but took a long breath instead. "You didn't answer my question." She knew the signs of someone deflecting. He didn't want to answer her question, so he pushed back on her.

"It's none of your business if I'm drinking."

"In fact, it is. When Gage calls me and tells me to come home because my father has been arrested, and when the family business is almost in the ground because somewhere a long time ago you stopped caring about it, your drinking becomes my business."

Her father turned his back and stood before Ava's dresser. She had kept a small wooden box and filled it with tokens that meant something to her. Keepsakes. Or junk, depending on Ava's mood. Her father ran his fingers over the lid. Right now, she was inclined to think of that tiny chest as junk.

He opened the box and pushed around its contents. She backed to the door. Whatever was inside could stay hidden. She would take this room apart whether he liked it or not.

"You can do what you want to the main house. I

don't care. But if you touch another thing in this room, I will never speak to you again." He kept his back to her. Ice ran through his voice.

He had never spoken to her in that tone before. The only other time she heard him use it was when he told her mother to get out of the house. He was upset. He didn't know what he was saying.

"You don't mean that." She held her breath and waited for him to say something.

"I mean it with every fiber of my body. If you take this room apart, we aren't related anymore."

"Dad, please. This is silly. You need to heal. We both do. But you can't do that it if you don't pack up her stuff."

He spun around to face her. "Stop telling me how to grieve. If I don't remember her, who will? Your mother? You? You left here minutes after the funeral. You just moved on without her, as if she didn't exist. You didn't care about her. My beautiful little daughter deprived of all the things she could have been. And what do you do? Do you try to live in her honor? No, you do nothing with your life. You wasted your life when your sister didn't even get a chance to live." His face bloomed red. A vein pulsed on the side of his neck.

A poisonous fury overpowered her. Her skin was hot, and her vision blurred. His words pushed her over the edge of sanity she'd been balancing above for years. Her legs moved forward of their own free will.

She shoved her dad with both hands. He fell against the dresser, and it bounced off the wall. The contents on top slid back and forth, as if they were on a ship fighting waves in a storm. The picture of her and Ava fell to the floor, and the glass shattered. The box of junk tipped over. The jewelry, lonely buttons that lost their rightful places, and dried flowers littered the dresser and mingled with the broken glass.

Her heart begged to be set free of the pain. "I wish this wasn't my family."

Tears slid from her eyes. Her father stared at her with his mouth hanging open, and as if he realized where he was for the first time, he dropped to the floor and gathered Ava's things without another word.

She ran from the lake house and up to the main house. The roaring in her ears drowned out all sound. She could still feel her father's small chest against her palms. Bile burned the back of her throat. She shoved open the door into the kitchen and gulped in air, but her heart refused to slow.

The bump on her forehead pounded. She poured water into a glass and paced the kitchen. She should leave now. Forget the Fourth and this house. Nothing she did mattered. Her father only loved Ava. He had stopped seeing her the day they put Ava in the ground. Instead of joining together in their loss, he wore his hurt and grief like the skin of a porcupine. She couldn't get near him, and she needed to. Just once she wanted her father to put his arms around her and tell her it would all be okay. She needed to hear that they would go on together and Ava's memory would be like a tide that rolled in and out. Instead, Ava's memory was a tsunami.

She grabbed her clothes and shoved them into her suitcase. She needed to forget Gage too. They would never work out. He was the enemy, and she had better stay on her side of the fighting line.

"Is anyone home?" Justin's voice vibrated through

the house and splintered her nerves further. Damn his punctuality. If Justin was here, Gage wouldn't be far behind. He wanted to ask Justin questions about the robbery at the pub, and he wouldn't be stopped, especially after what had happened between them last night and the fact she'd left this morning without even saying goodbye.

She rolled her shoulders and took a deep breath. "I'll be right there."

He waited by the front door with his hands in the pockets of his oversized pants. He wore his crooked smile and a blue T-shirt covered in bleach spots. He bounced on his toes, which made the baseball cap wobble on his head. His presence brought some light into her dark mood.

"Hey, Justin. I'm sorry. Were you waiting long?"

"What happened to your head?" The smile dropped. His eyes narrowed, and he inched closer.

She waved him away. Easier to keep things neutral. "I got in the way of a golf club. I'm okay now. Do you want some coffee?"

His reaction appeared natural. If he had been at the bar or involved with the robbers last night, he would have known what happened. He might have been outside, but he wasn't involved.

"Are you sure you're okay? Did you get into a fight or something?"

"Let's get that coffee. I need a strong cup." She led him into the kitchen and grabbed two mugs. She needed something stronger than coffee, but this would have to do. Justin eyed the cornbread on the counter. She cut him a large slice and slid the plate to him.

"Can I ask you something?" She poured milk into

her coffee and kept her gaze away from his.

"I guess so." He bit off a large piece of the cornbread. Crumbs tumbled back to the counter.

"Why were you at the pub last night?"

"What are you talking about?" He pushed the food away.

She took a deep breath. "The sheriff has video footage of you outside Kennedy's pub last night right before the bar was burglarized."

The color drained from his face. Her stomach twisted in knots. She rushed on. "He wants to ask you some questions. I asked him to wait until today. He's coming by this morning to talk to you."

"Is he charging me with something?"

"No."

"Then I've got nothing to say. He can arrest me or bring me in for questioning, but I'm not talking. He'll only pin this on me, and I didn't rob that bar. You believe me, don't you?"

"I do." The man who chased her into the office wasn't Justin. She was almost certain the other man wasn't either. Justin didn't rob anybody, but the tickle up her spine said he might know something. She didn't want Gage to be right about him. She needed Justin to be innocent.

"I'll be right here if you want. You can trust me when I say Sheriff Ryker is an honest man. I've known him my whole life. He would never accuse you of doing something you didn't. He just wants to ask you about being outside the bar. I kind of do too, Justin. What gives?"

He kept his gaze on the coffee he never touched. "I hung around town after work. I didn't want to go home.

141

You can get to the lake from there. I only wanted to sit on the dock for a little while. I didn't think it would matter. The place was closed, but I heard voices and I got back in my car and took off."

"Did anyone see you?" That would be what Gage would ask.

"I don't know."

"Was your brother home when you got there?"

He adjusted his cap. "No."

"Where are your parents?" She never heard him mention his family, and if this brother was responsible for him, he wasn't doing a very good job.

"My parents won't speak to me. They wanted me to go to college and then come back to the reservation and help my people. I don't want to go back. I'm tired of the struggle. They never have any money. There were times we didn't have any food. I want to make something of myself and bring them to live with me, but my father will never give up his heritage. Since I'm willing to give up mine, he said I was dead to him." He held her gaze and tilted up his chin.

"I'm so sorry." His father would never come around. The Indian people were proud, with every right. They had never wanted to be colonized, and the American government took away their chances for a prosperous life by owning their land. "And your brother agrees with them. May I ask how you and your brother are getting along?"

"I try to avoid him as much as possible. He doesn't like anything I do. Is this interrogation over?"

She hit too close to a deep wound. His life was his business. "If we don't talk to Gage now, he's only going to keep looking for you. I saw the video, Justin.

That's you on it. Whether you like it or not, you will have to answer some questions. My friend's bar was robbed, and she was hurt by whoever did it. They hit her over the head. I want Sheriff Ryker to make an arrest as much as anyone else."

"I didn't have anything to do with it."

"I know you didn't commit the robbery. I saw the two men. Your image outside the bar five minutes before the crime doesn't help your case. You might have wanted to sit by the lake, but you must've seen something that could be helpful."

"You know what? I just remembered an appointment I have. I'll be back tomorrow unless you're going to fire me. If you are, just do it now because I need a job. I'll have to start looking all over again." His black gaze never wavered.

She retreated. "I won't fire you."

"Thanks for breakfast." He marched out the front door.

She pulled out her phone and took a deep, meditative breath. Her fingers hovered over the screen. Gage would be furious. She had asked him to trust her, and she didn't produce. That would only confirm what he believed.

She sent the text and waited for his explosive response. The men in her life were ticking time bombs, and she stood in the middle of the minefield with no way out.

Chapter Thirteen

Gage slammed his fist on the desk. He knew it. Calista let Justin slip through her fingers. He should have gone to that kid's house last night and cornered him. Now he'd have to hunt him down, because Justin knew he would be questioned. He would have time to think about his answers and even get someone to give him an alibi.

If she hadn't looked up at him with those big brown eyes pleading with him to give her what she asked for... He was such an ass when it came to her. His foolish heart always got in the way. When would he learn?

"Sheriff Ryker, I don't have the budget to replace the furniture." Phyllis pointed to the desk with her pen from her spot outside his office. Her glasses sat on their perch at the top of her head.

"Not now." He tried to keep the growl out of his voice, but it slipped in. "I'm sorry. I don't mean to be disrespectful."

She came into his office and patted him on the shoulder. "You are a sweet boy. I hate to have to tell you this without the aid of a sugary treat."

He didn't want to hear it. "What now?"

She pressed her lips into a thin line. "The town is buzzing this morning about the robbery. People are concerned this is going to keep happening, and with the

Fourth right around the corner, they're worried the tourists won't come. A few of the stodgy old men are organizing a town meeting to discuss what to do."

"Because they think I'm not doing my job?"

She held her palms up.

"That robbery hasn't been more than eight hours ago. How fast do they think I can solve a crime? This isn't some television police show all wrapped up in an hour. This is real life. This stuff takes time. And the Fourth isn't for weeks." He raised his fist, but Phyllis grabbed his hand.

She shook her head. "I wouldn't. You might break something at your age, and this is your writing hand. Go to the meeting and tell them all to get their panties out of the wad they bunched them into. You'll solve this crime in no time. I'll text you the details of time and place so you don't miss it. Do you want me to order you lunch?"

"I don't have time to eat. I have a suspect to track down." He pushed away from his desk.

"Make sure to eat something on your travels. You're a bear when you miss a meal."

"Phyllis, why do you think you have to mother me? I don't pay you to do that." He shoved his phone in his pocket.

"No, but your mother does." She winked.

He kissed her cheek and headed to his cruiser. He drove through town with one eye on the road and one on the activities. People walked up and down Main Street, hopping in and out of stores. He would never allow something bad to happen to his town. The people who lived here were his people, and he would do what it took to keep them safe.

145

He beeped the horn as he went past the garage. When he realized where the noise was coming from, Kace held up a hand.

After he stopped at the B and B, he might swing by the ranch and check on Silver Bell. He hadn't been out to the barn for a few days. If he had any time or energy left, he'd go for a run.

He was supposed to go on that riding tour with the ranch guests for Jett tomorrow. He wished he could take his horse. *His horse.* Silver Bell could have been all their horse, but the reminders hurt too much for his other family members. Jett loved the horse. So did Lock. But his two brothers loved life on the ranch, and that included all the horses. Sometimes his mother would visit with Silver Bell, but not for long. She didn't want to cry. She said she'd done enough of that for Ajay. Silver Bell had become his. It was his way of taking care of Ajay when he couldn't.

The driveway for the B and B came into view, and he hit his signal director. A hole burned in his stomach. He wasn't ready to see Calista. She was gone this morning before he even woke up. If it hadn't been for the folded blanket on the edge of the couch, and the memory of her arms around him, he wouldn't have known she was even there. She wasn't ready to move on from the past. It was high time he did.

He shoved his way out of the cruiser and covered the area to the front door in about a second. He wanted answers, and he wanted them now.

The door flew open before he could reach the knob. Calista hurried out. "I need to talk to you. I don't want you going off half-cocked."

"I am here to interrogate a possible witness to a

crime in my jurisdiction. Please step aside."

She shoved her hands on her hips and tilted her chin. The wind went out of him. The glare in her dark eyes only created a hunger inside him. Her hair hung long over her shoulders. It came almost to her waist, and he wondered how she would look with nothing on and only her hair covering her breasts.

He pushed air out through his teeth. She was beautiful when she got fired up—especially at him. But she wasn't his. He needed to ignore the grip desire had on him and do his damn job.

"He isn't here."

"What do you mean he isn't here? I asked you to call him back." He searched for the beat-up old car Justin drove. Sure enough, the only vehicles in the driveway were the cruiser and hers.

"I will not allow you to browbeat him into saying something he shouldn't just because you don't like him. He told me he was outside the pub. He wanted to go to the lake. He didn't do this, Gage. He wasn't one of the men inside the bar."

"I don't force anyone into a confession. Is that what you think I would do? What kind of a police officer do you think I am?" His voice lifted and carried out to the lake.

Her words hurt more than what she'd said about his lack of love for Ajay. She didn't trust him. She never would again. He couldn't live with that. She was determined to make him pay for what Ajay had done every minute he took a breath.

She backed up and leaned against the clapboards. "I'm sorry. I didn't mean to imply…I wasn't thinking. Of course, you wouldn't do that. I'm worried about

Justin. Someone needs to look out for him."

He leaned against the railing to give them both more space. "Why do you think you should be that person?"

"I don't know."

He believed she did and didn't want to tell him. "Does this have something to do with Ava?"

"Of course not."

"You can't save the world, Calista."

"Why not?" She gave him a small smile. The breeze blew her hair off her neck.

His insides heated up again, and he couldn't blame the warm summer morning. He wanted to run his hands over her sides and pull her against him so he could ease the worry from her face. He also wanted to feel the way her curves softened his hard shell. Only she had ever been able to smooth his rough edges. He was never going to be able to stop his feelings for her no matter how hard he tried.

"Always the crusader. Stick to fixing what's wrong with your dad. He's an easier subject, and you have my mother on board if you want her. Leave Justin Crow to someone else."

"He's a good kid. He didn't rob Kennedy."

"You can trust me. I will follow procedure to the letter with him." He wanted to ask her to forgive him for the past, to allow that trust to flow into the wound in her soul. He never meant for anything bad to ever happen to her.

"I know you will. You always did. You're a good police officer. I'm sorry I said what I did." She dropped into the new rocking chair on the porch.

"Forget about it. I can't ignore the fact he was

there, though. He must have seen who did it. How could he have not seen something?"

"What if he's afraid of what he saw?"

"I can't help that. He has an obligation to tell us."

"Do you think for just five minutes you could operate from your heart and not your head?" She sprang from the chair and grabbed the doorknob.

"Where are you going?" He moved away from the railing before she could get any farther.

"I need some coffee if we're going to keep talking." She didn't wait for his response and hurried inside.

He caught the door before it slammed on his face. "Hang on a second. My job requires me to use my head. I can't treat every suspect like a stray cat. I'll leave the bleeding-heart stuff to you." He followed her into the kitchen.

Sun drenched the room. The board was still on the door from the robbery, but the window above the sink sparkled. The counters gleamed in the sunlight. A fresh bunch of bananas hung from a metal holder. A vase of flowers decorated the table. She'd made a little progress in here, and he was proud of her for it. Wasn't that his heart talking?

She had no idea how many times he wanted his heart to make decisions, but if he reacted from a place of emotion, people could get hurt. There wasn't time in the day to entertain emotions. Besides, he was raising a teenage girl. She wore enough emotions for the entire state of Montana.

"Gage, he's a kid who wants to break free from his past. You of all people should understand that." She pulled the coffee out of the fridge and slammed the door.

"Are you seriously comparing my not wanting to run the ranch to this kid? What do you even know about him?" He and this kid were not the same. He had never resorted to crime to change his life. He had just wanted something different than the family business. So had Kace. No one gave Kace any crap for his choices.

"He wanted off the rez to make a different life for himself. I know it's not the same thing. But you didn't want to end up like your dad. He doesn't either. You might have more in common than you realize."

"I doubt that, and at least I had the smarts not to get caught feeling up my date by her father."

"That was an honest mistake." She dumped the ground coffee into a filter and hit the start button.

"I don't care. He's trouble, and he's going to bring trouble to you. You shouldn't keep him working here. I don't want him near you."

"You don't need to protect me. He isn't going to hurt me."

"How do you know he won't hurt you or your dad? Did he give you his word?" He smirked. She didn't understand how easy it was for some people to wear a mask for the world. She wanted to believe the best in everyone, except him. That reality cut a little too deeply.

"Now you're just being an ass."

His temper sparked. "I am acting like the sheriff. I need to bring him in for questioning, and it's happening today. If he is involved, he's had too much time to get his story straight with the other men. They could be halfway across the country by now." He wanted justice served, but he wouldn't mind if those scum were gone and gone for good. Peace needed to be restored to his town.

"Can I stay while you talk to him?" She fingered the bandage on her head.

The stone wall around his heart cracked a little. How much pain was she in? "That's fine if he wants you to, but you can't say anything or lead him to answer. You're not his lawyer. I don't want a lawyer later saying you messed up this investigation."

"I won't. Thanks." The smile returned to her face.

It was barely lunchtime, and the day had worn him out already. "There's a meeting tonight. The town wants answers about these robberies."

"What are you going to tell them? You never said if you wanted coffee." She pulled two mugs from the cabinet.

Was she extending some kind of peace offering? He hesitated, but then the heart she didn't think he had gave in. "Sure. Thanks. I have to tell them the truth. I don't have any answers."

She poured coffee into the large mug and left plenty of room for milk. She remembered. A smile tugged at his lips. Something so small shouldn't mean so much, but it did. She slid the mug across the counter, and their fingers grazed as he reached for it. His gaze held hers while the warmth of their skin touching lapped over him and stopped his brain.

"Would you like to get something to eat with me after the meeting?"

He didn't know why he said that. He hadn't even thought about asking her out. In fact, he planned on doing very little speaking to her, and here he was running his mouth off.

She stared up at him with unreadable, wide eyes. She was going to say no. He tried to tamp down the disappointment churning in his stomach. Or maybe it was his bruised pride causing the acid reflux.

"My father and I had a big fight this morning. I don't know how much longer I can stay in Backwater."

Not an answer to the question. Well, maybe it was. She was leaving. There was no point in them spending time together, not even as friends. She wanted out of this town. That's why she never stayed for very long when she did come back. The pain was on every street corner for her. For him, the familiar grooves of this town were what kept him sane. "I understand you can't stick around. He's making it difficult for you. Probably better if you go. Then you won't need Justin working for you. I'll see you." He no longer wanted the coffee.

"Gage, wait."

He should continue walking, get in his car, and drive away. He couldn't keep going back and forth between the possibilities of being with her and not. He was tired of dragging around the hurt and the guilt and the hope.

He turned to her. "What's up?"

"That wasn't my answer to your question. I just wanted you to know things are pretty bad here. He didn't even ask me how I was feeling this morning. I guess I could use a friend who understands my situation. If the offer still stands, I'd like to go to dinner with you."

A shimmering self-assurance gripped him and held tight. He could hang on to hope a little longer. "I'll pick you up at seven."

Chapter Fourteen

Gage slipped into the main room of the community center and took a seat in the back. The room was filled with people in various stages of standing and sitting. The chatter of their voices echoed off the high ceiling. Metal chair legs scraped against the wood floor. The lack of fresh air hung in the room like a wet wool blanket. The air conditioning must have been on the fritz again because sweat beaded on his forehead and he had just arrived. It would only be a matter of time before someone noticed him, but he wanted a few minutes to assess the situation.

He had a few allies in the mix. His mother, Kace, and Jett were present. Barry Pearce, still wearing his uniform, spoke with a couple of old-timers up in the front corner. Phyllis sat two rows back from the front, deep in conversation with Margo. Probably about Margo's tomatoes and whoever had stuck their thumbs into them.

The mayor shuffled through papers at a table set before the crowd. David Moore's balding head reflected the overhead lights as he licked his finger and turned pages. Gage hoped that wasn't his speech. They'd be there for hours. He wanted to deal with the town's concerns and get home. He wanted to change out of his uniform before he picked up Calista and spend a few minutes with Izzi.

"Sheriff." Jodi Fry plopped down in the seat beside him. Her blonde hair hung to her shoulders in a puffy wave that wouldn't crash if Poseidon himself commanded it to. Her many bracelets jangled as she adjusted the sleeves of her suit.

"Evening, Jodi."

"Are you hiding back here?" She kept her voice low and looked at him through her thick eyelashes.

His mother would say Jodi's makeup was expertly applied. Makeup was something Karen Ryker didn't bother with, and he was glad about that. He preferred his women natural. Like Calista. Though he wouldn't mind seeing her in red lipstick.

"Guilty as charged."

"I'll make this quick because the lions are getting ready to feast on you."

He stifled a groan. "It's just a meeting."

"You can believe that if you want. What's your plan to catch these criminals? Because I've been pushing a marketing campaign to increase the number of new residents in our town. I don't want an uptick in the crime rate to sabotage me. My business can't survive without a healthy house market."

"Even small towns experience crime. The idea that they don't is a misconception. As a realtor, you must have come across that piece of information."

He hated that the people of his town thought they could go around without locking their doors or their cars. Crime happened everywhere, even in Backwater.

"I know that, but others don't. New residents want to feel safe when they choose a home. We're lucky here that our small-town businesses have foot traffic. Our schools are decent. We just need new people because we lose the young people to the big cities. I'm sure your Izzi is getting ready to put on her wings and fly as far away from Backwater as possible."

His spine snapped straight. Izzi wouldn't leave for good. Backwater was in her blood as it was in his. She would realize that once she had a taste of the outside world. He'd been plenty of places, and nothing was like home. He always came back to Backwater even though the space held as much pain for him as it did joy. Ajay was everywhere he looked.

He had told Izzi going to college was a non-discussable issue. She could go where she wanted. He pushed for the University of Montana, but he'd settle for something else. And then she would come back and live in Backwater like every other Ryker.

"I'll find whoever is committing these robberies." He pushed out of the chair before Jodi could say another word. He meant what he said. He would get to the bottom of things.

He marched up the middle aisle to his family. He needed to be around people who understood him, people he didn't have to explain himself to.

Kace patted him on the shoulder. "Hey. What's bothering you?"

"Nothing."

"That's why your face is twisted into a snarl." Jett laughed at his own joke.

"Hi, honey." His mother snuck in one of her hugs. "Did you have a bad day? I made some dinner for you and Izzi. Just heat it up when you get home. You'll feel better."

"What are you talking about? I'm not mad." He clenched his jaw.

He wasn't angry, but he would feel a lot better when he left and saw Calista. He had been looking forward to her smile all day. He was determined not to argue with her. Not after what was about to happen at this meeting, if the meeting would ever come to order.

"I'd be pissed off too, if I were you. The whole town is steaming mad about these robberies. That's all anyone is talking about downtown. They want to blame someone. That someone is you." Kace scratched at his jaw.

"I'm not pissed off. Will everyone stop staying that?" Sweat ran down his back. Damn broken AC. He'd need a shower before he picked up Calista.

"You keep believing that," Jett said.

"Honey, just relax. I know you'll solve these crimes. You're very good at what you do." His mother beamed at him.

"I am relaxed." He clenched his fists.

"Everyone, take your seats. Let's get this meeting started. We've wasted enough of your precious time." Mayor Moore's voice carried over the noise.

Gage searched for a seat between his brothers.

"Sheriff Ryker, would you join me up here?" The mayor arched an eyebrow.

Faces turned to stare at him. Nothing like going straight to the firing squad. Kace gave him a thumbs-up. His mother squeezed his arm. He took the place by the mayor.

David tapped on the table with his ruler. "All right, everyone. Let's quiet down. We're all concerned about the recent proliferation of crimes. I want to get to everyone's concerns. Make sure to raise your hand before calling out. Who wants to begin?"

Almost everyone's hand shot up. Gage bit his inner cheek. "Mayor, before you begin, may I say something?" He did not want to be on display, but he could at least steer this meeting his way.

David's mouth opened and closed as if he were a fish. "That wasn't the plan, but certainly. Everyone put your hands down until the sheriff speaks."

"I know you all want answers as to who is committing these robberies. I don't have those answers for you. Yet. I'm sorry you have to wait, but that's how police work goes. Your safety is my top priority. And the success of our Fourth of July is as important to me as everyone who owns a business. Keep your eyes open. If you see something, say something to me. Or Deputy Sheriff Pearce. Don't gossip about it to your neighbor. Lock your doors at night. As soon as I have answers, you will too. We can't rush this. It's too important. Thank you."

"Sheriff, I'd like to open the floor back up to questions," the mayor said.

"I don't think that's necessary. I don't have anything else to say. I can't reveal what evidence I do have. As far as I'm concerned, this discussion is over. You've all put your faith in me for years. I ask that you continue to do that now."

Marty Boseman stood up. "What if we want someone else to run this investigation? You don't have the experience. We've never had any problems like this in town. What do you know about solving real crimes?"

Marty was one of Backwater's oldest citizens. He had been here when most of the roads were made of dirt. He didn't like change, and he'd never liked Gage.

"Mr. Boseman, I've been the sheriff of this town

for quite a few years. I think I know what I'm doing."
He'd handled robberies before. They had been small
time. A few of the kids stealing bales of hay from some
of the farms. An ex-husband trying to steal jewelry
from his wife. But before he worked in Backwater, he'd
been on the police force as a patrolman in Missoula.
He'd worked robberies there.

"I'm with Boseman. I want someone else on this."
Roger Wilson joined in, pointing a finger toward him.

"Roger, are you deaf? I'm the damn sheriff. Who
do you think is going to come into our town and run an
investigation on a few robberies?"

"We can ask the county for help. I checked." Roger
puffed up his chest and searched the crowd for someone
to agree with him.

"I'm not calling the county for this." If he were
dealing with a murder investigation, then maybe.

"How are you going to keep the business in our
town? If tourists get wind of these crimes, they won't
come. We'll all go under," Marty said.

"That's not my job to bring foot traffic into your
stores. My job is to keep our town safe." He clenched
his fists at his sides again. His mother was right. He
needed to relax.

"If every other day another business is being
robbed, how the hell are we going to keep making
money? Who is going to come into our shops if they're
afraid of getting robbed? What if someone gets shot or
murdered? Look what happened to Kennedy. She's
lying in a hospital bed with her head busted up." Marty
pounded his chest.

"Marty, I understand your concerns, but I can't
catch the thieves any quicker. If someone comes into

your store to rob you, give them what they want. Don't argue. Especially if they have a gun. After they leave, call for help." He wished Kennedy had called sooner instead of going out into the bar area to check things out herself.

"I'm not giving up one damn thing." Marty held a finger in the air. "I have a shotgun under my register. I'm going to blow the face right off the bastard that comes into my place and tries to take what's mine. I've worked my entire life for what I have. Some no-good hoodlum is not going to steal from me, so help me God."

"I second that," Roger said.

"Me too." From someone in the back.

"And me," said Howard Hornsby.

"This is our town, and we're going to keep it safe when you can't." Marty waved an old, wrinkled fist in the air.

Clapping and jeers grew in volume until the ceiling shook.

Gage ran a hand over his face. What the hell was he going to do with a bunch of vigilantes? "Everyone. Everyone. Please settle down." He waved his hands in hopes they would follow his command.

The noise continued. He gripped his baton and slammed it on the table. "Shut the hell up. All of you." His voice challenged the chants and stomps.

The room settled down. Everyone stared at him with wide eyes and open mouths. He took a deep breath.

"You all need to listen to me. Don't go taking the law into your own hands. It's a crime. Do you understand me? I will have to arrest each and every one of you, and then your businesses will suffer for sure. Let me do my job."

"But you're not doing your job," Roger said. "We've had three burglaries in the last month. You can't protect us. We're going to protect ourselves."

It took all his self-control not to flip the table. He had spent over a decade keeping this town safe. He did his job twenty-four hours a day, making sure men like Roger and Marty could walk the streets at night without looking over their shoulders. In the blink of an eye, his people had turned on him.

Kace jumped up. "You two old coots need to sit down before your hearts give out. My brother is the best damn sheriff this town has ever seen. If anyone can solve this crime, it's Gage Ryker, and if anyone doesn't like that, they can come see me."

"I second that, and Lock told me to throw his vote in for Gage too, but he's at the ranch putting the horses to bed." Jett came halfway out of his chair, then sat back down.

His chest puffed up. He could always count on his brothers. His mother's smile spread to her ears. She gave him a nod and patted Kace's knee after he sat down.

"We want answers, Ryker," Marty Boseman said.

"And you'll have them. Until then you will respect the office of the sheriff of Backwater and allow us to do our jobs." He headed for the door and kept his head straight, avoiding stares, glances, and whispers.

He pushed out into the night air. The breeze did nothing to cool his heated skin. He took a deep breath. He would figure out who was committing these robberies. His gut told him Justin Crow was involved, and that had nothing to do with his antics on Gage's couch. He needed to figure out how to prove it was Justin and restore order to his town.

The problem was when he proved Justin was a criminal, Calista would hate him all over again. She wanted to save that boy, and he couldn't figure out why this kid meant so much. But it didn't matter. She'd have to find another disadvantaged child to rescue. She'd see her way clear to that decision. He hoped. Or the small chance he thought he had with her this time would evaporate like the sweat on his skin.

He wrestled his keys out of his pocket, ready to spend some time with the beautiful woman who had haunted his dreams for years.

"Hi, Gage." The voice stopped him in his tracks.

"What are you doing here? I was going to pick you up." He wanted to cross the parking spaces and pull Calista into his arms to wash away the hurt and anger still clinging to him, but he stayed put, unsure of what she wanted. Had she come to cancel because of their earlier disagreement? But she could have called or sent a text.

He swallowed the lump in his throat at the sight of her. Her floral summer dress floated over her body. She'd pulled back her long hair into a low ponytail that hung along her spine. Her toned legs went on forever to the strappy sandals on her feet. Her toenails were painted a pale color he couldn't make out in the dim light. But whatever color it was, his heart picked up speed taking all of her in.

"I couldn't stay another minute at home. The house feels too small, even though I have the whole place to myself. I'm afraid my dad will come up to the main house and start another fight." She waved her hand as if to dismiss her words. "Never mind. You don't need to hear about it. I hope it's all right that I came to you instead of waiting for you to pick me up."

"I planned on going home to change out of my uniform. I'm not exactly dressed to go out." He almost said for a date.

"I don't mind your uniform, but I understand if you want to freshen up. I could meet you at the restaurant. Or wherever you wanted to eat. We hadn't talked about that part." A rose flush colored her cheeks.

He moved closer, needing to be near her. Only she could ease the tension in his chest and help him shake off the memory of the people of this town staring at him with disappointment in their eyes. How could the town doubt him so much? It was as if they didn't know him at all. He was the person who came running when they called, even for things like a broken sprinkler they couldn't shut off. He'd found their dogs, walked their kids home from school, and driven a wagon around on Halloween when the trick-or-treaters didn't want to walk from house to house any longer. His townspeople had cut him in a way he didn't know could hurt so much.

"You could leave your car here and come with me. I'll stop home for a quick change, and then we can grab something in town. It will be less driving around like that. Or we could sneak into the kitchen at the ranch, and I could whip something up."

The ranch had guests this week. Four sets of couples. Two of whom were going on that tour. Jett and Mom would have closed down the kitchen by now, but family could reopen it.

"The ranch sounds nice. Do you still have that dining set outside? The sky is beautiful tonight." Her smile slid wide for him and danced in her eyes.

He dared to take another step toward her. Her warm, spicy scent drifted in the space between them. "Not as beautiful as the lady."

She shook her head. "I don't think so."

"Trust me. The view from here is better than any skyful of stars." He willed his heart to slow down.

She smoothed her dress against her waist. "Gage, the things you say sometimes…you throw me."

He didn't know if that was good or bad. He wanted to whisk her away before she thought too long and decided she didn't want his compliment.

"Let's go." He held out his hand. She slipped her soft one into his. He linked their fingers and hurried to his truck. If he could stop time, he would. Tonight would be about them. Not the town. Not the robberies.

Not the past.

Chapter Fifteen

Calista fought hard against the urge to run. Gage was changing in his bedroom, and all she could think about was him without his clothes on.

The ride over to the ranch and his cottage only made her hands shake and insides burn. She had tried not to stare at his chiseled face set in stone, but she couldn't stop. At least she controlled herself enough not to reach over and run her fingers through his black, silky hair.

His twitching jaw had said something bothered him. She hadn't wanted to ask what it was. She didn't want to fight with him, and she worried he was still figuring out how to pin the robberies on Justin. Tonight, she wanted to forget about all the things that had tied her up in knots recently, and Gage seemed to be the only one who could ease her tension.

"Hi, Calista. Are you waiting for my dad? That's a pretty dress." Izzi bounced into the room. Her hair was swept back. She wore leggings and what had to be Gage's shirt. The cotton fell to her knees, and the short sleeves hung at her elbows.

"Hi, Izzi. Yes, your dad is changing, and thank you for the compliment. I got it on sale."

"How's Justin?" Izzi's face lit up as she spoke the young man's name.

Calista remembered what being in love at that age

felt like. She doubted Gage would approve of his daughter being in love with anyone at this age or any other. "He's okay. Working hard around the B and B."

Izzi pulled a water bottle out of the fridge. "Do you want one?"

"I'm fine, thanks." She needed something a little stronger to calm her nerves.

Izzi held the bottle but didn't open it. "Justin wants to see the horses. I thought about bringing him over."

"Does your dad know?" There was no way Gage would allow that, but maybe she could talk him into it for Izzi.

"I haven't mentioned it yet. But it's not like we don't have people on the ranch all the time. We even offer riding lessons. Dad can't stop Justin from taking a lesson. Uncle Jett never turns away business."

She was pretty sure Gage would do his best to stop Justin from stepping foot on the ranch or anywhere else that involved Izzi, and if that meant fighting Jett or Lock with two fists, he'd do it. "You should talk to him first."

"Talk to who first?" Gage stepped into the living area with a smile on his face. His gaze searched for an answer.

She soaked him in. His black T-shirt accented his muscles. The collar had two small buttons left open to reveal his dark chest hair. Her memory could recall the soft texture of that hair against her fingers. She clenched her fists, and heat pooled between her legs. She needed to sit and calm her hormones. His daughter was only feet away.

"Dad, can I bring Justin here for a riding lesson?"

"Absolutely not."

165

As she figured. Calista dropped into a nearby chair.

Izzi's face fell. "Why not? What's the big deal? Plenty of people will be here. Uncle Jett or even Uncle Lock can chaperone. Or Gammy. She likes Justin. She told me."

"Or me." Was it so terrible to want to be liked by his daughter? "I don't mind being a chaperone if it helps. I'm sure Jett and Lock are busy."

He shot her a glare that froze her to her seat, but he turned back to Izzi. "I don't want you hanging around that boy. He's too old for you. I thought I made myself clear."

"You haven't tried to get to know him. He's nice and funny. Dad, you are so narrow-minded. You're judging Justin without giving him a chance." Izzi stomped out of the room. The slam of a door punctuated her exit.

Gage hung his head. "Be glad you don't have a teenager."

She sucked in a breath. She had wanted children for years but had to accept that the dream never worked out for her. Her chances of having a child at forty were near impossible. She didn't have a partner to share a child with. She hadn't been brave enough to have one on her own.

"She's lovely. You're doing a great job with her, though you might want to let up on some of those rules." She edged out of the chair and went to him.

"I like my rules, you know."

"I do know, and so does Izzi. You can be kind of inflexible at times." The space between them was charged with electricity.

He twisted a strand of her hair between his fingers.

166

"If I say you're right, can we table this discussion for another time? I just want to go up to the house and make you dinner. I don't want to fight crime or fight my daughter."

She had never been able to curb her attraction to him. That was why she always stayed away. But this time, because of the robbery, he had slipped in and stolen her breath again.

He gripped her shoulder as if he sensed somehow she was about to take flight.

"Calista, I know we don't have a future together any longer, but I need tonight. Would I be too much of a roughneck if I asked you to simply allow me to spend time with you and see where that takes us?"

Her head spun with conflicting emotions. She wanted to wrap herself around him and never let go, and she wanted to do the right thing for her sister and her heart.

Hadn't it been this morning she considered moving forward? Her father had made sure that couldn't happen. Did she need her father to change his mind in order for her to change hers? If she spent the night with Gage, would she be dishonoring Ava's memory?

"Please say something." His voice was low.

"I'm afraid. I keep trying to separate my feelings from what happened. How do I get involved with you knowing Ajay is the ghost in the room?" She stared at the center of his shirt, unable to look him in the eye. He was asking for one night to see where it would go. Why couldn't she give him that?

He tilted her chin up with his strong fingers. "I'm not asking for a relationship, darlin'. Tell me you don't still feel something between us. If you tell me that, I'll drive you right back to your car now, and I'll stay away from you."

She wanted to deny how much she wanted him, but that would be a lie. This was her chance to take a small step forward. She didn't have to be afraid, but every step closer to Gage made the ground crumble from under her. She would be looking down a large chasm soon if she wasn't careful. What would her father say if she went back to the only man she ever loved? Would his anger shake him enough he might wake up from his infatuation with the past? Or would he drink himself into oblivion?

"I still have feelings for you." Steamy heat ran over her skin. The uneven beads of her bracelet did nothing to calm her nerves as her fingers danced across the wood.

He cupped her face in his hands and pressed his lips against hers. Every nerve ending in her body tingled. She leaned into him and ran her fingers through the ends of his hair. He moaned against her lips. She wanted the kiss to go further, but he eased back before she had a chance to take them to another level.

"Let's start with dinner." He took her hand and led her outside.

Disappointment shoved its way into her belly. He was probably right. They should take small steps. She could handle small steps. They didn't have to lead anywhere.

Unless she wanted them to.

****

"The dinner was wonderful," Calista said. She leaned into Gage's embrace and closed her eyes. He took the moment to watch her. Her light skin against his darker complexion always made his heart gallop.

They had moved from the table in the main house's kitchen to the small settee by the firepit. When she was wrapped around him, he was complete. He tried not to think about what was under her dress and what was once his. He didn't want to embarrass himself with an uncontrollable erection.

"The meal was grilled cheese and a salad. Not exactly gourmet." He drank his beer and hoped to cool his hormones.

"I don't need anything gourmet. I came for the company. How was your meeting tonight?"

"I don't want to talk about it and ruin the night." The stars were out. The day had cooled down and added a slight breeze. He couldn't imagine being anywhere else.

"The town must be up to something." She looked at him.

He eased away from her, took his beer, and stood by the fire. "I have it under control."

She stood beside him. "Your spine is so straight it might snap."

"Those nuts are saying I'm not doing my job. Who do they think keeps them safe twenty-four seven? Not Barry Pearce." He wasn't being fair to Barry, but damn it, the town's attempt to take matters into their own hands brought about enough anger to make his blood boil.

He turned to her and twirled her hair between his fingers. "Let's talk about something else, okay?"

"The town is just scared. Once you solve the robberies, everything will go back to normal." She took his hand and laced her small fingers through his.

"So we're going to talk about it?"

"You probably should. It might make you feel better."

"What will you say if I prove Justin is involved?" He should stay away from the subject of Justin, but he couldn't seem to keep his mouth shut. And she wanted to talk.

"You won't, because he isn't." She pulled her hand away.

"If you're right about Justin, I'll eat my words, but don't count on it. That kid is trouble. If he isn't an accomplice to these robberies, it's only a matter of time before he does something else." He downed the rest of his beer.

"Why do you think he's so much trouble? What has he done that says he's no good? It can't only be what happened between him and Izzi."

He scratched the back of his neck. "His presence at every crime."

"He wasn't at the B and B when it got robbed." She dropped down onto the chair and tucked her legs under her.

"He was there earlier that day. I need to go back to the first two locations and try to find any evidence that puts him in proximity at the times of the robbery." He would take care of that first thing in the morning. He stopped. First thing after he took Jett's guests out for a ride.

"Does he remind you of Ajay?"

Her words cut through him. She was always able to call him on his shit. He loved that about her, yet that very trait frustrated the hell out of him.

"I don't know." Or he didn't want to admit it.

170

"Come on, Gage. Be honest."

He sat beside her and laced his fingers through hers. "Justin has that defiant glare in his eye Ajay always had. Ajay always thought he knew better. He wouldn't listen to anything I said."

"You can't accuse Justin of committing a crime to ease your conscience about not stopping Ajay."

"Calista, it's been too many years for me to be doing that. I don't like Justin. I don't like that he keeps turning up like a bad penny."

"I think you're too focused on one guy. You want to solve the crime, and you want to ease your guilt. Pinning this on Justin won't change the fact your brother murdered my sister."

He ran his hands through his hair. The ground between his feet stared up at him. "I wear my badge every day hoping I won't be the guy whose brother shot someone. Most days I can pull it off, but when you're standing next to me, I feel like I did when I walked up to you and you slapped me. I felt torn apart, ripped to shreds that night. My world was never going to be right again."

She snaked her arm through his and leaned her head against his shoulder. "I'm sorry I did that to you. I should have said that sooner."

He turned to look at her. Her lips were inches from his. Her eyes were wide and filled with tears.

"Take a walk with me."

"Where?"

"Back to my place." He wanted her in his bed.

At least one more time.

Chapter Sixteen

Gage held Calista's hand and let the warmth of her skin against his travel up his arm to the hollow of his chest. He led her off the patio and to the paved path that would take them to his cottage. He didn't know what would happen when they arrived, but he wanted to invite her in. She would probably push him away because she saw a different man from the one he was when she left him. But so far she followed him.

The big black sky offered them the backdrop of a million stars. He loved the Montana sky at night, unbroken by the light pollution big cities contended with. The air cooled his skin, but not enough. The only thing that might put out the slow burn in his belly would be feeling Calista under him. Or a cold shower. Which was more likely to be the thing that happened.

The walkway was lit with lanterns hung from poles. Jett had added the touch some years back. The golden glow allowed guests to take an evening stroll from their cottages to the main house. The light allowed him to see the set in her jaw and the straight line of her shoulders.

The cottage came into view with its front lamps welcoming them in. He stopped and faced her before they went any further. "The man I was when you left was young and naive. I've grown up since then. The world isn't filled with endless dreams and possibilities.

It's filled with hurt and disappointment. I just want to keep the people I care about from experiencing too much of both."

She placed a hand on his cheek. "Gage Ryker, if I can't save the world, neither can you."

He turned his face to press his lips against her palm. Her skin tasted salty. "I only want to save Backwater. The hell with the rest of the world."

If he could be the man he'd been before she left, he would be that man, but that young man disappeared the moment his youngest brother took a bullet to the chest. He pressed his hands against the small of her back and pulled her against him, wanting to feel her next to him.

She ran her fingers up his arms and tucked her hands under the sleeves of his shirt. Her soft touch left a trail of flames on his skin. She gripped his shoulders, keeping their bodies pressed together. "Will you look for other suspects besides Justin?"

"Is that the topic of conversation you want to have right now? Because I can think of a dozen other things I'd rather talk about. Or better yet, no talking at all."

"You're right. No more talking. Kiss me."

He leaned in, kissed her, and for the first time in sixteen years, he returned home.

****

Calista drowned in the force of his kiss. She clung to him, afraid she might topple over if she let go of his shoulders. Gage separated her lips with his tongue and set her world on end. She allowed reason to disappear. She would live in the moment, as she had practiced and preached in her yoga classes. She would not worry about tomorrow. Everything she needed stood in Gage's front yard.

What she had was the most confident, sexy, strong man she'd ever met, and he wanted her. She stood on her toes to deepen the kiss and dragged her fingers over the muscles in his back. She needed to touch him everywhere and allowed her fingers to dance across his skin. She rubbed her hands over his chest, and he groaned.

He tangled his hands in her hair and gave a tug. The heat exploded between her legs as she took the kiss deeper. She moved her hands under his shirt and traced the lines of every muscle on his stomach. The soft texture of his chest hair tickled her fingertips. He gripped her bottom and pulled her flat against him. His desire pressed into her belly.

He flicked the hook of her bra with ease. His calloused hands dipped down her dress and rubbed against her back. He slid his hands to her front and kneaded her breasts. The groan escaped her lips before she could stop it.

A light flashed behind her lids. Her hands froze on his waist. "What was that?" she said through the side of her mouth because her tongue was still tangled with his.

His chest heaved with hers. He pulled away and rested his forehead against hers. "The light went on inside the house. Izzi must be up. I don't want her to look out the window and see me undressing you on the front lawn."

"That would make you a bit of a hypocrite."

"At least we're consenting adults."

That she was. "I guess that's the end of our date." She smoothed his shirt back into place with regret.

He didn't let her go. "I'm taking a group of guests out for a ride tomorrow morning. Do you want to come?"

"You and me out in public together?" That would be another step forward. Would her feet obey?

"Would that be so bad?"

"I would like to, really. But I have to start taking down the kitchen cabinet doors tomorrow. I guess I'm going to stay in town until the end of the project. My dad will just have to deal with me around. How about you come by my place after your ride?" They would be alone there. They could pick up where they left off.

"I'll be there by noon, and I'll take you to lunch. I'd better bring you home before I change my mind and make love to you on the porch." His black eyes smoldered with lust.

She wanted to say to hell with principles. She was tired of denying her feelings. But they would have to wait one more day.

"Thank you for an unexpected evening, Sheriff Ryker." She brushed a kiss against his lips.

"You're welcome."

He kissed her until her head spun, and her knees went weak.

After he dropped her at the B and B, she stood on the porch watching his taillights fade to a speck of red and disappear. She locked the door and undressed. In the bathroom, she turned the shower to cold.

Tomorrow wouldn't come fast enough.

Chapter Seventeen

The sun hung full in the sky and dripped its heat all over everything. Gage wished for a breeze to come through the trees. Instead, he wiped the sweat off the back of his neck. The guided trail tour was almost over, and he couldn't wait. The guests had been courteous and willing to listen to him. Everyone except the guy named Ethan. Ethan had a long, pointy beard and a buzz cut. His narrowed gaze bounced around as if he were waiting for something to happen, and the guy never stopped bragging. Twice, Gage had to call him back to the trail.

He had planned to return to the ranch using a different route, but Ethan had taken off, and by the time Gage found him, they were too far from his original path. Now they would have to take the narrow passage near the cliff edge. They would go single file for three hundred yards. He wished one of his brothers were there to pull up the rear. This trail was safer with two guides.

He was anxious to see Calista. Sleep had evaded him most of the night because thoughts of her lips against his and the smooth texture of her back beneath his touch tortured him. She hadn't promised him anything, but she had been willing to be with him, and he would take that as a victory.

As soon as he finished the postride ritual, he had to

do more investigating, but then he would rush over and buy her lunch. After that, the rest of the day could unfold. He hoped it would be with her naked beside him.

He shook his head to stay focused. "Okay, everyone, we'll need to get into a single file here. I'll go first. The horses know the trail. All you have to do is sit back and relax. But make sure to glance a little to your right and see the river below. You don't want to miss the view, but please don't stop to take pictures."

"Is this safe?" The woman named Kathy called out from the back of the line. Kathy had packed her own riding helmet for this anniversary trip with her wife, Jane. Jane clucked at Kathy's wound-up questions and concerns.

Gage had to agree with the more carefree Jane. Real cowboys didn't wear helmets. He tired of city slickers who came to Montana to unwind from their hectic lives, hoping a week on the ranch would be enough to cure whatever was bothering them. Jett always reminded him to keep that to himself. He blew a long breath through his teeth. "Kathy, this trail is as safe as any. Just follow my instructions."

He rounded the corner of the big rock, and the land stretched and yawned in front of him. Relief renewed his energy. They would walk downhill from here and be back to the ranch in twenty minutes. He turned Kit Kat around to wait for the others.

The couple from Texas came around the turn first. Jett had said something about them celebrating a wedding anniversary too. They were followed by Jake, the brother of that pain in the ass, Ethan. Right on his tail were Kathy and Jane. Kathy's smile wavered, and her skin had a green tone to it, but she didn't appear any worse for having been so close to the edge. She adjusted the helmet and blew a kiss to Jane.

"Jake, where's Ethan?" The relief of making it past the narrow edge and to the open space was replaced with cold, slimy dread.

"Got me. I think he stopped to take a selfie."

"I gave one direction. Does he understand he jeopardizes everyone's safety when he doesn't listen? This isn't some damn joke." Fury boiled his blood. He flicked the reins and took off on Kit Kat. "Stay here. No one moves."

Jett would punch him in the face for talking to guests the way he just did. He'd deal with Jett after he found Ethan. He might not care a whole lot about wearing helmets, but he did want his guests to pay attention to the damn directions.

He slowed Kit Kat with a pull of the reins. The space narrowed again. The jagged mountain wall was inches away. The drop to the river below was only inches in the other direction. Ethan must have let the others go ahead of him. No one would have been able to pass him.

He navigated the path, wanting to hurry because every second could mean something bad for this guy who had been trouble from the onset. Jett would have to be called if anything happened. And if it was bad, they'd need a helicopter to the hospital. His sweaty hands gripped the reins with more force.

The path widened, and his stomach took a dive. The cliff edge was still close by. The rumble of the river below echoed up to him. Ethan's horse didn't have a rider. Marigold nosed the grass. Her tail swished without a care in the world.

He dismounted. "Ethan?"

The birds were the only ones answering back.

"Ethan? Where are you?" His pulse picked up speed. He eased closer to the cliff edge, but not close enough to see over. Still no one called back to him.

He cupped his hands around his mouth and shouted. "Ethan? Where the fuck are you?" Had the guy walked back the way they came?

"Help." A small voice broke the silence.

He hurried the rest of the way to the edge and peered over. Ethan stood on a small ledge that jutted out from the rock's side and looked up. His face and arms were scratched and bleeding. His left arm hung limp at his side.

"Are you okay?" The clock was ticking. He'd only have minutes to keep Ethan calm enough to get him back up the hill. He didn't have the right equipment to scale the rock or send a harness down to him.

"I think my arm is broken." Ethan's voice wobbled.

He wanted to ask what Ethan had been thinking when he got too close to the edge. "Did you fall on it?"

"I slipped off the edge trying to take a selfie with the water behind me. I'm sorry, man. Really. I didn't mean for this to happen. The ground crumbled under my feet."

No one ever meant for this stuff to happen. Ajay didn't mean to kill Ava, but he did. "I'm going to grab a rope. Don't move."

"No way."

He unsecured the rope from the saddle and made a bowline with a wide opening. "Ethan, I need you to listen carefully. Can you do that?"

If shock set in, Ethan might not be able to follow the directions that would save his life. Gage tied the other end of the rope around his waist.

"I'll do whatever you ask. Just get me out of here. My arm hurts." Ethan's voice shook more. He cradled his arm against his chest.

"I'm going to toss the rope down to you. You need to slip it over your head and pull the end so it's tight around your waist. I'll pull you up, but you're going to have to help. Are you with me so far?"

"But my arm. How am I going to pull myself up with one arm?"

"I'll do most of the work, but you're going to have to help. I can't get you up if you're dead weight. The rope won't hold long like that." They were wasting time. He tossed the rope over.

Ethan watched it dangle.

"Grab the rope."

It wasn't more than three feet away. Ethan stared back up at him.

"Ethan, stay with me. I need you to grab that rope. Just lean over."

"I can't."

He didn't waste time arguing. He recoiled the rope and tried to throw it closer. "You can reach that."

Ethan grabbed the rope and pressed his back against the rock face. "I'm going to fall. I don't want to die. Please don't let me die," he blubbered and wiped at his face with his good hand.

"You're not going to die. Put the rope around your waist. You can do it."

"I can't. You have to come down and get me. If

you don't, I'll fall off the edge." He hiccupped and cried harder.

"I have to stay up here and pull you to safety. Act like a damn man and put that fucking rope around your waist."

Ethan released the rope. It dangled only inches away from him. Gage ran a hand over his face. The ledge wasn't big enough for the two of them to stand on. If Ethan wouldn't put the rope around his waist, there wasn't anything else he could send him. He would have to scale the face and grab Ethan himself. He needed help.

"Ethan, I'm calling for backup. Don't move. Do you hear me? Just stay put. Ethan, say something."

"I hear you. I'll wait for backup."

He fumbled for his phone and called Jett. This would be a big issue for the ranch. They'd be sued, even though the incident was that jackass's fault. Jett would go batshit crazy when he heard a guest fell off the cliff, and blame him. He should have known someone like Ethan would go and do a fuck-up move. If he had been paying better attention and not thinking about where he wanted to be after the tour was over, this wouldn't have happened. He had trusted his guests, and he should have known better than to trust amateurs in a situation like this one. Safety should always be the number one priority. He was fucking up here the same way he was fucking up the investigation.

"What's up?" Jett's voice interrupted his internal raging.

"We've got a big problem."

****

The sun drooped behind the treetops, and the cool

mountain breeze froze the sweat on Gage's skin. He watched as Jett and his rancher rode off with Ethan. Jett had arrived with the climbing gear and the extra help to guide the other guests back.

Gage had been the one to go down the mountain face and rescue Ethan. The rocks cut his arms as he bounced off the side and missed his mark. The mountain used him for batting practice before his feet found their purchase. It took some convincing for Ethan to get in the gear and hold on to him. He hung suspended for the better part of an hour before Ethan finally moved. Jett and his rancher pulled them to safety.

"It's not your fault," Jett had whispered in his ear and surprised him. "Don't go beating yourself up for this. That's an order, big brother."

Now his muscles ached and his pride hurt as much as a rope burn. He wasn't sure if he had the energy to mount Kit Kat and make it home. He wanted to call Calista and explain, but the words only twisted in his head. He'd explain in person. Her smile would ease his pain. Unless she pushed him away again. He wanted to trust her to understand, but what if she didn't?

Chapter Eighteen

Calista turned off the sander and wiped the sweat from her brow. Her shoulders ached, and her back muscles twisted into a braid, but pride puffed up her lungs. She had spent the day sanding every kitchen cabinet and door.

Her father stayed away from the main house while she and Justin worked side by side. Not having to deal with her dad gave her the energy to keep going. Once the kitchen was done, she would start advertising for more guests. And try again to dismantle Ava's room.

"Calista, do you want to take a lunch break?" Justin carried a freshly stained cabinet door to the deck and leaned it against the rail with the others to dry.

She checked her phone for the third time. It was after noon. Her heart flipped. Gage would be there soon, which meant she wanted Justin to leave. Not because she didn't think he was a great helper and a good kid, but because Gage would scowl and become angry. She didn't want anything to ruin her afternoon plans. She was going to get Gage Ryker in her bed today.

"I forgot about an appointment I have this afternoon. Let's take off early. I'll pay you for the whole day. Go enjoy the sun." She wrapped up the sander cord.

He bounced down the deck steps to her. "Are you

sure? There's still a lot of work to be done. I don't mind doing it. I could keep working while you go to your appointment. Unless you don't want me here without you."

Of course he would think that. "Hey, that's not what I'm getting at. If you say you didn't have anything to do with the robbery at Kennedy's, then I believe you."

"Sheriff Ryker doesn't." Justin kicked the dirt.

"Once he finds a good lead, he'll realize he's been wrong."

"He'll never let me date his daughter. He doesn't think I'm good enough for her. He says it has nothing to do with me being from the rez, but I don't believe that."

She put a hand on his shoulder. "Gage's grandfather grew up on the reservation."

"Seriously?"

"Yup. His family was very poor. Grandpa Ryker always wanted to be a landowner. Both of his parents died when he was about sixteen, I think Gage said. So Grandpa Ryker left and joined the army."

"Izzi never mentioned it."

She lifted a shoulder. "I probably shouldn't say this, but I guess she has other things on her mind when she's with you."

Justin's face bloomed red. "What happened with Sheriff Ryker's grandfather?"

"His relatives were pretty mad about him joining the United States military, but he wanted a better life. He planned to bring his new skills back to the reservation, but he met a woman and fell in love." Kind of like what might be happening between Justin and Gage's daughter. Calista didn't know if such young love could last, but she did know there wasn't any point in fighting it.

"That would be Izzi's great-grandmother."

"That's right. She wasn't accepted on the reservation. So Grandpa Ryker left again with his new wife and bought the land, on a loan, that is the Ryker ranch now. Gage is very proud of his grandfather and his family. He would not judge you for being Indian."

"This great-grandfather and me have a lot in common. That's cool. My brother and parents want me to go back to the rez after school, but I won't. I've hurt my people, but I can't live like that anymore. I told Jamie he could live with me instead of our cousin, but he says no. We either all live together or not at all. I hope he changes his mind."

"I'd like to meet your brother sometime."

Justin smirked. "He won't come here, and he's not easy to get along with. He's angry all the time. I could never let him meet Izzi. He wouldn't like her. He'd see her as the reason I left home. Which isn't true, but that won't matter."

"You really like her, don't you?"

He shrugged. "Does it matter? Her father would rather skin me alive than allow us to date."

"Give him some time." She would try and talk to Gage about the kids. "Go get some lunch. I'll see you tomorrow."

"I'll just hang a few cabinets first."

"You don't have to do that. It can wait." She checked the phone again. They would probably have a little time before Gage arrived. The tour could always run late, and he'd have to put the horses away. He'd want everything in order before he left.

Justin narrowed his eyes. "I don't mind."

"Okay. Just a couple. I can make you lunch while you work." She wanted to take a quick shower and get the sweat and dust off her before Gage arrived, but that might not happen.

She hoped he wouldn't mind a little grit on her. Or they could shower together. That thought had her bouncing into the house.

Justin hung cabinet doors while she whipped together egg salad. She sliced fresh tomatoes and onions. The roll toasted and filled the kitchen with the smell of warm bread. Justin scoffed the food down and washed it away with a soda.

"That was great. Thanks. I guess I'll go now unless you want me to finish."

"No, that's fine. We've made some good progress. The place is really shaping up. Go do something fun this afternoon."

He went out the back door and into the warm afternoon. She watched as his car drove away. Gage was very late, and that wasn't like him. The man who thrived by the rules also made sure to run on time. Where was he? Had he changed his mind? Maybe something came up at work with the robberies.

She made a quick call to the hospital to check on Kennedy and see if Gage might have stopped there, but no one had seen him. She didn't want to bother him while he was out with guests. A call to him would have to wait.

She wanted to call the ranch, but she didn't want to speak with Gage's mother, and she didn't want to worry Izzi for any reason in case he hadn't been seen in a while. Instead, she left the door unlocked and jumped into the shower.

After drying off and dressing, she checked for a text or a call. Still no Gage. The sun hung low and painted the sky in pinks and oranges. He wasn't coming. That realization weighed down her shoulders. Standing on his lawn last night must have scared him off. He didn't want to be with her. She should have expected that. Still, she was a grown-up and not a teenager in love. She sent a quick text to see if he was okay.

She grabbed her yoga mat and went out to the dock. Maybe a few sun salutations would calm the nervous energy and disappointment stirring inside her. It was better to focus on why she came home in the first place and not on the reason she left. She and Gage were the past. That was the best place for them.

Yoga soothed her aching muscles and settled her mind. She flowed from pose to pose as the thoughts in her brain floated off and slid under the surface of the lake.

A truck's loud engine rumbled down the driveway, interrupting the quiet of the early evening. She stopped the flow of poses and turned toward the front yard. For a second, hope that Gage had arrived tapped on her heart, but it was more likely the overflow of guests from the Ryker ranch.

Jett had called the other day and said he was sending some guests her way. That call had surprised her. She expected everyone in Gage's family to hate her because she had broken his heart, but they were always ready to move forward. A lesson she should try and practice. She really was a terrible yogi. She rounded the garage and stopped.

A smile burst from her lips, but she pushed it off her face. He'd come after all, but who did he think he was showing up so late without a call? Did he expect her to just wait around for him? Even though she had.

Gage eased out of his truck. He stretched his back and rolled his head on his neck. His long stride was slow and deliberate as he favored one side. His shirt was ripped and covered in dirt. Long, bloody scratches punctuated his arms.

"What happened to you?" She ran to him, letting go of her earlier anger and hurt.

His smile lit up his eyes. He scratched the back of his neck. "I'm sorry I'm late. I should have sent a text, but I wanted to get here as fast as I could."

"Did you get into a fight? Never mind. Just come inside. I'll get you some ice."

"Hang on." He grabbed her and pulled her against him. "The only thing I have wanted all day was to hold you so I could smell your sweet scent. It's what kept me going."

"Gage, what happened?" She rested her head against his chest and listened to his heart pound.

"It's a long story, and I don't want to relive it."

"Was it on the tour? Did someone get hurt? Is it Izzi?" She eased back to see his face. His expression was neutral. He had closed down the wall over his emotions.

"It's not Izzi. She's fine. A guest on the tour this morning. I should've known."

Worry tried to strangle the next words. "Did someone die?"

He closed his eyes and shook his head. "I've made a lot of trouble for Jett and the ranch. I should've been paying better attention. It's all my fault."

She wrapped her arms around his neck and held him to her. Her fingers toyed with the ends of his hair. "I don't understand. Come inside. Let me help you get cleaned up."

He gripped her shoulders. "Someone almost died under my watch."

He explained about the man and the fall and kept his gaze off in the distance. Pain carved deep lines around his mouth, and dark circles hung under his eyes like half moons.

"That's not your fault. You told them to stay together."

"If he hadn't wandered off the first time, we would have taken the safer route. Those riders weren't experienced enough for that trail. If that guy sues us, we could be through. I may have destroyed my family's business in one afternoon."

"Let's go inside." She took his hand, led him into the house, and pulled out a chair at the kitchen table. "Do you want a beer?"

He stayed in the doorway. "No, thanks. I'm sorry. I'm not good company. I wanted to come over here and explain in person. I didn't want you thinking I was blowing you off. I thought about you all morning, but after today I should go."

"Please stay."

"Why?"

"Because I think you need someone to lean on and maybe some ibuprofen. Did anyone look at your injuries?"

"I can handle this. I just wanted to apologize."

She ran a dish towel under cold water. "Sit."

"Calista, please stop. I don't need you to pamper me. I only have a few scratches. That guy broke his arm and could've died. What if he died today? That man was my responsibility, and I let him and Jett down. I was so mad at that guest for not following my rules on the trail I wanted to punch him, and then when he cried like a baby because he was inches from death, I wanted to punch myself instead."

Things were starting to make some sense. Ajay was always in the room. Gage would never forgive himself and saw every opportunity to help someone as his chance for redemption. Had she had a part in that? What had she done to him while she was busy wallowing in her own grief? "Please sit down."

He plopped into the chair and stretched out his long legs. "I can go, if you want."

"I want you to stay and let me help you for a change." She dropped to her haunches and wiped the dried blood off his skin. The scratches weren't deep.

She held his gaze. What would she do if something terrible happened to him? She couldn't let him leave this earth without making sure he knew how she felt about him. She had wasted the past sixteen years thinking she could take all the time she wanted to forgive him and to get over losing Ava.

That wasn't true at all. They weren't given an unlimited amount of time. She had been selfish and arrogant to think she could hold out her feelings.

He cupped her face. "I'm fine. Thank you."

She wanted to kiss him. "Let me get you that ibuprofen. And maybe a shower to ease the tension in your muscles? Do you still keep a go bag?"

"You remembered that." His lips twitched in a

small smile.

She wiped the last of the blood from his arms and rinsed the towel out. She had remembered everything about him. She had hoped as time went by she would be able to forget the little details of their lives together, as if she were sweeping crumbs into the garbage, but every tiny grain of her memory remained.

"You can shower in my bathroom. Do you want me to get your bag?"

"I think I can handle that. If you're hungry, I can take you for dinner after." He pushed out of the chair and placed a kiss on her lips.

"Dinner would be great. I'm glad you're okay."

"I'll be right back." He went out the door.

She turned the shower up to high. The bathroom with its white-tiled floor and walls filled with steam. She grabbed fresh towels from the linen closet and tried not to think about Gage wrapping one around his waist.

"Calista, are you up here?" He stood inches from her in the hallway. His large frame took up most of the space and stole the breath from her lungs. Sweat glistened on his dark skin.

"I left some hydrogen peroxide and bandages on the counter for you. I can wash your clothes if you want." Her tongue tangled around the words and strangled their sound.

"I'll just stick them in my bag." He held up a black duffel. "Thanks for understanding."

"The accident wasn't your fault."

"Give me ten minutes. I'll be right out." He kissed her lips in a swift motion and closed the bathroom door.

She needed something to do while he showered in her house, or she would go right into that bathroom.

The image of his broad shoulders and long legs filling up her shower flooded her brain. His dark hair would be slicked back and pressed against his neck. Probably reaching his shoulders. She heaved a long breath. She loved his hair.

The hot water would run in rivulets over his toned muscles. She wanted to chase them with her tongue. Sweat pooled between her breasts.

She trotted down the steps to the kitchen and tugged open the refrigerator. The air cooled her down. "Get a grip," she said to herself.

He was probably hungry and tired, and the last thing he would want would be to start making out. They could make love another time. Ugh. Have sex. No one said anything about love.

"Shit." Gage's voice echoed through the ceiling.

She ran for the stairs and banged on the bathroom door. "Gage, are you okay?"

He didn't respond.

"Gage?"

She shoved the door open and stopped. He wore nothing but a towel around his thin waist. His black chest hair dusted his defined muscles and narrowed to a line that led to the top of that towel. She dragged her gaze back to his face, but his hair, wet and hanging, caught her attention. Her heart clogged her throat. She'd wanted to avoid him wet and sexy, and she walked right into her fantasy.

He pointed to the counter. "I spilled the whole bottle."

It took a second for the image to register. Hydrogen peroxide dripped off the counter and pooled onto the floor. Why was that important when Gage stood in her bathroom half-naked? "Oh. Hang on." She grabbed a towel from the hamper and mopped up the mess.

"I'm sorry. My hands were shaking. It was stupid." He ran his hands over his hair. His pec muscles flexed with the movement.

She tried to still her heart. "Maybe you're hurt worse than you thought. I could call Jett for you. Or take you to the hospital."

"I don't need the hospital. It's nerves."

She had never seen him get scared except for that night when everything went wrong. "Since when is Gage Ryker nervous about anything?"

"Honestly, not since the first time we made love." He held her gaze.

She swallowed her own nerves, still lodged in her throat. "We don't...if you don't want..." She couldn't finish the thought.

"I didn't plan on standing in your bathroom in a towel wishing you would have come in while I was in the shower. I planned to buy you lunch like a gentleman, take you for a walk, pick a wildflower, and hand it to you so you'd smile up at me. Then, and only then, if you would give me the honor, I would have tried to kiss you again. But there I was thinking about the mess of this afternoon and how I wanted you underneath me to ease some of the pain. Except I don't know if you still want me. What if you still hated me? That's when I dropped the bottle."

She didn't think she could go on talking to him as if this were any other conversation. She took a deep breath and tried a little faith. "I want you."

He cleared the small space in two steps and cupped

her face. His lips pressed against hers, and the room faded away. She wrapped her arms around his neck and curled her fingers in his wet hair. He parted her lips and intertwined their tongues. His mouth pressed harder, and his tongue moved in a frenzy. A galvanic energy ran across her skin, leaving goose bumps in its wake. She tried to keep up with him, wanting more of his almost-agitated kissing.

She could be the release he needed because that was what he was for her. He would be the pathway to a future that wasn't clouded by heartache and pain. He might be able to help her wipe clean the windows of her soul covered in dirt and grime and for the first time in sixteen years see the road ahead.

His hands ran up and down her back. The towel did nothing to hide his desire. She couldn't believe she and Gage were in this spot. She hadn't dreamed they would find their way back to each other after she sealed their fate with a slap. She wouldn't think about any of that now. Those memories would be muted by this one.

She ran her fingers over his chest and down the thin line of soft hair to his navel. Her hands explored his legs. The bumpy texture of the scar on his thigh was like finding an old forgotten treasure. He moaned as her hand went under the towel and rested on his hip. Joy burst her heart open and sent her home again.

He tugged her shirt over her head. She unhooked her bra and let it fall to the floor.

"Beautiful," he said on a long breath. "Now come back here." He tugged her closer.

His skin was still warm from the shower. She pressed against him, allowing his heat to mix with hers. His chest hair rubbed against her nipples and sent her head spinning. He pulled on the waist of her yoga pants, but the material stuck to her sweaty skin.

"Let me." She helped him and pushed her leggings to the floor. She stood naked before him, exposed, with nothing to shield her if this night turned on its head. She was ready to give herself to him again and possibly break her heart in so many pieces it could never be mended.

His hands sought all the places on her body that were once his. He dropped his mouth to her breast and brought the nub between his teeth. He nipped, and a prick of ecstatic pain shot through her. She brought her mouth to his neck and returned the favor.

"May I?" She tugged on the towel, and it dropped.

His desire-filled smile brightened his eyes.

"You are beautiful too." She took him in her hand and stroked the full length of him.

His kiss was hot and strong like the sun. His hands continued to search for something and everything at the same time. He broke the kiss, and their chests heaved.

"Do you want to go to the bedroom?" she said.

"Right here." He hiked her up on the counter and stood between her legs. "Unless you don't want to."

He had always made sure she was safe and taken care of. It was why the night of the tragedy she had depended on him to save her again. When he couldn't, she had fallen apart. "I have never wanted anything more than to be with you again."

His fingers gripped her hips. One hand slid over her side and dipped lower. She moaned as he found the place that longed for his touch the most. He set the pace she liked best without her having to remind him. The pleasure built inside her in a blissful agony. She wanted him to be hers again.

She pushed his hand out of the way to make room for what she really needed. "Now."

He kissed her again and thrust himself inside her. She wrapped her legs around him to take in all of him. She needed to be filled up the way a well needs water. She had stopped living and hadn't realized how much until now. No other man could drive her to the edge of ecstasy the way Gage could. It wasn't only his strong muscles and sexy smile but also his soft heart and protectiveness. He showed her a side of him he didn't share with anyone else.

They moved together in a rhythm meant for only them. She held on to his back as if she might drown if she let go. The desire curled inside her until it broke like a crashing tide against the sand. Her body shuddered as he continued to rock his hips.

He gripped her waist, plunged one more time, and met her on the other side of the sweet, dreamy pleasure.

"I think I need another shower," he said.

She placed kisses along his neck and shoulder. Her fingers caressed his chest and dropped lower.

He gripped her hand in his. "Hey."

She opened her eyes and with some regret pulled her lips from his skin. "What's the matter?"

He held her face in his hands and burned his gaze into hers. "You keep that up and I won't let you out of this bathroom."

"That was kind of the idea, stud. You can shower again later. For now, take me to bed."

He scooped her up and carried her into the bedroom. He made love to her until the sun set and the sky was filled with stars. Not that she saw them. The only view she wanted was the one of the man above her, beneath her, and beside her.

Chapter Nineteen

Gage held Calista close. Her sweet scent drifted around him while they lay entwined in her bed. Her breathing had deepened as he stroked her back. He didn't think he would be able to fall asleep. As long as she was wrapped around him naked, he would want to make love to her. He had lost time to make up for. He didn't care if he sounded like a teenager who couldn't control his hormones.

She had offered herself up to him today. She was ready to move forward. At least he hoped that was the case because she'd given him the few minutes of peace he needed. With Calista, he could catch his breath.

He wanted her to love him again and to understand what Ajay did wasn't his fault. In some ways, it had been. He should have been a better authority figure for his brother. He should have been able to give the right kind of advice. He hadn't known how to handle Ajay. His mother was busy with the ranch, and he was the oldest. The responsibility had been his, and he'd failed at it miserably, which was why he kept the reins tight on Izzi. He couldn't let anything happen to his daughter. He had no excuse this time. He wasn't young. He wasn't inexperienced.

With regret, he untangled himself from her beautiful body and shoved his legs into his boxer briefs. He found his phone in the bathroom and sent a text to

Izzi. He lied about working, but he'd be home soon. He shot a second text to Jett and asked him to sleep at his place. He didn't want Izzi to be alone all night, and there was no way he wanted to tell his mother he was at Calista's house. He might be forty and the sheriff of the town, but he still couldn't look his mother in the eye and admit he had sex.

"Gage?" Calista's voice drifted toward him.

He padded back into the bedroom. "I'm right here."

"I woke up and thought you left without saying goodbye."

"Hey, I would never do that." He climbed back into bed and gathered her to him. Her head rested against his shoulder. She snaked her arm around his waist.

"I was worried you regretted what happened." Her voice was low, and her breath warm against his skin.

"This is the only place I want to be." That was the truth, and hopefully not too much truth for her. They might have made love several times—he grinned—but they had not talked about what would happen between them. "I needed to check on Izzi."

If she asked him to leave, he would, but if she wanted him to stay the night, she wouldn't have to ask twice.

"Is she okay?" Her fingers skimmed his back. He leaned into the soft pressure of her touch with ease.

"I just didn't want her to worry about where I was."

"You're a good father. She's lucky to have you."

"Thanks." The compliment and the press of her breasts against his chest turned up the heat in his body several degrees. He started to grow hard again.

"Can you promise me something?" Her hands continued to entice him.

"Sure." He tangled his fingers in the ends of her long hair.

"Can you promise not to run away if I start to freak out about what's happening between us?"

"Are you sorry?" He stilled his hands and held his breath.

She gripped him tighter. "No. Never think that. I'm glad you're here and we did what we did. It's just when the sun comes up and we have to face the real world, I hope I don't get scared."

"Are you talking about your father not wanting us to be together or about your feelings for me?" He shifted up on an elbow to see her better.

He could handle Andy Hartman, who would be unhappy about this arrangement, but if she backpedaled and left him again because of the past, he might not recover from that.

"I never thought we'd be in this situation, but when I'm with you, I want to stop living in the past, and when I'm in Backwater, all I can do is relive it. Ava is everywhere in this house and around every corner. Your family fills in all the other crevices she isn't. It's hard to breathe sometimes."

"Can I ask you to promise me something?" He wanted to make things easier for her, but until she was ready, the past would haunt her. He'd try, though. He didn't want her hurting anymore because of his brother.

"Of course."

"Tell me if you're frightened. Don't push me away this time. If you're leaving me, I want it to be for something other than Ajay. If I'm not the man you want today, I can live with that. Please don't judge me for the man I was before." Because he'd been trying for sixteen years to be better.

She placed a warm hand on his cheek. "I'll be honest with you. I promise."

He brushed his lips against hers. His insides burned for more of her. He had years of missed chances to love her to make up for. She laced her fingers in his hair and returned the kiss.

He ran his hand down her back and cupped her bottom. She gripped his hand and eased away from the kiss.

"Did I do something wrong?" he said.

"The opposite, but I'm starving. You never took me to lunch or dinner." Even with only the moonlight spilling through the curtains, he could see the sparkle in her eye.

Relief spread through his chest, and he laughed. "I can take care of your empty stomach. I can run into town and pick something up at the café." He checked his phone. "I have about thirty minutes before they close. If I call, they'll wait for me."

"Or we could whip up something here." She ran a finger down his chest and stopped right before the good part.

"I like that idea." He kissed her nose.

His phone went off. He wanted to ignore it but stole a glance anyway. Barry Pearce was calling. He could let his deputy handle whatever was happening. Tonight was about Calista.

"You should get that. I don't mind. It could be important." She gathered the sheet around her.

On a long breath, he sat up and swiped at the

screen. "Sheriff Ryker."

"Sorry to disturb you, Sheriff, but we have another robbery. And this time someone's been shot."

****

Gage jumped from the truck and ran down Main Street. The ambulance and the tanker truck blocked the road. Bystanders, some in their pajamas, huddled on the sidewalk. His heart throbbed in his ears as his boots stampeded the ground. Someone blocked the entrance to the florist. He shoved them aside.

"Where is she?" He gulped in air.

Faces turned toward him. His deputy was there. Luke Patterson from the EMS squad knelt on the floor, packing up his bag. John Granger from the fire department spoke into his phone.

Barry took a step forward. The lines around his mouth deepened, and his cheeks had sunken. His eyes were bloodshot. Marty Boseman stared at him with glassy eyes, then averted his gaze back to the floor. He was handcuffed.

"I'm sorry, boss."

He pushed Barry aside and went behind the tall display case of flower arrangements. Anger seared his blood. Nyx Blackwood knelt by the gurney and held the hand of the woman who acted like his other mother.

"Phyllis…" His voice stuck in his throat. He couldn't lose someone else he cared about to a damn gunshot wound.

Nyx turned and blocked his path. "Gage, you should—"

"Get the hell out of the way, Nyx." He stepped around her to get to Phyllis.

She was so small on the gurney. His heart ached.

Her eyes were closed, but Nyx hadn't removed the oxygen yet. A brace was secured around her neck. "Phyllis?"

Her eyelids fluttered open. Her lips moved into a small smile. "Sheriff, I was waiting for you." Her voice was like tires over gravel. She closed her eyes, and he held his breath.

She opened them again, and the air left his lungs. He took her hand in both of his. "If you wanted a day off, you should have just asked."

Her grip on his hand was weak. "Don't smartmouth me. And don't you worry about a thing. My office is a tightly run ship. You'll find everything you need." She squeezed her eyes shut and groaned. "This one hurts, Gage."

He kept his gaze on Phyllis and said, "Nyx, what's the assessment?"

"GSW to the abdominal area. We need to go, Gage. She insisted we wait for you, but she could be bleeding internally."

Of course she had insisted, because that was Phyllis. He leaned closer to her ear and whispered, "Don't die on me."

"I love you too," she whispered back.

He helped Nyx get Phyllis in the ambulance. He slammed the back doors, and they sped off with lights flashing and sirens blaring.

He waited until the sirens couldn't be heard and turned on Marty Boseman. He grabbed him by the collar and lifted him up. "You stupid idiot. I warned you something like this would happen. If she dies, so help me, I will nail your ass to the wall." He shook Boseman until drool ran down his face.

"Sheriff, stop." Barry's hands were on him, but he threw Barry off.

This was all his fault because he hadn't solved the robberies. His town didn't trust him. Another person he loved was slipping away from him, and he could have done something to stop it. How was he going to walk into his department and not find Phyllis standing there with her glasses on her head and bossing him around?

"Sheriff," Barry yelled.

He wanted to shake Marty Boseman until his eyes fell out of his head. Until all the pain and hurt and anger could slink back under its rock and stay there forever.

"He's an old man, Gage." Kace's voice cut through the confused noise in his head. He pulled Gage's hands free from Boseman's shirt, and Boseman slumped against the storefront.

He held his brother's gaze. The same black eyes as his stared at him, but he didn't see Kace at all.

"When did you get here?" He hadn't seen or heard Kace arrive.

"I came as soon as I heard."

As always, one of his brothers was there when he needed them, but he continued to let them down. First Ajay in the worst way possible. And today with Jett. Jett could lose the ranch because of him. The only thing Jett loved more than his family was his ranch. What about Kace? How many times had he let Kace down? Or Lock? They were residents of the town. Hadn't he let the whole town down too?

"Barry, what happened?" He needed answers to feel in control of something.

Barry read from his notebook. "She was helping Marty with the night shift and making some flower arrangements. Someone banged on the front door. He went out front to see who it was. They argued. Marty had his gun pointed at one of the suspects. The kid ran, and Phyllis ran after him. Marty pulled the trigger. She was in the way."

For once he'd taken good notes.

"Did you get a look at who came in your store, Marty?"

Marty looked up at him with a watery gaze. "Two Indian boys. Young. One of them looked like the boy that Howard hired to paint his fence. I'm sorry, Gage. I didn't mean for this to happen."

"Shut up. No one wants to hear you're sorry."

He marched away with Kace calling after him.

Chapter Twenty

"Thanks, Lincoln. Anything you can find out about Justin Crow and his brother would be a big help." Gage pulled his tie from the rack in his bedroom closet and laid it on the bed beside his only black suit.

"My pleasure. I'll run his name through every program I have. Something will come up. It always does. What did this kid do anyway?" Lincoln Smith was a private bodyguard with connections and skills not too many other people had.

Gage had met Lincoln through an old police academy friend during a Christmas party some years back. He had liked the man instantly and often hosted him on the ranch. "He's involved in a string of robberies. I just can't prove it yet."

And if he could find a way, he'd pin murder on Justin Crow too.

"I'll call you back when I find something. And hey, I'm sorry for your loss."

"Thanks." He ended the call before he embarrassed himself and started crying. He'd save it for the funeral. Then no more.

He slid the tie around his neck, but his hands shook. He wasn't ready to do this. Wasn't even sure if he could. He hadn't been to the cemetery in a very long time. His mother always gave him her disapproving look when she asked him about it. But he wouldn't go.

Couldn't go. Those gravestones weren't his family. His father and brother had moved on. Their spirits lived someplace else. Maybe that was his Kootenai heritage speaking, but he liked to believe they were more than just bones in a rotting coffin. When he wanted to talk to his dad, he stood in the middle of the field.

He would have to watch as Phyllis's coffin was lowered into the ground. His heart fractured, and his legs buckled under the weight of the broken pieces. He dropped onto the corner of the bed and held his head in his hands.

"Gage, it's almost time." Calista's voice forced him to look up. She stood in the doorway of his bedroom in a black dress. She had pulled her hair up in a knot at the back of her head and had swept a gloss across her lips.

His breath caught in his throat at the sight of her. "I need a few minutes." He wrestled with the tie and lost.

"Let me." She untangled the fabric from his grip and smiled up at him.

"I can tie my own tie." If he could hear the growl in his voice, she wouldn't have missed it.

She kept smiling at him. "I know you can, but I can also see the anguish on your face. There's no crime in getting a little help today. Plus, I want to touch you. It makes me feel better." She finished knotting the tie and flattened her palms against his chest.

Her touch melted some of the ice around his heart. "I went for a five-mile run this morning, but it didn't do anything to make the anger stop. I want to punch something." Once he found something out on Justin, he was going to find a way to get that kid alone and beat the shit out of him.

He'd spoken to Justin after the robbery at the flower shop. His alibi checked out, which just pissed him off because he wanted a reason to arrest the kid. Marty's identification of a person that looked like Justin wasn't enough, and there hadn't been any surveillance footage because men like Marty Boseman refused to listen to him when he told them to update their security.

If the kid Marty saw wasn't Justin, Gage hoped it was the brother. He needed more information. If Lincoln came through, this would all be over. He wasn't going to let Phyllis die in vain the way Ajay had.

"Give yourself time." Calista's voice dragged him from his runaway thoughts.

"I'm out of time. Four robberies and now a death. The residents want answers, and so do I."

"The residents can wait. Today their sheriff needs to be with family and friends."

"Thank you for being here. It's the only thing keeping me together." He wrapped his fingers around hers.

"I'll be here for as long as you want."

He wanted to say he wished she'd never leave. He wanted to ask her to stay and make a life with him, but the words stuck in his throat. He'd ask her later, after they made love again and some of the edges of the hurt softened.

"Dad, Uncle Kace and Gammy are here. They're ready to go." Izzi stood in the doorway in her gray skirt and white top. The cuts on her legs had healed.

The interruption had Calista pulling away from him. He wanted to pull her back.

"I'll follow in my car." She smoothed back her already-neat hair.

He shrugged into his suit jacket. "You don't want to drive with me and Izzi?"

"You two need some time together. I'll be right behind you."

"Izzi, tell Uncle Kace and Gammy we'll be right out." He waited for her to disappear down the hall and took Calista's hand again.

"I want you beside me today. I don't care what anyone thinks about us. Not my family, not your father. Izzi loves you. That's all that matters to me."

"Are you sure? Today is going to be hard for everyone. I know I'm here right now, but anyone would understand my stopping by considering the circumstances. You and I together as a couple in public, without warning, might be too much for your family. It's going to send my dad over the edge."

"My family doesn't hate you, and I will handle your father."

"Your family has every right to hate me for the pain I caused you."

"You were just reacting to losing your sister. The only thing that matters is we're past it now. I don't want to focus on that night anymore. Ride with me, Calista."

****

Everyone was gone. Gage hadn't moved from the metal folding chair sinking in the grass. Sweat ran down his neck into the collar of his dress shirt. The heat from the sun was unbearable. His body ached. The woman he loved like a second mother was gone because of him. He couldn't save Ajay, and now his incompetence had taken away another person he held dear. This wasn't supposed to happen. His job was to keep everyone safe. If he couldn't do his job, he shouldn't be the sheriff anymore. And what if he couldn't keep Izzi safe? Just the idea of her hurting because of him nearly stopped his heart.

The chair beside him creaked with the weight of a person sliding on it. Her spicy scent drifted toward him and eased some of the hurt. "I thought you left," he said.

"I couldn't. My ride is still here." Calista gripped his knee.

He closed his eyes and fought back the emotions. Her tenderness, the thing he'd needed sixteen years ago, she gave so willingly today. He wanted to drown in it and forget. "Can we go to your place? I can't go to the restaurant and see Phyllis's husband and kids. They would have every right to spit in my face."

"Gage, look at me."

His neck burned with the weight of his heavy head as he met her gaze.

She placed a cool palm on his hot cheek. "It's not your fault. Phyllis's family knows that. Marty Boseman behaved badly, and because of that, a tragedy happened. You warned them all not to take matters into their own hands. He didn't listen to you. You could not have known Phyllis would be anywhere near him."

"If I solved the robberies. If I could prove who did it. She'd still be here giving me a bad time about everything."

"It might do you some good to go to the restaurant and tell good stories about Phyllis. Remembering her that way and not like this." She pointed to the coffin.

"No." He had no right to tell stories about her to make himself feel better. He would sit here and sear this image into his brain.

"Do you want to visit with your brother and dad for a while? Your mom is over there."

"Absolutely not."

"Tell me how I can help you." She grabbed his hand and squeezed.

The back of his throat ached. He gathered Calista in his arms because he didn't want to feel the pain anymore.

And cried.

Chapter Twenty-One

Calista unlocked the front door of the B and B. The smell of fresh paint met her in the living room. The place was shaping up, thanks to Justin. A name she would not bring up while Gage was with her.

He hadn't said a word on the ride from the cemetery to her house. He'd kept his jaw set and his hands on the wheel. His knuckles had been white the whole time. She wanted to ease the pain for him and didn't have a clue how to begin. She had let him cry on her shoulder but struggled with seeing him fall apart. It had reminded her of that night. He had been crying then too, and she had not helped him. The echo of that slap on his face haunted her at night. She hoped she was making up for that just a little now.

"Do you want a drink? I have some wine and a couple of beers." She kicked off her strappy sandals. She hadn't worn them since Fox's funeral a few weeks ago. After today, she was going to burn those shoes. They only brought bad energy and aching feet.

He tossed his suit jacket on the couch and tugged his tie off his neck. "A beer would be great."

She handed him the bottle. He held it to his head. She wasn't expecting that. "Do you have a headache?"

"I guess so." He twisted off the cap and took a swig.

"Are you hungry?"

"All I want to do is hold you." He put the bottle on the counter and wrapped his arms around her.

She sank into him and inhaled his woodsy scent. She relaxed to his heartbeat. This was the only place she wanted to be.

The kitchen door banged open. "What's going on here?" Her father's voice rattled her nerves and made her jump.

"Dad, I didn't know you were home." His presence had her saying stupid things. As if she were a teenager again and had been caught drinking or making out.

"Where else would I be? The funeral was over hours ago. Calista, do you realize what you're doing here?"

She eased out of Gage's embrace and squared her shoulders. "I'm pretty sure I do."

"Andy, you need to know Calista and I are working through our issues. We're going to be together." Gage stood his full height.

Her heart filled up her chest. Strength rolled off him. He was protecting her in that way he always had. His presence and the glare in his eye told everyone to back off. She was his, and he would take care of her. She had missed his protectiveness. It didn't matter that she could take care of herself. Knowing he was there for her gave her extra courage.

"Yes, Dad. Gage and I are back together."

Her father's eyes grew wide behind his glasses. "The Rykers aren't welcomed in my house." He slammed the door behind him.

She wilted against the counter. "I'm sorry. He's impossible this time because of all the changes I'm making. He's mad at me. Not you. He likes you. He wasn't even all that mad you arrested him."

"I should go. I've caused enough pain for one week. It might be better if we meet at my place instead of here until your dad comes around."

The weight of the day pressed on her. She didn't want him to go, especially if he needed her, but she could use a few hours to recharge her battery and find a way to make her father understand that she was moving on and he would have to as well.

"Are you going to be okay?" she said.

"I'm going to take Silver Bell out for a ride, and then I'll go for a run or something like that. I have work to do. I can stay busy. Can you come by later?" He gripped her hips and tugged her closer.

She snaked her arms around his neck and relished in his hard chest pressed to hers. "I'm working at the pub tonight to help Kennedy. She's just about ready to start working again. Can I come after that? It will be late."

"I don't care what time it is. I just want you in my bed tonight." He kissed her lips.

"Izzi will be across the hall. A sleepover won't be respectable behavior for her father to partake in." She undid the top button of his shirt and drew circles with her finger on the soft skin.

"I'll send her up to the main house for the night." He nipped at her earlobe. "We'll finish this later."

"I hope that's a promise."

"Oh, believe me, it is."

****

Calista changed out of her funeral clothes and threw them in a heap with the sandals. She never wanted to wear them again. She would always be reminded of the pain on the faces of the people hurting at the loss of their loved ones. Death was a part of life, but that didn't make it any easier.

She debated on talking to her father about her and Gage, but by the time she got the nerve up, he had gone out and didn't tell her where.

That gave her an opportunity to do what she'd wanted to do since she stepped foot in Backwater. She opened the door to the lake house. Of course, it wasn't locked. Her father hadn't learned a thing since the robbery. They hadn't replaced any of the stolen items, and the back door in the kitchen still had the wood nailed over the broken window. She'd have Justin fix that this week.

She wished she could make Gage see that Justin wasn't involved in these robberies, but how to do that escaped her as much as how to push her father forward did. Packing up Ava's room was going to end badly for her. That didn't stop her from dropping cardboard boxes on the floor of Ava's room.

The wooden box with Ava's trinkets was gone. Her father probably moved it into his room. That could be his keepsake. She wouldn't touch it if it was there, and she wouldn't look for it.

She didn't know how much time she had before her father returned. She couldn't afford to be particular with how items went into the boxes. She would start with the clothes in the closet.

She ripped dresses and shirts from the hangers and tossed them in the box. She didn't stop to look or remember times when Ava wore them. If she wasted even a second, she might not finish before her father came back. The dust flew around the room in angry swirls, as if to protest her actions as well. She threw open the window for fresh air.

The dresser was still full of undergarments, socks, and T-shirts that now smelled stale and old. Her hands flew over the worn fabrics and tossed them. Some of them hung suspended in the air before they floated to the ground. Many of them missed the box.

Tears spilled down her cheeks. She wiped her nose with the back of her hand. She had never thought this trip would turn out the way it had so far. Could she finally be at a place in her life she thought would never come? She had been waiting for years for the moment she would feel like herself again. Her yoga practice told her it would come, but she didn't know when and had started believing it never would. How would she put the pieces of her life together again? But she finally saw the light to guide her. Not everything was fixed between her and Gage, but they were so close. They would make it, and she would be able to close the wound with Ava's name on it. She would always miss her sister, but the pain could lessen.

"What the hell is going on in here?" Her father's bellow shook the open window.

She jumped. "Dad. When did you get back?"

"Never mind that. What are you doing?"

"I'm packing up." She held his gaze. "I want to clean this place up and start renting it out again. You can move back to the main house with me. You need to rent this house out to guests now. You need the money to pay the mortgage and continue the upkeep. Since you allowed the insurance to lapse, you also need the money to replace the stolen items."

"First I find you in the arms of Gage Ryker. Now

this. You only care about yourself. If you loved me at all, you would leave this room alone. I hate you. Get out of my house. Forever."

His words were a slap on her face. Her body shook with disbelief. He couldn't mean it, but the cold, dead stare in his blue eyes said he did. Her bottom lip trembled, but she wouldn't cry. Her father had been sending that message to her from the moment Ava died. He secretly blamed her for Ava's death.

If she hadn't been dating Gage, Ava would be alive. Ava would never have been friends with Ajay if it wasn't for her and Gage. Their relationship made a friendship with Ajay safe for Ava to explore. Except it had been anything but safe.

Her father had never said those exact words to her, but he didn't have to. He stopped looking at her the same way after. And when her mother left without her, the door to his heart shut forever. He didn't want her around as a reminder of what he lost. Not long after Ava died, she had packed her bags and moved away.

Without another word, because there was nothing left to say, she turned and walked out. She returned to the main house and packed her bags. She loaded her old SUV and drove away.

She stole a glance in the rearview mirror and said a final goodbye.

Chapter Twenty-Two

Gage pulled onto the ranch's property and took a deep breath. This day had torn him to pieces, but knowing Calista would be with him later gave him hope. He would change out of his suit and go for a run through the wooded trails, then take Silver Bell out for a short ride. He hoped he'd be able to breathe again by then.

He passed the main house. Jett's truck was there. Maybe Jett would saddle up a horse and come with him. He'd like to have his brother with him today.

His phone buzzed and connected through the truck's Bluetooth. Lincoln's number popped up on the screen. He hit the brakes. That was faster than he expected, but he had called Linc because of his skills.

"Hey, Linc, what did you find?"

"I don't know if this is what you want to hear, but there's nothing about Justin Crow you don't already know. He's clean. I even managed to get some outside footage of your town. He never spoke to anyone on those nights in question. He was nowhere near the flower shop the night of the shooting."

His heart sank. "What about the brother?"

"Jamie Crow is a little different. He has a history of doing some petty drug stuff. He was arrested once, but nothing stuck. He doesn't have a job. It appears he has a drinking problem too. There's no connection to the robberies, though. He could be stealing to keep up the drug habit, but I can't give you anything to pin on him. I'm sorry."

"I need to arrest someone." He had to tell his residents something. They were relying on him. He didn't care that Lincoln couldn't find anything. Justin was involved somehow. He could feel it in his gut.

"I'll keep poking around if you want, but turn your investigation away from this Justin Crow kid. He's not one of the unsubs."

"Please keep checking. Thanks. I'll be in touch." He ended the call and pounded the steering wheel until his hand hurt.

Fury shook him. He had no other leads besides Justin. He kept showing up at every robbery in one way or another. He had to be connected, and Gage was going to find out how.

He followed the road past the barns and slammed on the brakes. He threw the truck in park and bolted out the door. He ran like mad and tripped in his dress shoes. He righted himself and continued without further thought. Justin's beat-up sedan sat by the horse stable. Izzi had disobeyed him again and brought that criminal onto his property.

He bounded into the barn. They stood at the end of the aisle by Silver Bell's stall. White-hot rage blinded him. He had to shake his head to see clearly. He forced his legs to sprint harder, as if he were about to tackle his sworn enemy. His arms reached out. He grabbed Justin by the back of his shirt collar and threw him against a stall door. Justin bounced forward. His eyes rolled into the back of his head.

"Daddy," Izzi screamed.

He pushed Justin against the wall and fisted Justin's collar in his hands. He yanked Justin onto his toes to look him in the eye. "Who robbed the flower shop?"

Justin opened his mouth, but he couldn't bear to hear a lie. He shook Justin. "Tell me, or I swear I will shake it out of you."

"Daddy, stop. You're hurting him."

"Isabelle, go inside. Now." He never took his gaze off Justin. "Tell me who robbed the flower shop. You know. Do you realize that woman died because of you? She had a family who loved her." He shoved Justin against the wall again.

He slid to the ground, but Gage wrenched him back up.

"I don't know, Mr. Ryker. I wasn't there."

"You're lying." He hated liars. "Tell me." His voice blew Justin's hair back. The kid tried to squirm away, but there was nowhere to go.

"I don't know. I'm sorry."

Gage grabbed Justin's neck. His vision narrowed to a pinhole. He wanted answers because someone he loved had been murdered.

"Uncle Jett. Uncle Jett. Come quick." Izzi ran to the barn entrance and screamed.

Justin's fingers scratched at his hands. The kid tried to kick him, but Gage moved out of the way. His height gave him the advantage he needed. "Tell me who robbed that store, damn it."

Hands gripped his arms like a vice and dragged him away from Justin. Justin's neck slipped from his grasp.

"Jesus Christ, Gage, let go." Jett's deep voice

startled him.

The black around the edge of his vision retreated, and more of the barn came into view. Justin slid to the ground, holding his neck. His face was red, and he gasped for air. Izzi dropped down beside him.

Gage stared at Jett. His heart pounded in his ears. The hot rage continued to burn inside him.

"Have you lost your mind? You're the damn sheriff of this town. You were going to kill him. Don't we have enough trouble in our lives at the moment?" Jett wiped his face with his hands.

"I'm sorry."

"Daddy, how could you?" Izzi helped Justin stand.

Gage took a step forward, and Justin jumped back. "Stay the fuck away from me."

"I'm sleeping at Gammy's." Izzi led Justin out of the stables.

He turned to Jett. "He knows something about those robberies."

"Choking him to death isn't going to give you the answers. Do you think that's what Phyllis would want you to do? Pull your shit together and fast. I don't have time for this." Jett marched away.

He tugged his phone out his pants pocket and dialed Barry Pearce.

Barry answered on the first ring. "Everything okay, Sheriff?"

"You're the sheriff now. I quit."

****

Gage downed the last of his beer and crumpled the can in his fist. He threw it against the wall and knocked over the picture of him and his brothers taken on the Mother's Day before Ajay died. The glass shattered as it hit the corner of the cement hearth. He didn't move.

Calista wouldn't be there for several hours. He didn't know if he could wait until after her shift to see her. She made him feel better, and he needed that now. But he wouldn't go to the pub tonight. Not feeling as if he could tear someone in two.

He had really fucked things up today. He couldn't be the sheriff any longer if he was willing to hurt a suspect. Or hurt anyone. He'd shown his daughter the absolute worst part of him. He was a lousy father. His whole family would be disappointed in him, and that would include Phyllis.

The doorbell shattered the silence. He hung his head. It was probably his mother or Jett or even Barry. He couldn't deal with any of them at the moment, so he stayed on the couch. Like a scream in the night, the bell rang again.

His phone buzzed. Without thought, he glanced down. Calista had sent a text.

—Are you home? I'm at the door. I'm early.—

He jumped up and tore open the door. The breath left his lungs at the sight of her. He gathered her in his arms and inhaled her spicy scent. "God, it's good to see you."

She snuggled up against him. "I appreciate that, but what's the matter?"

He pulled back and looked down at her. "What makes you say that?"

She gave him a half shrug and a grin. "Well, it's all over your face."

"What is?" He pulled her into the house, then checked the area outside for anyone else. More habit than worry, but he did not want an unexpected guest to interrupt them.

"The anguish. Something happened since I left you."

"I don't want to talk about it now. I just want to hold you." He dropped down on the couch with her and wrapped his arms around her so she was tucked against him.

"Gage, you shouldn't keep it inside. Let me help you." Her fingers tapped against his chest.

Emotions he wanted buried deep bubbled up to the surface. He fought to keep them from spilling over. He had cried already. He wouldn't do it again. Move forward. That was what a Ryker did.

"I quit my job."

She jumped out of his arms. "No way is that possible. Please tell me you're joking." She dropped her gaze as if to consider what he said, but looked back at him. "You're not, are you?"

He hesitated. He wouldn't be able to stand her disappointment when she heard what he'd done to Justin. It would be like it had been with Ajay. Even if she didn't slap him this time, if the way she looked at him changed, he would crumble.

"I can't be the sheriff anymore."

"You're scaring me."

He took her hands in his and told her the whole story from the moment he called Lincoln. She sat there silent as the words spilled out on the wave of emotion he had desperately wanted kept inside.

"Hey, it's okay." She placed a hand on his face. Her touch lessened his pain.

"If Jett hadn't come in, I would've killed him." He was as certain of that as he was of sitting on the couch with Calista. He was also disgusted with himself.

"No, you wouldn't have. That's not who you are. I know you."

"How can you be so sure when I'm not sure?"

"Gage, you might be a lot of things, like a control freak pain in the ass, but you aren't a killer." She flopped against the back of the sofa with a wave of her hand.

A laugh broke open in his throat. He leaned back on the cushions beside her and stared at the ceiling. He reached for her hand, and she laced her fingers through his. His lungs worked again.

"I'm going to have to apologize to him." He needed to do that a lot lately.

"Yes."

"Why are you here so early? I should've asked you that sooner." He straightened and met her gaze. He really looked at her for the first time since she arrived.

Dark half circles draped under her eyes like a saddle blanket. Her hair was pulled back but hung in pieces around her face. She unhooked her hand from his and played with her beaded bracelet.

"My father threw me out." Her bottom lip trembled, and she worked it under her teeth.

"He's gone too far this time. I'll talk to him." He started to get up, but her hand on his thigh stopped him. "Babe, I'll take care of your father. He can't throw you out. Was he drunk?"

"I don't know if he had been drinking. Maybe, but it doesn't matter. He's made his point. He doesn't love me. Not the way I want him to. I can't stay in this small town. As long as he hangs on to the past with two tight fists, there isn't any place for me in his life. I don't want to live there anymore."

"What about us?" He'd just gotten her back, and now she was leaving again. He couldn't let that happen.

"I was hoping I could stay here for a couple of days. I'm working at the pub tonight still and tomorrow night. Then Kennedy comes back to work. After that, maybe we could try the long-distance thing?"

"After all the years we missed out on, I don't want two hours between us. How are we going to spend time together?"

"It doesn't have to be forever. Just until I figure out my next move. My lease is up in a few months. I can bartend and teach yoga anywhere. Maybe I can move to Missoula. That's not as far."

"If you leave town, I'm leaving too." The words hung in the air. He tasted them for a second to see if they felt sour on his tongue.

"Gage, get real. You're the sheriff."

"Not anymore."

"You're just upset right now. When things calm down a little, you'll want to go back to work. It's in your blood. This town is in your blood. You can't leave here. You can't leave Izzi, and she shouldn't move. She needs her family and stability. Our time will come."

"There aren't any guarantees, and you know that. I won't waste another minute without you. If you tell me you don't want me, that's one thing. But if you're willing to be by my side, then I want to be together. For everyone to see."

"I do want you, but we have a lot of things to work out. We've both been through so much recently."

"You're pushing me away."

"No." She sat back.

"Yes, damn it. You are. Again. Just say it this time. Look me in the eye, and tell me you don't love me, and I'll walk you straight to your car and never bother you. But you're going to say it. You're not getting off easy again." He pushed off the couch and picked up the broken picture frame. Everything in his life was like this glass covering the photo. He wanted to get to the place where the picture was, but he didn't know how to anymore.

He had played by the rules. He'd promised his father's memory he would take care of his brothers, and he failed. He had tried to make a good and honest life with Calista, but life laughed at his plans. He'd tried to do right by Izzi's mother when he hadn't really loved her enough to spend his life with her, and she left him to care for their child alone, only concerned about her own feelings. He followed the law to the letter, and the residents of his town took that law in their own hands, and now he lost Phyllis. Playing by the rules didn't pay off. Kace was right about that.

Calista eased the picture out of his hands and placed it on the table. He held his breath for what was about to come. She was going to say goodbye for good. She had just said as much not two minutes ago. At least this time she would look him in the eye and be honest. He wanted that much.

"I love you. I always have. I—"

He intercepted her last words with his kiss. He didn't care about the rest. She said she loved him. That was all he needed to hear.

He cupped the back of her head to deepen the kiss. She opened her mouth and let him in. His blood roared like the rapids. His other hand went under her shirt to feel her soft skin against his fingers.

She tangled her hands in his hair. He wanted her hands on his body to squelch some of the fire. He couldn't wait. Those three simple words broke the dam holding him together. He yanked her shirt over her head, tossed it aside, and eased her hair free from the holder.

"I want to see it spill over your shoulders."

She fanned her hair out so it floated down in a brown cascade. He wrapped the ends around his fingers.

He took her mouth again because he needed to keep tasting her. The living room wasn't the place he wanted to make love to her. He doubted Izzi would return or anyone would show up now, but he wanted to shut the door and lock it on the world.

He scooped her up and carried her to the bedroom.

"Gage, I can walk." Her laughter ended the kiss.

"I love the sound of my name on your lips. You have a way of making it sexy." He eased her down on the bed. She belonged with him in this space. It was as if this cabin had been waiting for her to join him.

"You are sexy all by yourself." She held her arms out to him.

He lay down beside her and kissed her again. His heart galloped as she fumbled with the buttons of his dress shirt. He would help her, but he wanted to touch her instead. He ran his hand over her breast. The black lace scratched at his skin. He reached around and unhooked it because he wanted nothing between them. She arched into his touch and moaned. He might not be able to make it to the end. She was wreaking havoc on his stamina.

She shoved his shirt from his shoulders, and he shrugged out of it.

"This too." She tugged at the bottom of his undershirt.

Reluctantly, he slid far enough away to do as she asked. Her hands explored his chest, setting his skin on fire, a fire that could burn down a forest. He left a trail of wet kisses on her neck and shoulder. She tasted like summertime.

Her hands continued to run lines down his front and over the erection pressing against his zipper. The heat was too much. He stood and removed his pants. She smiled up at him, and his heart bounced off his ribs.

"I love the sight of you in your boxer briefs." She slid off her shorts and invited him back into her arms.

The only place he wanted to be was wrapped up in her. She was the only one who could patch up the hole in his chest enough he could stand the dull ache left behind. Their families would have to get on board. He wanted this woman beside him every day. She couldn't leave Backwater just yet. Or he would leave with her.

Her hand gripped him and stroked. His head spun. He didn't need to think about anything except them in his bed. He tested her readiness because he wanted her and couldn't wait. She moaned again and moved her hips to the pace he set. His chest filled with pride. She trusted him to share herself in this way.

"Are you ready?" He positioned himself between her legs.

"Oh yes."

He entered her, and white light flashed behind his eyes. He pushed up on his forearms and let his mind go blank and just feel her hands on his ass and her legs around his waist. Her teeth nipped at the skin below his collarbone. A frenzy coiled inside him. He drove into her, searching for the release, but he held off to wait for her.

"Gage."

His name on her lips brought his gaze to hers. She laced her fingers in his hair and smiled.

"Yeah?"

"I need you."

Her body shuddered with her orgasm. Her muscles flexed around him, and that was all he needed for his heart to tumble along with the sweet explosive release only she could give him.

He gathered her to him as his breath slowed. "I'm all yours."

Chapter Twenty-Three

Calista closed her eyes and relished in her body's satisfied vibrations. Her head rested against Gage's chest, where she could listen to his rapid heartbeat slowing down like a love song. She tangled her legs around his strong ones. She'd never be able to rid her soul of him now. How were they going to work through the sticky web their lives had become? She could have him forever, but she had to give up her father. He would never forgive her for packing up Ava's stuff, and he certainly wouldn't forgive her for loving Gage. She couldn't help who she loved. She didn't want to fight it anymore. Gage was the only good thing left in her life, flaws and all. Because he had them.

"Babe, you hungry?" He stroked her back and sent shivers along her skin.

"Not if it means I have to get up from this bed." But she was going to have to leave soon. She had her shift at Kennedy's in an hour.

"About that."

She moved to see his face. His eyes were closed. "Do you regret what we just did? Because you seemed pretty into it a minute ago."

He looked right at her. "Are you kidding me? I can breathe when I'm next to you. My life makes some sense when we're together. I only meant you can spend the night tonight, but I don't know if it's a good idea if you move in here just yet. Because of Izzi."

"I'll stay tonight because I want to wake up in your arms, but I would never do anything that could hurt Izzi."

He turned to her. His smile was all over his face. "Then we'll have to talk about making this more permanent."

Panic pierced her heart. "After tomorrow, I'm leaving town. I can't stay here now. We're doing the long-distance thing, remember? Please don't fight me on this."

"I can't stay in town without you. It doesn't feel right anymore."

She flopped back. It was nice to imagine for a second a life with Gage that shut out everyone else. "You can't leave. Your family and the town need you."

"The only person I owe is Izzi."

She propped up on an elbow and brushed his hair away from his face. "You're a man of honor. You'd be gone five minutes and want to be back here. I love that about you. You can't go."

He grabbed her hand and kissed her fingers. His soft lips sent shivers over her skin. She could toss this whole conversation aside and get lost in making love.

"I have to clean up some of my mess. I have to set a good example for Izzi. But after that, I could get away for a little while. Maybe the rest of the summer. I could come with you, if you want. Izzi can stay with my mom and brother as long as I'm back before the school year starts."

She did want him with her, but she couldn't allow him to leave town now. Not after what had just happened. He was hurt, but in time he'd see where he belonged. And she belonged with him.

"If I walk away, the B and B won't get fixed up. My dad will run the business straight into the ground. Even though he told me he hated me, I should try and stay, shouldn't I?" Staying for Gage might be the right thing to do, but the idea of staying to finish the B and B made her stomach clench. There had to be a way to fix up the B and B without living there.

"I'm probably not the right person to ask for advice at the moment." He gathered her to him. "When we're like this, the noise in my head quiets down. You don't have to stay after how your dad treated you. He isn't ready to change. Forcing him to move on isn't a fight you can win. I don't want to say this out loud, but we'll do the long-distance thing for now."

Her heart soared. Selfishly. The B and B would have to wait until she could work things without her dad. She just wasn't ready to tackle that after today. "You mean that? You'll try the long-distance thing with me?"

"I love you, Calista. I only want you to be happy. We'll work through all our baggage, and then we'll live in the same town again."

"Can I ask you something?"

"Anything."

"Are you really going to apologize to Justin?"

"For nearly beating the shit out of him? Yes. But I still think he knows something."

She sat up and gathered the sheets around her. "I was afraid you'd say that."

He pushed up on his elbow. "Hey, don't pull away from me."

"Gage, you have to let this go and find another

suspect."

"I've already let it go. I quit, remember?"

"You aren't going to quit." She swung her legs over the bed. She'd steal a quick shower before she went to work. Her stomach growled as if to remind her she hadn't eaten in hours. Okay, she'd also grab a bite before her shift began. The real world always had a way of sneaking in on the moments she hoped would help her forget about her problems.

He followed her out of the bed. She tried not to take in his long, lean body, but she failed. His muscles rippled under the dark skin that she loved so much. He was her opposite, and yet he was still the other piece of her that fit so perfectly.

"I did something stupid today. The town would have a right to ask for my resignation. I'm just giving it to them first. I can't walk into that department and not see Phyllis. And I don't trust myself right now to do the right thing where the robberies are concerned. I need time to figure things out." He wrapped his arms around her, and she went willingly.

She understood he was knocked sideways. He'd been through a lot, and she was throwing more at him by asking him to accept Justin wasn't involved. He'd have to figure that out for himself as she'd have to figure out what to do about her father. Maybe she could stay in town a little longer. "Does your family have a room up at the main house I could rent?"

He kissed the top of her head. "I know one of the guest cottages isn't being rented right now because Jett wanted to fix up a few things. You could stay there. It's closer to my place. I can sneak over after Izzi goes to bed each night."

"At least through the Fourth. I want to be in town for the anniversary and visit with Ava that day. After that, we'll see what happens and where I land."

"Knowing we're going to be apart is too much reality. Take your shower. I'll make you something to eat before you go to work." He shoved his legs into his briefs.

She sashayed away, hoping his gaze stayed glued to her butt. "Unless you want to join me."

And he did just that.

****

Gage sent a text to his mother to check on Izzi.

—She's sleeping. You went too far today. She's very upset.—

—I'll take care of it.—

Because that's what he did even when he didn't want to. He sent another text to Calista telling her the front door was unlocked and to come in when she got back from work. He'd wait up for her. And if she wasn't too tired, maybe they could pick up where they'd left off in the shower.

He replayed the image of her standing under the showerhead as water ran over her body. She stole his breath at every turn. He hoped they'd make it this time, but the odds were against them.

He slid the picture of him and his brothers out of the broken frame and tossed the glass. His heart swelled with the love and pride he had for his family. Where would he be today without Kace, Jett, and Lock? He'd have to find a way to make up for his mistakes on the trail.

The smile on Ajay's face in the picture hid all the hurt he'd caused with his antics. He'd been pulled over in another town not two months before for speeding and arrested for having enough pot and paraphernalia on him to sell. His mother had begged him to get Ajay and straighten it out. She hadn't wanted Ajay to end up in jail. He hadn't either, but maybe a few nights behind bars would have done him some good.

"I'm sorry I wasn't there for you the way you needed me to be," he said to the picture and hoped wherever Ajay was he could hear him.

His phone vibrated in his pocket. Calista's name popped up on the screen.

"Hey, babe. Are you on a break?"

"Gage, I need you to come here right away. My father is drunk and starting a fight. He won't leave." She had to yell into the phone over the loud music and voices filling up the space in the background.

"Did you call Barry? He's on duty." Because he certainly wasn't. Barry could handle a drunk Andy Hartman. He could send Barry a text and tell him to arrest Andy if Barry wasn't entirely sure what to do with the disorderly man.

"I don't want Barry to handle him. I need you. Please." The pleading in her voice hit him in the gut.

He would do anything for her. Except believe her where Justin Crow was concerned. He let out a long breath. "I'll be right there."

****

Gage pushed through the door of Kennedy's Pub and was met with the thumping of the band playing, glasses clinking, and the booming voice of Andy Hartman rising above the crowd.

Calista swiped the glass from her father and shoved her finger in the other bartender's face, Jimmy Collins.

Jimmy hung his head and took the glass. She smacked the bar in front of her father and pointed to the door.

She met his gaze at that moment, and relief filled her eyes. Andy turned to see what had caught her attention and scowled.

Feelings are mutual right now.

She wiped her hands on a towel and ran around the bar to meet him.

"What's he doing?" He leaned down to yell in her ear and to get a whiff of her spicy scent that sent shivers over his skin.

She put a hand on his shoulder to pull him closer. Her lips brushed his ear. "Besides yelling at everyone who comes near him and telling them life isn't worth living sober when your daughter's been murdered by the sheriff's brother?"

He stifled a groan. When was Andy going to give this a rest? "Has anyone complained?"

"I lost three customers because of him. I told him to leave, but he won't listen to me. Says I'm not part of this town. Jimmy won't bounce him. He feels sorry for him. Can you just take him outside and talk to him? Maybe you can convince him to go home."

Andy wasn't going to listen to him either and would have to give up his keys to him, which he doubted Andy would agree to. "I'll try."

She gave him a soft kiss on the lips and punctuated it with a sweet smile that stretched wide. "Thank you for taking care of this. I'll see you later tonight, okay?"

His heart tumbled around in his chest. He wanted to take her in his arms and kiss the hell out of her right here in the bar, but shattering glass stopped him.

A hush fell over the crowd, though the band kept

playing.

"Get your stupid hands off me." Andy pushed the man standing next to him.

"I'll take care of it. Go back to work." Gage didn't wait for her to answer. He straightened his shoulders and moved through the crowd gathering at the end of the bar.

"Don't push me, old man." The guy shoved Andy, and he slipped off the stool into the person behind him. The woman knocked Andy forward into the guy he had shoved.

This guy had Andy by thirty years. His small frame was muscular. His arms were covered in tattoos. He wore a silver chain from his belt to his back pants pocket. Probably attached to his wallet. His work boots were beat up like the skin on his face.

The scrappy guy grabbed Andy by the shoulders and shook him. Andy's glasses tumbled off his face, and his eyes rolled back into his head. Calista yelled for the man to stop.

Gage grabbed the guy by the back of the collar and pulled him away from Andy. "That's enough."

"Who are you? His son or something?" The scrappy guy stood toe to toe with him.

"Step back." He placed his hand on the butt of his gun to give this guy the message that he was for real. "My name is Sheriff Ryker. This is my town."

"Well, arrest this guy. He shoved me for no reason." Scrappy leaned around him to point at Andy.

"Gage, I did no such thing." Andy retrieved his glasses from the floor.

"Andy, shut up." He kept his gaze fixed on Scrappy.

Scrappy was an outsider. A tourist maybe, but more likely someone just passing through. He didn't want an outsider thinking he could throw his weight around in this town. And he wanted a chance to show his residents he could take care of them.

"You were assaulting this man. I should arrest you." Nothing would give him greater pleasure than to prove a point at the moment.

"I only touched him because he put his hands on me first. I don't want any trouble. I'm sorry, okay? No harm." Scrappy raised his hands in surrender.

Gage turned to Andy. "Apologize to the man."

"I will not."

"You will. Now." He'd be happy to arrest Andy if he couldn't bring Scrappy in.

Andy lifted his glass. "Apologies."

"Whatever," Scrappy said and signaled for another drink.

"Let's go." He grabbed Andy by the elbow.

"I'm not going with you." Andy tried to pull away from his grasp, but he held tighter.

He leaned in to make sure Andy didn't miss what he said. "You will come with me right now, or I will arrest you again for anything that can keep you in my jail for as long as possible. Pay your tab."

Andy threw some bills on the bar. If it wasn't enough, he'd settle up with Calista later. He walked Andy outside, where his ears rang with the deafening silence. He stopped at his truck.

"What's wrong with you, Andy?"

"I don't know what you're talking about." He swayed on his feet.

"You're drunk again. You threw Calista out of the

house, and now you come to where she's working and cause trouble for her. That young guy could have beaten you senseless. When are you going to learn?"

"I don't need to be lectured by you. You don't understand anything. I lost my little girl because of your family."

He grabbed Andy's shirt with his fists and yanked him closer. "That doesn't give you the right to act like an asshole all the time." He shoved him away and took a deep breath. He couldn't lose it again tonight. He'd be no better than Andy.

Andy took a swing, but his arm moved as if he were in slow motion. His feet tangled up in themselves, and he fell forward. Gage caught him before he hit the ground, then positioned him against the truck.

"Hitting me isn't going to make you feel any better." Even though sometimes punching something did ease some of the tension.

"Your brother killed my baby."

He fisted his hands to keep them from shaking Andy. "I know. Christ, I live with that every fucking day. Do you think that's easy for me or my family? It was an accident. He didn't mean to hurt her. When are you going to figure that out? Ajay liked Ava. Ava walked into the path of that bullet because she was trying to stop him."

"Shut up. Shut up. You're a Ryker. You don't understand. None of you take the blame for what Ajay did."

"Because Ajay was the one who did it. Damn it, we all live with the guilt of what he did. If any one of us could go back and stop him, we would. Me especially." He'd replayed that night a million times, always

239

rewriting the ending. If he'd turned just a second sooner, he might have been able to yell to Ava. Or he might have been able to grab Ajay.

If only he'd stopped to talk to Ajay earlier in the day when he came by to ask him for help, none of this would have happened. He had thrown Ajay out of his house because he reeked of pot again, and that time he found track lines on Ajay's arm. He grabbed Ajay by the wrist and yanked him to the gun safe.

"Do it." He screamed at Ajay.

"Do what, Gage?" Ajay's eyes grew wide, and his lip trembled. Gage thought he was probably high, but maybe he was about to cry.

"Kill yourself already. You're doing it now with the drugs and the assholes you run around with. Save yourself and everyone a lot of time and open the fucking safe." He shoved Ajay into the six-foot metal safe.

"I'm not going to shoot myself."

"Why the fuck not? Don't be a coward. Act like a man and kill yourself quick and fast."

"I don't want to die, you asshole. I need your help. Please help me, Gage. I don't know what to do." A tear fell from Ajay's eye, but Gage turned his back on his brother.

"Go ask Lock for advice. He's the sensitive one." He had marched back to the main house without looking back. If Gage had known later that night Ajay would be faced with a decision he couldn't handle, he wouldn't have been such a jerk to him.

"I want someone to hurt as much as I do." Andy's voice dragged him away from the past and right back to Kennedy's parking lot.

"Calista does. When are you going to see that?"

"She doesn't care about Ava. She moved away and left me." Andy pulled off his glasses and cleaned the lenses on the hem of his shirt before securing them to his face.

"She moved away because you don't see what's right in front of you. You're still here. She needs you. I wish my dad was here to be a shoulder to lean on now and again. You're missing out on a chance to have a relationship with Calista with all your drinking and living in the past. It's time to take care of the daughter that's still alive."

He could use his father's advice now about how to handle the investigation or to ask for guidance on raising a daughter. He'd like to sit with his dad and tell him about his feelings for Calista.

When his dad was still here, he would find him in the barn fixing something or whittling a piece of wood. He'd stand there quietly until his dad noticed his twelve-year-old boy had taken a place at his side.

"Do you have something on your mind, son?" His father's deep voice had been soft and smooth, like a lake on a windless day.

He'd take the knife from his dad sometimes and start whittling too. He never whittled now. But he could talk to his dad about his problems and keep his gaze on the wood so his dad wouldn't see the pain that might be in his eyes. He could never hide his feelings from his dad. He learned how to do that after his father died and there was no one else to whittle with anymore. His heart ached with the hole his father's absence made.

Andy slid down the side of the truck and plopped on the ground. He removed his glasses again and wiped at his face. "I've been a lousy father."

Gage sat beside him. "I won't argue with that. You need to pull your act together. Your daughter needs you to tell her you love her. She lost her whole family when Ava died. Have you ever thought about that, or have you been too busy feeling sorry for yourself?"

"I do love her. Of course, I do. I just want the pain to stop."

"It doesn't. It changes so you can go on living. You could have a good life with Calista. She might even stay in town permanently. Wouldn't it be nice to have her work with you at the B and B and not have to tend bar?" He didn't care what she did for a living as long as she was happy, but he would much rather have her in bed with him at night instead of pouring drinks for strangers.

"I said some bad things." Andy wiped his nose with the back of his hand.

"You can apologize. If you stay sober and out of trouble, you might have a chance with her. I want her happy, Andy, and I will do whatever it takes to see that happen. If you can't straighten out, I'll see to it you're driven out of Backwater and she stays. Am I making myself clear?" He pushed off the ground and wiped the back of his pants.

"Are you threatening me?"

"Yes."

Andy nodded. "She still loves you. I don't understand why."

He half shrugged and grinned. Calista's feelings for him were so obvious even Andy noticed. "I don't either, but I'm lucky that she does. And you're lucky she loves you. I'm sorry Ajay hurt you, and I'm sorry

Ava is gone, but Calista is still here. Fix your relationship while you still have the chance." He would always be apologizing for Ajay. Some wounds might heal, but the scars were so big they could be seen from the Montana sky.

"I'll talk to her when she gets home."

"She's not going to live with you until you're sober. You can call her at my place. In fact, if you can stay sober, you can come to our pre-Fourth barbeque my mother has been planning. She'd love to see you. And that's something I don't understand."

"Your mother is a charm. Thank you. I'd like to be at your party."

"Good. Now give me your keys. I'll get you a ride home." He sent a text to Barry.

Andy staggered to his feet. "You're a good man. Your father would be proud of you."

"I'd like to think so."

He'd made plenty of mistakes in his life, but he wanted his dad to be proud of the man he turned out to be. Without him around, Gage had to be proud of himself. He needed to start doing that again.

Barry pulled into the parking lot with the cruiser's lights flashing. Gage shook his head and helped Andy into the front seat.

"See that he gets inside safely." He gave the car keys to Barry.

"Sheriff, about what you said to me earlier…" Barry kicked the dirt.

"Forget I said it. I was mad about Phyllis."

"I understand. I'm pretty broken up too. Won't be the same without her."

He clapped Barry on the shoulder. "No, it won't."

"Wouldn't be the same without you either. Glad you're not quitting."

"Yeah, me too." And he meant that.

Chapter Twenty-Four

Calista met Justin in the driveway of the B and B. She had waited in her car until he arrived for work that morning. She could have texted him, but she wanted to explain in person. She owed him that much, especially after what happened between him and Gage. She wasn't going to stay and finish the project she started. If her father wanted his business to continue, he'd have to manage that without her. Being without her was what he wanted, and she finally understood that. She wished it were different, but a broken family was easier to accept than begging him to love her.

She took a deep breath and ran her fingers over her bracelet. "Hi."

He stopped in his tracks. "You're firing me because of what happened at the Ryker Ranch. I knew it. You're on his side."

"I'm not on anyone's side. This isn't about Gage." But she hoped he would apologize soon. He promised her last night he would speak to Justin right after he talked with Izzi.

Justin leaned against the hood of the car and crossed his ankles. "What's it about, then?"

"My dad. He doesn't want me here anymore, and I don't think I belong here. I can't fix the place up. I'm sorry. I'd be happy to be a reference for you, and..." She dug inside her tote. "Here's the pay for the next week."

He hesitated.

"Take it. It's the least I can do. You're out of a job because of me. I probably shouldn't have hired you in the first place. I was taking a big chance here, and you got caught up in my mess. I really am sorry." She meant that in more ways than one. She was also sorry Gage hadn't believed him and had tried to hurt him.

He pocketed the money. "I wouldn't take it except I'm trying to get a place of my own before the fall semester."

"You don't have to explain. Hey, what happened at the ranch...that's not really Gage. He was upset about losing Phyllis."

He rubbed at his neck. "It seemed just like him to me." He turned his gaze off toward the lake and took a deep breath. "I think I should stop hanging around with Izzi." The thin line of his lips and the hurt in his eyes said telling her that and actually doing it cost him. He must have cared deeply for Izzi.

"Maybe it's for the best right now. She should focus on school." She wouldn't give him the "they were young" speech. But if they were meant to be, they would be. She was starting to believe that.

"Yeah. I guess. Are you leaving town?"

She would have been if it wasn't for Gage. "I'm staying through the Fourth. After that, I'm not sure what I'm doing."

"I liked having you around. You're one of the few people who don't judge an Indian kid like me."

"Don't listen to anyone, okay? You're a good person with a lot to offer. It doesn't matter where you're from or where you land. Your brother will understand eventually." Not that he'd mentioned his brother, but what little she knew about Justin and his family life worried her. No one was really looking out for him.

"I'll always be judged by either my family or the people who don't look like me. My family doesn't understand why I want to leave the rez, and white people can't understand what it's like to be me. Not even Sheriff Ryker. He has that big family on that ranch, and everyone in town accepts them. He doesn't know what it's like to worry about where you're going to live or how to survive. I only want a place to fit in."

Her heart broke for him. He was right about the Rykers. "Just be yourself. You'll find the place you belong."

"Have you?"

She gnawed on her lip. She hadn't found that place, and she'd been looking for a long time. She'd been hanging in limbo since Ava's death. That needed to stop. She'd figured out a few things, at least. She couldn't find a home at the B and B and probably not in Backwater, but she might be able to find peace and purpose with Gage back in her life.

"I'm working on it. Life is a process. Much like the practice of yoga. Some days you show up and things go great, and other days you fall on your butt."

"I don't think all that yoga stuff is for me, but thanks. If you take off, come say goodbye, okay?"

"Sure." She wanted to hug him but didn't know if he would want that, so she stayed put. "Take care."

"Yeah. You too." He hitched his leg into the car, shut the door, and drove away.

Tears burned the back of her throat. She wanted to

get out of there before her father realized she was home. Well, it wasn't home anymore. She didn't know where home was going to be. For now, Gage's ranch was as close to home as she was going to get. She was unsure about being there. And though she knew how she felt about him, she still worried she'd wake up and think she'd be unable to look at him and not see Ajay pulling that trigger. Was that memory ever going to get shoved far enough away she didn't run her fingers over it like a scab?

She fumbled for her keys in her tote. The tears spilled down her cheeks. Love wasn't supposed to be hard.

"Calista, wait." Her father's voice rang out from the side of the house.

She wasn't ready to see him, not after what he'd said to her or last night at the bar. She hurried to her car. "I have to go, Dad." Her tote slipped from her shoulder, and her gum, hair ties, wallet, keys, lip balm, yoga therapy balls, all her essentials, spilled on the ground.

She dropped down to gather her things. The tears came harder. After everything, now was going to be the moment she lost it. Her father knelt beside her and scooped up her wallet and keys. His familiar pine scent drifted toward her. Her heart tugged to go to him, as it had when she was little, but she fought it.

"Are you okay?" He handed over her belongings.

"I'm fine. Thanks. I have to go. Gage is expecting me." She shoved her stuff back in her tote.

He adjusted his glasses. His white hair fell forward over his brow. His smile was small, but it reached his eyes for the first time in a long time. He might actually be sober today. "Can we talk for a minute?"

"I don't think so. There isn't anything to say." She didn't want to hear the awful things he thought about her. Not now, after she had to tell Justin goodbye. Letting go hurt as much as hanging on.

"I'm sorry."

"What?" She couldn't have heard him right.

He drew in a breath. "I'm sorry for what I said the other day. I don't feel that way."

"But you said it." And he couldn't take it back that easily.

"I know I did, and I was wrong. I was shocked when I walked into Ava's room. I go in there every day at that time to sit for a little while. When I saw you boxing up her things, I got angry. It's no excuse. I should never have said what I did because it isn't true."

"Okay." She wasn't sure it was okay, but what else could she say? She wanted to get in her car and drive away. Agreeing would make that happen faster.

"I want us to be okay someday. I'm going back to meetings. I'm going to make things better here and between us."

"Why do you go into Ava's room every day at the same time?" That seemed like torture, but so did living with her room untouched for the past sixteen years.

He kicked a stone. "That was the last time I spoke to her. I had walked past her room, and she was standing in front of her mirror in that pretty yellow dress with the flowers."

That was the dress she had worn the night of the tragedy. "I remember it. She looked lovely in it."

"It was a little low cut for my liking. I told her that. She just smiled at me and said, 'Oh, Daddy. You worry too much.' She gave me a kiss on the cheek and said she'd see me later. I wish I knew the next time I'd see her was inside a body bag." His hands shook as he removed his glasses and wiped the tears away.

She held her breath. He had never told her that story before. "You couldn't know, Dad. No one knew what was coming."

"I spoke with Gage last night. Did he tell you?"

"No."

"He cares a lot about you. He told me I needed to get my act together, and he was right. I've behaved badly for a very long time. I think it was when he said he wished his dad was still around that it hit me. Those boys lost their father at a young age. If Jim Ryker had still been alive, Ajay might've turned out differently. But I'm here, and you still lost me. I'm sorry. I didn't stop to think about what you lost that night."

The breeze picked up and brushed her hair away from her neck. A black-and-gold butterfly flew out of the bush and flapped its wings but hovered as if to say hello before it dashed away.

She had ignored her yoga practice since her return to Backwater because she'd been hurt by Fox's death, the robbery, and the decay of her childhood home. But she would not ignore the sign of that butterfly. Ava was telling her to forgive their father.

"Thanks, Dad. I appreciate you saying that." She would still need time, but this was the first step in the right direction. "I really do have to go. I'm staying in town through the Fourth."

"You won't finish fixing up the B and B?"

"You want me to?"

"I think so, yes. It's time to let go of the past. If

you'd let me, I'd like to help you with Ava's room."

"I'm not sure if I want to stay around for the rest of the summer, but I will help you with Ava's room before I go." She wanted to take small steps first. An apology was one thing, but her father doing what he said would go far to convince her he meant he wanted to change.

"I can live with that. Oh, before you do go, I have something for you." He fumbled around in his shirt pocket and pulled out a gold necklace with a charm of four floating hearts.

Her breath caught in her throat.

"You should have this." He handed over the delicate piece of jewelry that had belonged to Ava. It was her favorite necklace. She'd been wearing it that night.

"I thought this was gone." The chain dangled from her fingers, catching the glint of the sun.

"I kept it. I shouldn't have. You should have been wearing it all these years. Ava would've wanted you to have it, but I couldn't let it go. Unfortunately, I couldn't let anything go. I lost too much by hanging on too tightly. I hope you'll forgive me someday, sweetie. I want to make up for what I've done."

She blinked away the tears and bit down on her lip to stop the trembling. Her hand grasped the necklace. "Thank you."

"I love you, Calista."

"I love you, Daddy."

Chapter Twenty-Five

Gage didn't know where to begin. His daughter sat slumped on the couch with her arms crossed and a scowl on her pretty face. He perched on the edge of the coffee table in their living room and faced her. She hadn't said a word to him since the incident in the barn. She had only agreed to speak to him now because his mother ran interference. He had lost complete control of his relationship with Izzi.

"I'm sorry," he said. Sorry didn't need an explanation. There was no point in following that with the excuses for his behavior the other night.

She glanced up through her long lashes. "What for?"

"A lot of things, but most importantly for how I behaved with Justin. That was wrong. I shouldn't have put my hands on him like that."

She scooted to the opposite end of the couch. "You've always said violence isn't the answer. You said if Uncle Ajay hadn't had a gun that night, he would still be alive. I don't understand why you were choking Justin. You scared me."

He let out a long breath. Ajay should have lived long enough to hear Izzi call him uncle. "I'm sorry I scared you. I don't want to be that person. I was upset about Phyllis. That's no excuse. I know better, but in that moment, I couldn't stop myself. We all make mistakes, Izzi. Even me. I hope you'll forgive me."

He'd be sorry for a long time. Sorrier than she'd ever know.

"I don't understand why you hate him so much."

Because Justin reminded him of Ajay and that meant a path of destruction that he didn't want his daughter near. "I don't hate him, but I do suspect he knows what's going down with the robberies. That makes me leery of him. He might not be committing the crimes, but he's aiding the criminals who are. And there was that couch incident."

She looked away with cheeks that bloomed red. "I like him, Daddy."

Daddy. He missed the days when she climbed into his lap and pounded her little fists on his cheeks so he'd blow bubbles made from gum. She'd stick her finger in the center until it popped, and her big, bright laugh would escape into the room, filling it with love for him.

Now she liked some kid who was probably headed for federal prison. Ajay would have had a good laugh at this one.

"He's too old for you."

"Can I invite him to the Fourth barbeque?"

She was killing him. For once, he didn't want to be the only parent involved in major decisions. How could he allow his daughter to associate with a possible criminal? And yet what if he was wrong and Calista was right about Justin? Even if Calista was right, which he wasn't ready to admit, he still didn't like the age difference. His head hurt. "I'll think about it."

"Why can you live with Calista, but I can't invite Justin to a party where my whole family will be watching? We won't do anything inappropriate."

"For starters, I'm not living with her. She's in the cottage next door, and that's temporary until she can work things out with her father. Secondly, I'm forty and the dad. When you're forty and I'm dead, you can date Justin as long as you want." He pushed off the table and went into the kitchen.

She cracked a smile. His heart swelled. Maybe they'd be okay in the end.

"I like Calista. I'd be okay with it if you keep dating her." She jumped to her feet and swiped at her phone.

"Thanks, sweetie. I like her too." A lot.

"It's nice to see you dating. You deserve to be happy."

"I'm happy. I have you and Gammy and all your uncles. I have a great job."

"You're a single dad in a small town who lives with his mother and should be getting some."

"Isabelle, I didn't teach you to talk like that." Heat flushed his cheeks. His little girl was anything but.

"Nope, Uncle Kace did." She giggled.

He was going to beat the shit out of his brother.

"Hey, Izzi?" He pulled meat and vegetables out of the fridge for dinner.

"Yes?"

"I'll try to go a little easier on the rules." He needed to face the reality she was growing up. If he wanted to keep their relationship strong, he would have to let go a little. She wasn't Ajay.

"Thanks, Daddy." She skipped down the hall.

His phone vibrated against the counter. He hoped it was Calista saying she was on her way back. He missed her. A glance at the screen made the blood drain from his head. Jett had sent a text.

—*Come now. Silver Bell.*—

****

Gage held Izzi against his chest while she cried. "It's going to be okay," he whispered.

She pushed away from him and wiped her eyes. "I need to go for a walk."

He let her go. He needed some time to catch his breath. "We'll change Silver Bell's food," he said to Jett, who stood by and watched the scene with Izzi unfold.

Jett shoved his hands in his back pockets and stared up at the blue sky. His T-shirt was covered in pieces of hay from lying on the ground with Bell. "It might not make a difference."

"But you're going to try, right?" Keeping his emotions under lock and key grew harder and harder. He had experienced too much suffering recently. He couldn't watch Silver Bell die too.

"I will change her food and lessen the time she's out in the pasture. That should get rid of the laminitis. It's going to come back. It never shows up once, and she's old."

"I know she's old, damn it. You don't have to keep reminding me."

"I want you to be ready. It might not be now or tomorrow or even six months from now, but it's coming. You need to be ready for the possibility you won't be here when it happens. You could be at work, at the store, anywhere. And be ready for Izzi. She's never lost an animal before, and she's attached to Silver Bell as much as you are."

"You think I won't know how to handle my

daughter? What the hell are you getting at?"

"I'm not getting at anything. I know when Silver Bell finally goes, it's going to hit you a lot harder than you realize."

"What are you some kind of shrink now?"

Jett crossed his arms over his chest. "I was the one pulling you off that kid the other night. I've watched you for sixteen years shove everything you feel down your throat. It's bound to blow up eventually."

"Don't go psychoanalyzing me, little brother. You don't let your emotions out either. You pour all your feelings into these animals."

"But I'm not the one trying to beat the shit out of a kid because I lost someone else I love."

"You don't know how you'll feel when someone else you love dies. You can't be bothered to get close to anyone. You—and Lock, for that matter. At least Lock lets someone in his bed. When was the last time you even got laid?"

"This isn't about me or Lock. It's about you and how close you are to losing it once and for all. I'll take care of Silver Bell, and I hope she lives a few more years, but you need to be ready when it happens. It's going to be like losing Ajay all over again. I don't know if you're going to be able to bounce back from that." Jett marched away without another word.

He picked up a bale of hay and threw it. A couple of horses lifted their heads and whinnied. Jett was right, and that made his blood turn to ice. He couldn't lose Silver Bell now.

"Hey, girl." He dropped his forehead to Silver Bell's nose. She trembled and shifted her weight because the laminitis caused swelling in her front feet.

It could lead to her being unable to stand.

"We're going to get you better." And if they couldn't, then he would be right by her side in the end. Losing her caused his chest to burn. A tear threatened to push its way out.

He moved away from the stall and out into the fresh air. The midday sun heated his skin and made sweat break out on his neck. A run would do him good or a five-mile hike. He'd call Calista and tell her where he went so she wouldn't worry. Maybe by the time he got back, his mind would be clearer.

He cut through the field to his house and stopped as he rounded the front. The pain in his head came back. Justin Crow held Izzi in his arms while she cried. They sat on the front steps of the cabin. Izzi's hair fell over her face, but her shoulders shook, and she gripped Justin's shirt in her fist.

No matter what he said, she went against him. He didn't understand what it was about this kid his daughter liked so much. She could not continue to break his rules without there being a consequence.

He marched ahead but stopped again and scratched at the back of his neck. They still hadn't noticed his arrival. He could turn around and go anywhere else on the ranch. But he didn't.

"Isabelle."

She jumped from Justin's embrace and rubbed her face. Justin backed up, wiping his hands on his pants as if he'd been playing in the dirt.

"Daddy, I called Justin. He's here because I told him about Silver Bell. Don't get mad." She sniffled and brushed her hair away from her face.

Justin held his hands up. "I'll go. She was upset on

the phone, and I was nearby."

"You came by to help her?"

"Yes, sir. I wanted to give Izzi some comfort. I'm sorry Silver Bell is sick. She mentioned you've had the horse a very long time."

"Thank you." He cleared his throat. "Justin, I'm sorry I assaulted you the other night. You would be in your right to press charges." There, he'd said it and it didn't taste as dry as he thought it would.

Justin's eyes grew to the size of the Montana sky. "Press charges? Against you? No way. It's all good now." He took a deep breath. "Sheriff, I know you don't think I'm good enough for Izzi. I understand why you think I might be involved in those robberies, but I'm not a criminal."

"I don't like it that my daughter has feelings for you, and it's not because you're a poor college kid whose family lives on the reservation. I know Calista told you about my father's family. I wouldn't judge my own people. What I don't like is you keep showing up at those robberies. You tell me you're not a criminal, and I want to believe you because Izzi and Calista do, but I still don't."

"Daddy, you're being unreasonable."

"Give me a second." He turned back to Justin. "You can be friends with Izzi until she's sixteen. Then we'll talk about dating. But if I find out you know one thing about what's happening at these robberies and you've been lying to me, what I did to you in the barn will be nothing. Am I clear?"

Justin's gaze bounced from him to Izzi and back. "Yes, sir."

"Good. We're having a barbeque as an early Fourth

celebration. Would you like to come?"

Izzi threw herself into his arms. He held her and swallowed the emotions gripping his chest.

"Thank you, Dad."

He kissed her head and set her on her feet.

"Thank you, Sheriff Ryker. Yes, I'd like to come by."

Calista's car rolled down the driveway to the cabin. His heart swelled. He'd had enough of his problems over the last weeks. All he wanted now was to wrap his woman in his arms and drown in the sweet scent of her.

"Behave," he said to Izzi and went to Calista.

He met her as she opened the car door, and swept her into his arms. She circled her arms around his neck. He couldn't wait and didn't care that his daughter might be yards away. He pressed his lips against Calista's and sighed when she yielded and opened her mouth to his.

He laced his fingers in her soft hair and tilted her head back to deepen the kiss. This was the place he needed to be. With her in his arms, he could handle all the things coming at him at top speed. With her, the pain went away.

She eased out of the kiss and looked up at him with wide eyes. "Did you miss me?"

"Always. How was your morning?"

"I had to let Justin go, but Dad apologized."

"Hire Justin back."

"Excuse me? Did something hit you in the head while I was gone?" She narrowed her eyes.

"If you can move forward, so can I. I won't rule Justin out, but I'll look for another suspect."

"I don't understand what prompted this change of heart."

He told her about Silver Bell and his conversation with Justin. "Babe, I'm tired of fighting everything all the time. I need peace in my life. If your dad apologized, stay in town and finish fixing the B and B. I'm better when you're around."

"Gage Ryker, you know how to sweep a woman off her feet."

He scooped her up into his arms and marched her over to the cabin she was renting. She laughed and told him to put her down. He kicked the front door of her cabin shut, eased her onto the bed, and all afternoon showed her exactly how much better she made him.

Chapter Twenty-Six

The morning of the Ryker Fourth of July celebration came wrapped in a big blue sky, a slight breeze through the pines, and the sun nudging the flowers open with its warmth. Calista stirred pasta salad in the kitchen of the rental cabin as the birds wished her good morning at the window.

She checked her phone. Izzi was supposed to arrive soon to make mala bracelets. Only a short time ago, she had been afraid to get to know Gage's daughter. Now they were becoming friends. This trip home had surprised her in many ways. The biggest being her father.

The doorbell interrupted her mixing. She wiped her hands on a towel and went to the door. She should have just yelled to come in. Izzi didn't have to knock anymore. She would be sure to tell her that.

Her mouth hung open halfway as she stared at the woman on the doorstep. "Hi, Karen. I wasn't expecting you. Come on in."

Gage's mother offered a small smile that didn't reach her eyes behind her black glasses. They hadn't spoken much since she moved in. Part of her wanted to avoid Karen because she wasn't ready to discuss her relationship with Gage yet.

"I won't stay long. I know Izzi will be here soon, and I have a ton of things to accomplish back at the main house before this afternoon's festivities. I wanted to see how you were settling in." Karen peered over her shoulder as if in search of something.

She wasn't sure what Karen expected to see. Possibly Gage?

"The cabin is lovely. Thank you for allowing me to stay here. Can I get you something to drink?" She went back into the kitchen, and Karen followed.

"No, thank you. I'm glad you're comfortable. You can stay as long as you'd like. We aren't renting this cabin this summer." She slid onto the chair at the table. Her fingers fluttered by her glasses as if she were trying to rearrange something on the stems. "I won't overstay my welcome."

Even though Calista had insisted on paying the fee for the cabin, Gage hadn't wanted her to. But Jett had no problem giving her a rental contract to sign. She didn't blame him. Living here was a business deal with some perks. Heat filled her cheeks as she remembered the perks of Gage carrying her to bed.

"How are things with your dad?" Karen rearranged the napkins in the holder.

"Okay, I think." She hoped. They had spoken a couple of times since he apologized. He'd helped Justin finish hanging the kitchen cabinets.

"Can I talk to you about something important?" Karen folded and unfolded the top napkin.

She wanted to take the napkins away from her. Instead, she gripped the wooden spoon she used to mix the pasta salad. "I guess. Sure."

"Do you love my son?" Karen's set jaw and stern look filled in all the things she didn't say.

That one direct statement drew a line between

them. No matter how nice Karen Ryker was, she wanted Calista to know Gage would always belong to her. Karen wouldn't allow her to hurt Gage a second time.

"That's kind of personal." She didn't know how to answer that question. She had loved Gage her whole life, but that wasn't what Karen wanted to hear.

"Does that mean no?"

"Gage and I are figuring things out right now." She busied herself with wrapping the pasta salad and sticking it in the fridge.

"He doesn't know I'm here. I don't care if you tell him I was. I always liked you and at one time wished very much you and Gage would get married…" Her hands went back to her glasses.

"But?"

"But after that night, too many hearts were broken to go on as usual. I will always be sorry for the pain Ajay caused, but you blamed the wrong man."

"I had never planned to hurt him, but I didn't know how to be with him and handle my own grief."

"Right after you left town, he did too. The boundaries of this town made him feel like a caged animal. He never said a word, but I could tell. A mother always knows when her child is hurting." Karen looked off into the distance. "Well, maybe not always. But I did with him because he's my first. He had to go find something that would bring him peace. It broke my heart to watch him leave. I thought I had lost another son for good. But not long after he was back with Izzi. I was thrilled to have them both, but the hurt it cost him to have failed at his marriage and to struggle as a father had etched itself deep within him."

She had caused that pain too. He wouldn't have run off and married some other woman if they had tried to work through the tragedy together. But he wouldn't have Izzi, and she doubted he regretted that one beautiful thing in the midst of the misery.

"He's a good father," she said.

Karen's smile found her eyes. "Yes, he is. Once he got his legs under him, he rose to the challenge of being a single parent. He's tough on himself and Izzi, but he loves her with his whole heart. You shattered Gage by leaving him when he was at his worst."

"I hope you can forgive me for the pain I caused him. I never want to do that to him again." Hearing Gage's mother tell her how hurt he was by her actions scratched out her heart. The accusation stung more coming from Karen.

"Okay, then. I'm glad to hear it." She slid from the chair. "I'll see you later, and thank you, Calista."

"For what?"

"For letting me be a meddlesome mother. I should mind my own business. My sons are grown men who live their lives by their choices, but of all my boys Gage is the most fragile. Now don't you tell any of them I said it. Gage will be hurt, and Jett, Lock, and Kace will never let him live that down. But he can't afford to be hurt again the same way. Losing Phyllis almost destroyed him. Losing you a second time will be something he'll never come back from."

****

Calista locked the door to the cabin and with her pasta salad headed over to the main house. She could drive, but the late afternoon air was filled with sweet scents and a light breeze. She would walk and appreciate all the good things around her. She ran her fingers over the new bracelet she'd made with Izzi today. It had been a good time, and her heart filled with ease knowing Gage's daughter accepted her in her father's life.

Karen's last words before she left still vibrated in her mind. If things ended between her and Gage, it would be his doing this time. She was right where she wanted to be. She would not hurt him again.

The sound of voices and laughter drifted toward her as she approached the house. All the guests at the ranch were invited as well as some people from town. Gage had been assigned to man the grill this year. She looked forward to seeing him in his apron.

A volleyball net had been set up in the back. Kace, Lock, and some of the guys who worked at the garage had a game going. Kace spiked the ball, and Lock missed it. Kace high-fived the guy next to him. Lock gave him the middle finger. Of all of Gage's brothers, Lockwood Ryker was the most mysterious. Always had been.

Guests sat around some of the picnic tables or played boccie. Her father stood by the patio and talked with Mable and Howard. Dad's face was clear today, and his eyes bright. Izzi sat on the patio swing, deep in her phone. Jett came out the back door holding a plate of hamburgers, hot dogs, and steaks. He sent her a quick wave. Her gaze followed him to the person she wanted to see most.

Gage stood at the grill, rotating corn on the cob. He wiped his brow and took the plate from Jett. His black T-shirt hugged his muscles. His shorts outlined his butt and made her stomach flip. He turned, as if he could feel her stare on his back, and awarded her with his high-voltage smile. The apron did look good on him. He handed the plate back to Jett, who rolled his eyes.

"You made it." He leaned down and kissed her lips. He smelled like grilled beef and the woods. She wanted to take a bite out of him.

"I'll take that." Jett grabbed the pasta salad. "Gage, don't let the food burn. I have people counting on this meal as part of their vacation. Thanks for coming, Calista." He nodded and put the pasta on the table with all the side food. He started talking to some of the guests, leaving them alone.

"He seems a little grumpy." She kept her hands planted on Gage's shoulders.

"He's mad at me for the way I dealt with Justin. He also doesn't trust my reaction when Silver Bell goes."

"Oh, Gage, I'm sorry. You two are so close. He'll come around."

"I'm not worried about Jett. With you here, nothing can go wrong today. But I do have to get back to the grill. Are you hungry?"

She stood on her toes to be near his ear. "Not for food."

He grabbed her bottom and pulled her to him. "Later." He kissed her lips and returned to work.

She mingled with the guests as the sun set and the stars dotted the sky. Fireflies danced and spread their green light like brush strokes on a dark canvas. Droplets of condensation ran off her iced tea glass. Izzi sat on a lounge chair she must have dragged away from the party.

"Hey, can I join you?" Calista waited for the invite to sit down.

"Sure." Izzi tucked her legs under her to make room on the chair.

"I thought Justin was coming." She took the seat and sipped her drink.

"Me too. He said he'd be here hours ago. I've texted him, but he hasn't responded."

That didn't sound good, but she wouldn't say that to a fifteen-year-old girl waiting for her crush to arrive. "Maybe he got caught up in something. I'm sure he'll text or show up soon."

"Whatever. If this is how he's going to act, my dad will never let us date. Justin needed to impress my dad, not blow me off." She dropped her phone in her lap.

"Well, at least wait to hear what he says. Maybe he had to stop by his parents' house or something."

"That's not it. It doesn't matter. Are you having fun?"

Izzi had learned the skill of changing the subject the way her father would. Gage had lived his life with his emotions close in order to keep himself safe. But his beautiful daughter had nothing to fear. Hopefully, someday Izzi would learn that. "I am having a lot of fun. It's a nice celebration."

"Uncle Jett has fireworks planned. He lets Uncle Kace set them off every year, or they get into a fistfight my dad has to break up. One year he dragged them both to jail before the fireworks were done. Gammy wouldn't bail them out. Uncle Lock stole the keys from Dad's desk and set them free."

"You have a wonderful family." She had been foolish to stay away from the Rykers. She'd had a place here once. They would have been a family that could have helped her deal with Ava's death when her own family fell apart. How foolish her young heart had been, thinking it knew all the answers.

She searched the crowd for Gage. He stood with his brothers, talking and laughing. Her heart tapped on her shoulder. The heart did know best sometimes.

"My dad and my uncles are a lot to take sometimes, but they're okay, I guess. I wish my uncles would date or get married so I'm not the only girl around. It might've been nice to have cousins."

"That could still happen. Your uncles are young enough."

"Will you and my dad have any more children?"

She choked on her drink and shook her head. "Um, I don't think so. We're older. Definitely not planning that far ahead. One day at a time. Living in the moment kind of thing." Out of the mouths of babes.

"That's dumb. You two have wasted enough time. You should just get married and have babies."

"Izzi, Calista, come here." Gage's voice held a note of impatience.

Gage had saved her from responding to that comment by whatever was bothering him. She and Izzi jumped from the chair and ran toward the grill. Justin swayed on his feet. He had a cut on his head over his two black eyes. Blood was caked under his nose, and his lip was swollen.

"What happened?" Calista tilted Justin's chin with her fingers.

He stepped back and waved her away. "Nothing. I need to talk to you and Sheriff Ryker."

"Justin, did you get in a fight? I was texting you all day," Izzi said.

"I need to talk to Calista and the sheriff. Alone."

His words made Izzi back up.

"Fine. I don't care if you talk to them all night." She turned and marched away with her arms flapping in the air.

"This better be good because your face doesn't look like 'nothing,' " Gage said.

"We need to get him to a doctor." Whatever Justin needed to tell them could wait. His injuries looked significant enough to warrant help.

"No." Justin swayed again, but his voice was strong and confident.

He walked to the front of the main house and into the driveway. He kept going until he was far away from any guests before he stopped and faced them. She took Gage's hand. The tension sizzled in the air like heat lightning.

Justin looked off into the distance. "You need to get everyone out of here."

"What?" Gage said.

"I don't understand," she said.

Justin's glare met hers. "Your ranch is going to get hit tonight."

Gage dropped her hand. Her heart stuck in her throat. This couldn't be happening. "Please take a second and explain."

"My brother and his friend have been committing the robberies. You were right. I did know. I've been trying to stop him, but he's a lot stronger than I am." Justin pointed to the gash on his head. "He found out I was invited here today. Thinks he's going to teach me a lesson by hurting you. He's coming here with guns to steal from everyone. I'm sorry. I don't want anyone else to get hurt. Especially not Izzi. Please get everyone out of here before they get here."

Gage grabbed Justin by the collar of his shirt and yanked him off his feet. "I'm going to make sure you pay for this for a very long time." He dropped Justin and ran.

****

"Everyone inside. Now," Gage yelled over the conversations and laughter. His insides shook with adrenaline. He had to act without hesitation and save these people.

The crowd silenced and stared.

"Don't ask questions. Jett, take everyone into the basement safe room. You all need to stay inside until I tell you to come out. Kace, get the guns."

But it was too late. He should have known they weren't going to have enough time. Five men with pistols and masks over their faces surrounded the house. They must have been in the woods waiting for the right moment, the moment when the sheriff wasn't paying attention.

Someone screamed. Guests ran. Mable took off toward the walking path. Kace bolted for the house. Andy hurried his mother out of the way. One of the robbers fired a shot into the air. Everyone stopped.

"Nobody move, and no one gets hurt. Give us your money, and we'll be out of here."

"We don't want trouble." Gage took a tentative step forward with his hands raised. He'd tucked his gun in the holster under his shirt, but he would have to wait for the right moment to pull it.

"We just want your money and valuables." The same man spoke. He had a deep voice with a Montana accent. His frame was slim but tall. His skin was the color of wet sand. He could be Jamie Crow.

"Gage, what do we do?" Kace said.

"Shut up." The man at the back of the group pointed his gun at the guests.

"Gage?" From Kace, because no one was ever going to tell Kace to keep quiet. Not even a man with a gun.

"I said to shut up." The man with the gun shot Howard in the leg. Howard bellowed like a dying animal.

"Do as I say, Kace. Do you hear me?" It was a code for Kace to wait until he gave the direction. He hoped his brother would listen.

Kace nodded.

That didn't stop the pounding of his heart making it difficult to breathe. Gage assessed the crowd. He wasn't sure where Izzi or Calista was. Probably behind him, but he hoped they found somewhere safe to hide. He took a step back.

"Everyone on the ground." The man who appeared to be the leader of the group stood ahead of the other two. His gun was steady, but his gaze jumped from either fear, adrenaline, or worse, drugs.

A guest started to cry. One of the robbers shoved her and shouted for her to quiet down. Everyone dropped down except for Jett and Kace. Lock looked at him from the ground, anger in his eyes. He tried to will Lock to stay put. Lock wouldn't like this any more than Kace did.

Kace had a rifle in his truck, but how was he going to tell his brother to grab it? He would never risk Kace's life anyway. Inside the garage, Jett had three rifle safes. All that armory and no way to access it. His

Glock wasn't going to be enough against five lunatics with guns.

Izzi peeked out from the side of the house. Damn it. The criminal at the back of the group fired a shot in her direction. She screamed and disappeared behind the house. He bolted toward her, but the leader of the group stepped in his path and blocked his way with a gun pointed at his face. Lock jumped up, but one of the criminals pointed the gun at his head. Lock raised his hands and dropped to his knees.

"Let me get to my daughter. You don't want a murder on your hands. We'll give you our stuff. Just let me get to my child."

The man didn't move.

Jett eased to the side with the slightest of nods. Gage stayed still, but his heart slammed his ribs and begged his legs to run after Izzi. He would let his brother get to Izzi. He needed to keep his wits about him and save everyone.

"You get down." A third man clocked Kace in the back of the head with his pistol. Kace crumbled.

His mother screamed and lunged. Andy grabbed her arm and yanked her back to the ground. She let out a whoosh, and her glasses went flying. He needed to regain control of the situation before someone ended up dead.

"You too." The leader indicated him with the gun.

He would not get on the ground. That would take away his only chance. He still didn't know where Calista was. Maybe she had run away with Justin and called for help. Two of the men patted pockets of the victims and pulled phones and wallets out. One man kicked some of the guests as he went by. Rage strangled him.

Jett eased back another few steps. Like a rabbit on the run for his life, he took off for the side of the house. One of the gunmen fired a shot, and someone screamed. The leader turned his head in the direction Jett went.

Gage had a second to act. He tucked his head and rammed into the leader's solar plexus. The man let go of the gun, which tumbled into the air. Gage knocked the leader to the ground and punched his face until the man stopped fighting back.

Lock grabbed the errant firearm and pointed it at a remaining robber.

The other gunmen ran into the woods with the items belonging to the guests. Jett bolted from the side of the house and sprinted after them.

"Jett, come back." Gage didn't need his brother getting hurt.

Some of the guests jumped up and scurried for the house. Lock waved them on, checking to make sure they were safe.

"I'll call for help," Andy said.

Gage hoisted the leader of the group onto his feet. "Who are you?"

The man shook his head and pulled off the mask. The resemblance to Justin was unmistakable. Jamie Crow stared at him with vacant, black eyes.

He had been right and wished he wasn't. "You are under arrest. You have the right—"

Jamie's fist collided with his jaw like an attack from a rattlesnake. His head snapped back, and he lost his grip on the man. His knees buckled, and he went down, skimming his legs on the concrete patio.

"Gage." Calista's voice pierced the air.

Footsteps thudded against the ground and disappeared into the night.

Someone stood over him. His blurred vision masked their face. He opened his mouth, but only a garble of sounds came out. He needed to get the robbers before they were gone. Someone grabbed his hand. He tried to get up, but someone pressed on his chest. Too many people around him. He couldn't breathe. He couldn't talk. He couldn't save anyone.

Chapter Twenty-Seven

Calista held Gage's hand in her cold, shaking one. Her whole body trembled, no matter how hard she tried to stop it. Her father had put a blanket around her shoulders, but it did nothing to make the shakes stop.

The ambulance and Barry Pearce were on their way. The shot fired at Izzi hit the side of the house and ricocheted. It nicked her leg. Jett bandaged her up, and Karen held her granddaughter. Jett cared for the other guests as well. He had wrapped a bandage around Kace's head only after Jett threatened to hit him again. Kace reluctantly agreed, saying he'd been hit by a car harder. Now Kace assisted Jett helping those injured. A knot lodged in her throat. It was too close to what happened sixteen years ago.

"Calista?" Gage's voice dragged her from her thoughts.

"Are you okay?" She helped him sit up.

He rubbed at his jaw. "Did I black out?"

"I think so. Don't get up. The ambulance is coming."

"Where's Izzi?" He pushed her hands away from his arms and tried to stand.

"She just went inside with your mother." She tried to swallow the knot in her throat. "She was hurt, but Jett took care of it."

"What do you mean? I have to get to her." He

stumbled.

"Wait a second." She grabbed his arm. "You took a hit to the head. You need to sit down."

He shrugged her off. "Don't tell me what I need to do. It's because of you my daughter is hurt. And these people." He pointed to the scattered guests. "Shit, look at Kace. Why did I ever listen to you? Where is Justin? I'm going to arrest him and throw the book at him."

He didn't wait for her to answer. He marched off inside the house in search of Izzi. Her legs called it quits, and she dropped to the ground. What had she done to this family? She had insisted that Justin was not a part of those robberies. She should have listened to Gage because if she had, none of this would have happened. Now the people she had hurt and loved were hurt again. Her heart shattered into a million pieces cutting into her lungs. Tears pooled in her eyes and ran down her face.

"Lissa, let's go home." Her father extended his hand.

She slid hers into his rough and aged one and allowed him to pull her to her feet. He wrapped an arm around her shoulders. "It's going to be okay, sweet pea."

"It's never going to be okay again. I broke his heart. He's never going to forgive me. I allowed these people to be hurt. I should check on Izzi."

Her father shook his head. "We don't belong here."

"We should stay and talk to Barry. We need to give them our statements."

"They know who did it. They don't need us. It's time to go. I'll drive you home. You can come get your car and your things tomorrow."

She took in the scene one final time. This was the end. She never thought it would have happened so quickly and with so much blood.

She wanted to go back in time and tell Gage he was right about Justin, but she had been so convinced because Justin had reminded her of Fox. She didn't want another boy to be caught up in the middle of something he had nothing to do with. She had been stupid. Justin had been involved and probably playing them the whole time. To think she'd even tried to convince Gage to allow Justin to date Izzi. A moan escaped from her lips. He had every right to hate her.

She hated herself about now.

"Let's go. I don't belong here." She never had.

Chapter Twenty-Eight

Gage held a cold beer can to his jaw. Jamie Crow had a mean punch. His head still reeled. He had refused Nyx Blackwood's assistance when the ambulance finally arrived because other people were hurt worse than he was. Instead, he helped her tend to anyone who needed medical attention and helped Barry get everyone's statement. No one had seen Justin leave.

Now he was alone in his cabin sitting in the dark. Izzi stayed with his mother. He wanted her home, but she refused to leave. Kace had decided to stay home too. He slept on the couch, only yards from Izzi, with a rifle in reach. Lock had promised to sleep on the chair next to Kace. Jett wouldn't sleep at all.

Some of the guests had checked out as soon as he and Barry finished getting their statements. One couple had decided to stay. This incident was going to kill their business. He could never make this up to Jett, Lock, and his mother. Their lives were the ranch, and he destroyed that. What he wanted to know was why did Justin's brother hit the ranch?

How could he have been so gullible? He wiped a hand over his face, avoiding his bruised jaw. He had allowed his emotions for Calista to get in the way of his police work. He had been right about Justin all along. That didn't make him feel any better. He would never allow his emotions to get in the way again. He and

Calista couldn't be together. He didn't trust himself around her.

His phone buzzed. He swiped it up. "Are you okay?"

"Dad, I can't sleep. I wanted to check on you."

"I'm fine. I can come get you if you want to sleep in your own bed."

"No, I'm in the sewing room. I like it here. It makes me feel safe."

"And you don't feel safe here?" He'd kill anyone who would try to hurt her. He thought she would know that.

"I do, but I want to stay. I think Gammy likes having everyone around, even if the uncles are armed and dangerous. Are you going to get any sleep?"

His mother knew how to make Izzi feel needed— and that was important at her age. Considering Izzi's mother never made her feel needed or wanted, Karen Ryker filled a void in Izzi's life. "I don't think so. Izzi, do you know where Justin is?"

"No. He won't answer my texts. Are you going to arrest him when you find him?"

"Yes."

"Dad, don't you think Justin deserves a second chance? It's not his fault his brother committed those crimes."

"You don't understand. He had knowledge about the crimes being committed, and he didn't tell me. That's a crime in and of itself. If we had a lead, maybe Phyllis would still be alive. You wouldn't have been shot." The thought of losing Izzi to a bullet sent a sharp pain through his chest. He would gladly give up his life to save hers.

"It's just a small cut."

"That bullet could have killed you." He didn't mean to raise his voice. The panic clutched his throat and shoved the words out with force.

"I'm fine. You always said it's okay if we make mistakes as long as we own up to them. Justin tried to do that tonight. And haven't you said Uncle Ajay had deserved another chance from you?"

He closed his eyes and took a deep breath. "So you do listen when I speak."

Her giggle reached through the phone and soothed some of the hurt. "Of course, I listen to you. You talk all the time."

"Only when I have something to say."

"When it comes to giving orders, that's all the time."

"You've also been talking to Uncle Kace too much."

"Did you know he snores? I can hear him all the way up here. Uncle Jett has yelled at him like three times."

A bubble of laughter from someplace deep inside him soothed his hurt more. Ajay had deserved another chance from him. If he had given it to him, his little brother would be alive and giving their family the layer of love it needed. He pushed out another long breath. Justin had come to the ranch to confess. That couldn't have been easy for him. The scratches and cuts on his face were from a fight. A fight with his brother. He hated to admit it, but he and Justin had a lot in common.

"I don't tell you enough how proud I am of you," he said.

"Sure you do. And I'm proud of you too, Daddy.

I'm going to get some sleep now. Night."

"Night."

He placed the phone down, and the screen lit back up.

Someone was calling, and he didn't recognize the number.

He hesitated for a second but swiped at the screen. "Sheriff Ryker."

Silence met him on the other side.

"Hello? This is Sheriff Ryker. Is someone there?"

"It's Justin. I need your help."

Chapter Twenty-Nine

Calista dried her hair on a towel and sipped at the wine. She stared out the window of her room back in the B and B and fought the urge to cry. The moonlight glistened on the lake's surface like black diamonds. The view could be any other night, but it was one of the worst nights she'd ever lived through.

Justin had hurt her in a way she couldn't have seen coming. She had wanted so badly to believe he had told the truth. She had begged Gage to listen to her. Because of her, all those people were hurt. And she and Gage were through. He blamed her for what happened. The irony wasn't lost on her.

Maybe in the light of morning...no. Maybe nothing. In the morning, she would pack her belongings and go back to Billings. She would get rid of her apartment and find another city to live in where she could tend bar and practice yoga. Yoga might be the only thing left that could save her.

Her heart ached for Gage. She didn't want him upset, and she wanted to check on Izzi. She missed his strong embrace. His arms around her would also be the one thing that could save her. Except he would never allow her that luxury. He would shut his emotions right down where she was concerned.

She debated on calling him. He would be awake. If she could just hear his voice one more time, she might be able to tuck the memory away for safekeeping with the other memories of this trip.

Her silent phone mocked her from the bed. She wished he had called and told her he was wrong for being mad at her, that he would never do to her what she had done to him. But he would never call. He would spend his time hunting down Justin and his brother until justice was served. By then, too much time would have passed.

She picked up the phone anyway. Someone had called. Justin. She fumbled through the screen until she arrived at the voice mail.

"Calista, it's me. I need help. I'm at my apartment, and I'm hurt. Jamie beat me up. I can't call anyone else. Please come."

Her blood roared in her ears. She tried to call Justin back, but the phone rang and rang. A voice said his mailbox was full. She threw on jeans and a T-shirt but stopped. She shouldn't go alone. She dialed Gage. The call went to voice mail.

"Gage, it's me. Justin called. He's at his apartment, and his brother beat him. Please meet me there...and I'm sorry."

She grabbed her keys and ran.

****

Calista tried to call Justin while she stood outside his apartment building, but he didn't answer. She dialed Gage again too, but his voice mail still picked up. She would rather go inside with him. Was he so furious with her he wouldn't answer her calls?

A car horn went off someplace. A cat screeched in the distance. She jumped, and her heart knocked on her ribs. "Shit." She ran her fingers over her bracelet.

"Gage, where are you?"

She couldn't waste any more time. Justin needed her help, and she would give it. He hadn't meant to hurt anyone. He was just a kid who missed love and guidance. What kind of a person would she be if she turned him away now?

Headlights turned down the street. She hesitated. Had Gage come after all? She waited to see if it was him.

A black car rolled to a stop. Her mind caught up to the image in front of her. A car, not Gage's truck. Her stomach heaved. Her feet froze in place. The back window slid down, and the barrel of a gun pointed at her.

"Look what I found. Don't think about moving."

Chapter Thirty

Gage pulled open the door to Justin's apartment building. A car horn blew open the night somewhere down the street. The lobby smelled of fish and fried food. He removed his gun from the holster and kept it at the ready.

He opted for the stairs instead of the elevator. At the entrance to the second floor, he gripped the handle of the metal door and shoved it open but didn't leave the stairway. He glanced into the hall but jumped back. No one was in the hall. He was safe to continue.

Backup would be good about now, but Barry Pearce wasn't going to be much help in this situation. He could have asked one of his brothers to come with him, but he wouldn't endanger them even if he wanted the company. He would have to do this alone and pray for a little help. Except he didn't believe in God.

Justin's apartment was at the end of the long hall. What if he was lying again and this was a trick? He didn't want to die tonight and leave Izzi without a parent.

He banged on the apartment door. His heart galloped in his chest. "Police. Open up."

A door behind him opened. He swung around and pointed the gun. A large woman in a pink bathrobe and curlers threw her hands up. "Ooh. Don't shoot. I didn't do nothing."

"Go back inside, ma'am. This is official police business."

The lady slammed the door shut. He banged on Justin's door again.

The door opened a crack.

He kept his gun pointed.

"Sheriff Ryker?"

He lowered his gun. "Yeah, Justin. Can you let me in?"

Justin opened the door wide enough for him to slip through. The apartment was dark, except for a small lamp on in the corner of the crowded living space. The tiny area smelled of stale smoke and dirty bodies. A lonely table was covered in used food wrappers. The sofa sagged in the middle. A big-screen television sat on an old pockmarked dresser. Several long wires dangled from the television and snaked to a video-game machine.

The kitchen was not much bigger than a postage stamp. Food-covered dishes filled the sink. Cereal boxes, spotted glasses, and used cigarettes in a makeshift ashtray littered the kitchen table.

Justin's face was swollen and purple, his eyes mere slits. Blood caked on the side of his head. He engaged the chain and slid to the ground with his back to the door. "Thank you for coming."

"Did your brother do this to you?"

Justin nodded. He guessed if he lifted Justin's shirt, he'd find bruising along his torso too.

"Why?" He checked out the window, but the only thing out there was a fire escape.

"He thinks I've traded my family for yours. He thinks I snitched, and that's unforgivable to him." Justin clutched his side.

"He sees you leaving the rez for something else as a betrayal. Where is he?"

"I don't know."

"Let's get you to the hospital." He leaned down to help Justin.

"Wait. I'm sorry. I didn't know how to stop him from committing those crimes. He's got a drug problem. He wasn't always like this." His breath came out in short bursts.

"Don't talk so much. Can you walk?" He understood Jamie Crow better than he wanted to. Ajay wasn't always in a gang. He was once a good kid who got tangled up with the wrong crowd.

"I think so. If I go to the hospital, he'll kill me for telling on him." Justin struggled to stand.

"If you don't, he has killed you for sure. You could be bleeding internally. I'll keep you safe." He took Justin's elbow to steady him.

"I really am sorry."

"Yeah, me too." He gripped Justin around the waist because the kid looked as if he were about to fall over.

"I called Calista to come too." Justin wrapped an arm around his shoulder and leaned into him.

"You did? Is she coming?" He didn't want her here alone. This was not the safest neighborhood, and he had no idea where Jamie Crow was.

"She never called back."

That didn't sound like her. "Hang on." He pulled his phone from his pocket. Three missed calls from her. He helped Justin lean against the wall. "I want to reach her."

His phone went off in his hand. Calista's name

appeared. "Where are you?" he said.

"Gage." Her voice was strangled with tears.

"Babe, are you all right?" He strained to hear her over the sound of a car horn in the background.

"He got me. Please come." Her voice trailed away as if the phone were pulled from her mouth.

"Calista," he yelled.

"We're on the roof, Sheriff. Bring my brother, or I kill your girl." Jamie Crow hung up.

****

Calista knelt on the roof of Justin's apartment building. The cement bored into her knees. Her hands were clasped behind her head, and Jamie Crow pointed a large gun at her face. The wind lifted the hair off her neck and blew strands across her face like tiny whips. "Why are you doing this?" She forced her trembling lip still.

"To teach my brother a lesson." He glanced over his shoulder at the rooftop door.

"Gage is never going to let you get away with this." She would not cry in front of this monster and show her fear. She wanted to take back every awful thought she ever had of Ajay Ryker. He hadn't meant to kill Ava the way Jamie meant to hurt her tonight on this roof.

"My brother dishonored my family by leaving us for you and that white girl he likes. Now I'm going to show him the mistake he made." Jamie tapped his foot in an erratic beat.

"By hurting me?"

"He needs to learn."

"Gage is going to arrest you." She needed him to stay calm somehow, or he might accidentally pull that trigger.

"Not while I have a gun pointed at your head."

The door to the roof swung open. Gage held a large black pistol in both hands. He stepped forward as if he were a panther about to pounce on its prey. The forbidding stare in his eyes chilled her. He was alone.

"Put that gun down, and we all go home." His voice held more ice than a Montana winter.

"Can't do that, Sheriff. Where is my brother?"

"He comes out when you let Calista go." Gage kept the gun pointed at Jamie.

"This ain't no trade. My brother gave me up for you. He's going to give something up for me. Justin? You here?" Jamie craned his neck. If he was looking for Justin behind Gage, the hall was too dark to see into.

"Calista, are you okay?" Gage's gaze never wavered off Jamie.

"I've been better." The gun was an inch from her head. She kept her gaze on Gage, not wanting to see the black barrel any longer.

"Shut up, both of you. Justin?" Jamie's voice carried over the rooftop and blew away in the wind. "Come out here and watch your friends die."

Justin hobbled out.

"No." Gage groaned.

A cry died in her throat. Justin was barely walking, and his face was a mess.

"It's a party. Yeehaw!" Jamie said.

Justin leaned against the door and held his side. "Jamie, put that gun away." His chest heaved with each word.

"Can't. I want you to see what it's like to lose your

family." Jamie cut his words with a sneer.

"You're going to jail," Gage said.

"You need help, Jamie. Gage and Calista can get you cleaned up." Justin held himself up with one arm against the door.

"They are nothing to me. They aren't my family. Only family can help me, and that's not you anymore." Jamie grabbed her hair and dragged her toward the edge of the roof.

She tried to pry his hands from her hair, but his hold was like a vice. Her heels dragged along the concrete roof, gripping nothing. "Let go of me." She yelled and twisted to get free as her heart pounded against her ribs, but she didn't have the power to stop Jamie.

"Okay. Okay. Whatever you want." Gage's voice shook. He holstered his gun and held up his hands.

Jamie dropped her on her ass but kept the gun on her. "That's better."

Her gaze bounced from Justin, covered in blood, to Gage with his hands in the air. He couldn't allow this night to end the way things had ended for Ajay and Ava, could he? She didn't care about herself. She wanted Gage to save Justin from his brother.

"Son, put the gun down before someone gets hurt," Gage said.

"I'm not your son." Jamie shoved the cold metal of the gun against her head.

A scream escaped her lips. Gage lunged. Jamie swung the gun in his direction. Gage backed up.

"Easy now." Gage kept his hands raised. "We can talk about this. You don't want anyone else killed."

"This is all your fault, Justin. You wanted them as

your family instead of your own. If you just accepted your life, but no, you traded us in for them. They aren't your people."

Justin doubled over and spit out blood. He was going to die because no one was helping him. Just like Ava. She couldn't let that happen.

The blood roared in her ears. Her body moved as if she were under water. Justin needed her. He caught her movement and shook his head. Gage reached for her with both hands. His lips moved, but no sound came out. The solid crack of metal against her head made her eyes roll back. The concrete slammed into her face and knocked her out.

Chapter Thirty-One

Gage wanted to kill Jamie Crow. Blood ran from Calista's head, and he stood there helpless. If he drew his gun back out, Jamie would only shoot him and probably Justin and Calista too. Real life wasn't the same as the movies. He didn't have some trick up his sleeve, like another gun taped to his back. He was a sheriff in a small town with his heart in his throat and the woman he loved and this kid who needed him in grave danger. He should have called his brothers earlier.

"Jamie," Justin said, but his brother ignored him.

"If she dies, that's going to be two murders on your hands." Gage's hands shook. He made fists to stop the shaking. "Let me call for help. You can still have me, but you let Justin and Calista go to the hospital."

"We all stay together." Sweat beaded on Jamie's head. He shifted from one foot to the other.

Time was running out. If Jamie had been high, that high was ending. He was going to be edgy, skittish, and even more desperate. Gage had to figure out a way to get them all out of this alive.

"He's your brother. You need to let him get some medical attention. I know you love him. I love my kid brothers. There's nothing I wouldn't do for them." He stole a glance at Calista. She hadn't moved. He needed to get to her. He inched forward.

"Don't talk to me like we're friends, 'cause we ain't. You hate me 'cause of my skin and where I'm from. Back up." He waved the gun.

Gage didn't move.

"Justin, they don't care about you. Why did you snitch on me for them?" Jamie wiped his nose with the back of his shaking hand.

Justin held his side and coughed up more blood. "I don't want to live in that shitty apartment anymore. I don't want to live on the rez with empty cabinets and my belly twisting in knots because of hunger."

"Sheriff, there's a change of plans. I want you to call for a helicopter or something. We're getting out of here." Jamie dug in his pocket and tossed over his phone. It skipped across the concrete.

"Where am I supposed to get a helicopter?" This guy had to be high.

Jamie fired a shot in the air. Gage took the chance and drew his gun. Jamie pointed his gun at him. They were at a stalemate.

"Wait." Justin grabbed his arm. "Don't shoot him."

Calista stirred. She pushed off the ground and shook her head. "Gage?"

"Don't move, babe." He kept his gun drawn on Jamie. He wouldn't put it away again. As long as she stayed on the ground, he'd have a clean shot to the chest.

"Sheriff Ryker, please put your gun away," Justin said. "I'll go with you, Jamie, but you have to let the sheriff and Calista go. I'm sorry I hurt you. You are my family. Not them. I see that now." Tears slid down his face.

Tears ran down Jamie's face too. "He'll arrest me.

I robbed his ranch and those other places."

Justin shuffled forward. "No, he won't. Sheriff Ryker is a good man. A fair man. He'll let you go, but you have to let them go. Put the gun down, okay?"

"Justin, what are you doing?" Gage said.

"Trust me, Sheriff. This is what's best. Jamie, put your gun down." Justin moved closer to his brother.

"Why did you snitch on me?" The tears continued to spill down Jamie's face.

"I was afraid. I didn't want you to kill anyone. You're all the family I have left. I thought I could fit in off the reservation, but I can't. You showed me that tonight when you found me on the street." Justin cried too.

Gage tilted his chin, indicating she slide to the side. He kept the gun on Jamie, but Justin had moved into his path and blocked any chance of a clean shot.

"I don't belong in their world." Justin stopped inches from his brother.

"No, you don't. You've always been a dumb shit brother. I guess that beating finally knocked some sense into you."

He tried not to think about the times he wanted to beat the shit out of Ajay in hopes of turning him around. He had never been gladder that he hadn't.

"Let me come home, Jamie."

Jamie tucked the gun behind his back with still shaking hands. Justin grabbed him in a hug. Jamie pounded on his back. Justin groaned from the slaps. Calista crawled out of the way. Gage kept the gun poised. He didn't know what was going to happen, but he wasn't about to leave Justin behind.

Jamie's eyes grew wide. His hands hovered over

Justin's back in mid-slap. Justin jumped away. Jamie grabbed for Justin's hands.

Justin had the gun. And he pointed it at Jamie.

"Gage," Calista yelled.

He still didn't have a clear shot. The brothers struggled for the gun. He risked hitting Justin, who still stood in front of Jamie even though they fought.

Calista ran behind him and grabbed on to his shirt.

The wind picked up. A fire burned somewhere in the distance. Time slowed down.

"Drop the gun, Justin," Gage said.

But Justin didn't let go. And neither did Jamie as they continued to struggle and fight. No one was going to win this battle. "Drop the damn gun, Justin," he shouted.

The gun went off. Justin stumbled away from his brother. Jamie's mouth formed a large circle, but no sound came out. Gage's ears rang from the gunshot. Calista's scream came to him as if she were down a long tunnel. The wind continued to blow.

Justin turned to him with narrowed eyes. He clutched his stomach. A dark, red circle grew on his shirt. He fell to his knees. Jamie dropped the gun and ran for the stairs.

Gage begged his legs to work. Time stalled. It was sixteen years ago, and he had to get to Ajay. The dash across the roof seemed to take hours. Justin was on his side. Blood spilled over his long, tan fingers as he clutched his stomach.

"Help. Don't let me die," Justin said.

The same thing Ajay had said to him.

He threw the phone at Calista. "Call nine-one-one." He knelt down by Justin and turned him on his back.

The gunshot wound was big. He was losing a lot of blood. He might not make it.

His throat closed, but he forced a swallow and tore off his shirt to press against the wound. He pulled Justin's hands over the shirt. "Hold on to this. Press hard. Help is coming. You need to hang on, okay?"

Justin opened his mouth to speak.

"Don't talk. Keep looking at me. I'm right here. I won't let anything happen to you. You're going to be fine." Justin needed to believe him if he had any chance to survive.

Calista dropped down beside him and gripped Justin's arm. "Help is on the way. Hang in there. You're going to be okay."

"Please don't let me die." Tears ran down his face.

He hadn't had the power to save his brother. He was the last person this young man should rely on to save him. "You aren't going to die tonight."

It was the same lie he'd told Ajay.

Chapter Thirty-Two

The doctors and nurses ran alongside Justin on a stretcher. They shoved through the operating room doors and shut Calista out. She heaved a breath and wiped the sweat from her brow. All she could do now was pray. Praying hadn't helped the last time she was in this hospital.

She had left Gage filling out paperwork for Justin. He didn't know the information the hospital needed, but because he was the sheriff, the person working at admittance allowed him to try. He needed to do something. The helplessness had been in his eyes.

In the waiting room, Gage sat on the edge of the plastic seat, holding his head in his hands, the clipboard forgotten. His fingers raked through his hair. She took the seat beside him and placed a hand on his shoulder.

He turned to face her. The pain of sixteen years carved lines in his face and darkened his eyes. "This is my fault."

"No, it isn't. It's Jamie's fault. He committed the crimes, beat up Justin, and threatened to kill me and you and his brother. You did all you could do."

"That young boy tried to save us all and will probably end up dead because of it. If I had listened to you from the beginning and searched someplace else for the people robbing my town, I would have found Jamie Crow. Shit, even Lincoln Smith told me to look into Jamie as a possibility, but I was hell bent on it being Justin."

He shoved out of the chair and paced the small area. She went to him and grabbed his arms to keep him from moving. Her heart ached for what he'd been carrying around inside him for so long. "What happened tonight is not the same thing. You couldn't have saved Ajay no matter what you did. Someone should have told you that. I should've told you that, but even as recent as a few days ago, I still blamed you for not knowing. How can you possibly still love me?"

His eyes filled with unexpected tears. She held him tighter.

"He needed me, and I let him down."

She didn't have to ask him who he was talking about. "It's time to forgive yourself."

"If Justin dies, I won't be able to do that." He removed her grip on his arm and went to the window. The dark night and the parking lot with scattered lights offered no explanations.

"Saving Justin isn't your salvation, Gage."

"Oh really? Isn't that exactly what you were doing with him?"

She had been. Justin was the stand-in for Fox and Ava. Until recently, she'd been too afraid to love someone as she'd loved her sister, and then Fox stole her heart and died, taking a piece with him. If she lost Justin too, nothing would be left of her. She might not even be able to go on loving Gage. So much pain surrounded them.

"Why don't you go home and get some rest? I'll stay until the surgery is over." She dropped into the chair and leaned her head against the wall.

"Do you need a doctor to look at you?" He took the seat beside her and laced his fingers through hers.

His touch was warm and safe. No matter what happened, where they ended up, he would be a part of her. "I'm fine. I'm also sorry about what happened at the ranch. I should've listened to you too."

"Don't do that. You were just opening your heart in the way I love about you. You have that soft side I can't find in me. You see the best in people when I only see the worst. This isn't your fault."

"Thank you for coming to the apartment building to help Justin."

He shrugged. "You should be the one to go home and rest. I can call Kace to come and get you."

"If it's okay with you, I'd like to stay."

"Why wouldn't it be okay with me?"

"What's going to happen to us?"

He sat up and faced her. "No matter what, I will always love you."

"Sheriff Ryker?" A tall, thin man dressed in blue scrubs with a paper cap on his head stood in the doorway. His arms were crossed over his chest. He averted his gaze. The thin line his lips made said more than he needed to.

Her heart splintered.

Gage stood. "Yes. Is Justin okay?"

"Why don't you have a seat?"

Chapter Thirty-Three

The sun climbed into the bright, blue sky and warmed the fourth day of July. Calista always loved the vast Montana sky, especially from Gage's ranch where nothing blocked the view. She closed her eyes and took a deep breath. Today was the anniversary. They had all come so far.

"Ready?" Her father's voice brought her attention back to what they were doing today.

She smoothed the dress she'd chosen. A far cry from her wide-legged gauzy pants. But today deserved something nicer than the clothes she threw on without thinking about it.

She slid her hand into her dad's, as she had when she was little and life hadn't worn the dark coat of trauma and loss. He smiled down. His eyes were clear behind his glasses, and his skin was smooth again. Through all the recent tragedies, she had her father back.

"I'm ready." She looked over her shoulder.

Gage leaned against his truck with his ankles crossed. He looked great in his khakis with the sharp crease and white button-down shirt against his dark skin. He'd rolled the sleeves up to his elbows and showed off his roped forearms. Arms that held her night after night, keeping her safe and as warm as the Montana sun.

"You'll be right here?" she said to him.

"Like I promised." He gifted her his smile.

She hadn't been sure if he would come today. He was making progress since the incident with Justin and Jamie, but he wasn't totally healed.

She stepped off the walkway and onto the grass. Justin survived the gunshot and the surgery. It had been touch-and-go for the first forty-eight hours, but he was young and strong. Gage hadn't had the heart to charge Justin with anything. After he was released from the hospital, she moved him into the family cottage with her dad on the lake. They were a family now. Jamie and his accomplices were still on the run, but Gage hadn't given up. His friend Lincoln was helping him look.

She and her dad navigated the headstones until they came to the place they wanted. With a sniffle, her father placed the bouquet of flowers on the top of Ava's gravestone. No one had been here in quite some time. Weeds poked out of the ground. It seemed nature tried to take back its spot and wanted to cover Ava's headstone. She bent to pull some of the weeds out.

"Leave it. I'll come back tomorrow and clean this place up. She deserves that much out of me." Dad wiped tears away from his cheeks.

"We can do it together." Ava deserved that much from her too.

They stood there for a while not saying anything. Her father took a long breath. "I think I'm ready to go."

They walked back, and Gage still leaned against his truck, waiting as he'd promised. He'd been waiting for her for a long time. Her chest filled with the joy of knowing he never stopped loving her.

"Your turn," she said.

He took her hand and gave it a squeeze. "Thank you for doing this with me. I wouldn't have come alone."

"I know." His mother had cried and held her tightly when she told Karen about this plan. Gage deserved some peace too.

They walked in the opposite direction of Ava's grave and up the hill to the large stone that read Ryker. Three plots had been secured for this site. One spot was for Mr. Ryker, and the second spot was left open for the day Karen would join him. The stone to the right was the one added for Ajay.

Gage ran a hand over Ajay's name. "Hey, bro." He blew out a loud breath and hung his head.

She gave him some space to let whatever he needed to happen, happen. But that didn't stop the tears from spilling down her cheeks. The weight of this visit pressed against her lungs.

"I don't know what to do or say." He took her hand and pulled her closer.

"You don't have to do anything." She squeezed his hand to let him know she would never be far if that's what he wanted.

"But I want him to know I was here, and talking doesn't seem like enough."

She fished inside the pocket of her dress and pulled out Ava's necklace her father had given her. She dangled it from her fingers so the sun caught the gold. The chain flickered in the light. Gage narrowed his eyes.

"This is my gift to Ajay." She placed it on the top of the headstone.

"Leaving something on the grave is my family's

tradition. I should've thought of that."

"I hope you don't mind that I'm doing this. It's Ava's necklace. I hoped having something of Ava's might help Ajay know he's forgiven so his spirit can find its way home. More importantly, that I'm asking for his forgiveness." Her heart clamored against her ribs. She hadn't told him about the necklace.

He remained still but looked off in the other direction.

"I should've checked with you first," she said.

He grabbed her hands. His eyes glistened as his gaze met hers. "Thank you for this. It's exactly what Ajay needs. It's exactly what I need. He will be able to go home now and be in peace. Maybe even sit beside my father again."

"I love you, Gage. I've loved you always. You are woven into the fabric of my life. I can't imagine another minute without you. If you can forgive me for allowing my hurt to keep us apart for too long, I want to spend the rest of my life with you and only you."

He placed a kiss on her lips. "I love you. You showed me how to let go of the pain I carried around for too long. If you really want me—and I'd be the luckiest bastard in the world if you do—then I promise to be the best man I can each and every day for you."

He kissed her again long and hard.

She laced her fingers through his, and together they found their way back, and their way home.

Enjoy this excerpt from

A Second Chance House

by

Stacey Wilk

Heritage River Series, Book One

Chapter One

Grace Starr turned her Subaru Impreza into the driveway of her two-story gray colonial with black shutters and matching black double doors. She loved this house with its oversized deck she sat on at night catching the breeze and drinking tea, the big kitchen with plenty of cabinets, and the gas fireplace that burned clean. Twenty-Five Tudor Drive was the place she started a family with her husband and raised her daughter, Chloe.

She hated the For Sale sign in the front yard.

She had an hour before she had to be back at the library. She should get some lunch, take a walk, clean a bathroom. The bathroom would win, and if she had time, she'd throw in a load of laundry, wipe down the counters, sort the mail into piles. Her favorite pile being the one that went into the garbage.

The extra car was parked in the driveway too. What was Chloe doing home from school in the middle of the afternoon? Had there been a half day Grace had forgotten about? Some kind of teacher in-service thing? Possibly. Lately, she kept returning to the bathroom to touch her toothbrush just to see if it was wet. Her mind couldn't hold a thought if it were a vault. Problem was, she didn't know if the absentmindedness was her age or the stress of the divorce. Better to blame it on the divorce. She wasn't that old...yet. Maybe Chloe felt the effects of senior year ending and was ditching.

The garage door yawned open, and Chloe came out in bare feet, her blue-streaked hair bouncing off her shoulders. Her nose piercing sparkled in the sun, mocking Grace from its coveted place on Chloe's face. Her shorts barely covered the necessary parts, and her shirt showed too much skin.

Grace cringed at the uncontrolled appearance of her almost-eighteen-year-old. She tried to arrange her face in a way that said she was used to seeing Chloe this way. Larry had let her get the piercing. He had bought her the blue dye. Grace was always the bad guy. The boring parent.

Chloe waved something in her hand. "Mom, you've got to see this."

Please don't let it be a letter from the guidance counselor.

"What are you doing home?" Chloe said, slightly out of breath, through the open car window. "I thought you were volunteering at the library today."

"I am, later. I was wondering what you were doing home on a Wednesday. Did you get in trouble for wearing that outfit to school?" What was the point in fighting? But she couldn't keep her mouth shut.

Chloe rolled her eyes with the skill of a seasoned pro. "No one dress codes in June. School's boring. We're not doing anything. They won't even notice I'm gone."

The same arguments about doing the right thing bubbled inside Grace and died on her tongue. Did it really matter? And look what doing the right thing did for her. She had followed the rules and planned for all possible outcomes. She was the dutiful wife, and she had still been evicted from her life. "Don't make skipping a habit. I don't care that there's only two weeks of school left."

Ignoring her last remark, Chloe shoved the white paper at Grace. "This came in the mail today. I didn't open it, but it looks interesting. Did Dad get new lawyers or something? Did he move out of state and not tell us? It would be just like him, the jerk."

"Chloe, don't call your father names." Even if Larry was a big fat jerk. Grace inspected the envelope addressed to her. A postmark she didn't recognize. A law firm's name and address in the top corner. Pretty official. What had Larry gone and done? She shoved her way out of the Impreza, gripping the envelope. She took a closer look. Tennessee? "This must be a mistake." She handed the envelope back.

"Are you kidding? You've got to open this." Chloe shoved the envelope at her. "Maybe we won something."

"Wishful thinking. I've never even been to Tennessee. Take it inside, please."

"No, Mom. Open it." Chloe gripped Grace's hand and shoved the envelope in her grasp.

Why was this so important? "Oh, all right." She ripped the envelope open and scanned its contents.

A letter on the firm's letterhead. Her hand began to shake. She had to read it twice to make sure she was seeing things correctly.

"Well, what is it?" Chloe's blue eyes had grown to the size of sunflowers. Her face sagged when she stared at Grace. "Dad did something bad, didn't he? He's keeping all his money or not letting me go to college, right?"

Grace shook her head and searched for her voice. "Surprisingly, Dad has nothing to do with this, but it must be a mistake. There's no way this is real." She looked back at the letter. "It says someone has left me a house. Who would do such a crazy thing?" A laugh bubbled up into her throat.

"That's great. Now we have a place to live. You can tell Dad you don't need him anymore."

Grace thrust the letter back in the envelope. Chloe's loyalty was sweet, but it might not last. These days they got along one minute, and the next Grace had said or done something wrong. Having a teenage daughter could be wonderful and exhausting at the same time. "The house is in Tennessee. You don't want to live there. I don't want to live in Tennessee. I like it here, in this town. Like I said, I'm sure it's a mistake. You want to get some lunch?"

"Wait. Who does it say gave you the house?"

Grace folded the envelope. "I don't know. They don't want to be identified."

"And you don't think that's mysterious and want to find out more?" Chloe raised her eyebrows.

She envied Chloe's ability to still believe amazing things happened at random moments. That was a blessing of youth. "Even if it's legitimate, which I highly doubt it is, nothing good can come from an unidentified person giving you a house. It's unheard of and ridiculous. People don't do things like that." Well, not practical people anyway.

****

The darkness covered Grace like a cocoon. The only light spilling into the kitchen was the dim one over the sink. She liked this time of night when Chloe either was out or barricaded in her room and she sat in the protection of the dark.

She sipped the white tea with citrus and stared at her computer. The law firm on the envelope had an impressive website. They certainly looked legit. But it still didn't make any sense. Who would leave her a house, especially one in Tennessee? No one she knew, and no one she knew had recently died. She had no relatives except Chloe. Her father had walked out of her life when she was too young to remember him, and her mother passed away when Grace was in her twenties. Both of her parents had no siblings.

What would it hurt to call? And what if someone had left her a house? The idea began to buzz around inside her head. She could sell it and buy something nicer up here. She had been planning to rent, but with extra money she could maybe buy sooner. Renting left a lot of unknowns, but buying at least would allow her to settle in and make the place her own.

She shook her head. What was she thinking? She had to stick to the plan. She and Chloe would move in with Grace's long-time friend, Jenn, until she found a place. She would have to find a job at some point too. The alimony was enough, but it wasn't her money. Never was.

She gripped the letter, ready to tear it in half. Her cell vibrated and interrupted her thoughts. Who would call at that hour? She checked the screen, and her heart sank.

"Hello, Larry."

"Sorry to call so late." His voice was low and raspy, as if he might have been speaking for a long time or didn't want anyone to hear him. "I haven't had another chance all day, and I wanted to reach you as soon as I could."

He had stood in their kitchen on a night not much different from this one and leaning against the gas range, confessed feelings for someone else. He had used words like *controlling, obsessive, cold,* and *buttoned up.*

She was controlling, but she wasn't buttoned up. She thought they were in a rut. Didn't all marriages have those after nineteen years? How excited could you get when you knew all of the other person's moves? It wasn't as if Larry was creative. While she was busy running their home, raising their child, and volunteering at the library, he was busy being creative with someone else, though. Someone younger than she was. Grace was the quintessential cliché. He had packed up and moved in with his young hottie whose skin still stayed in all the right places and who hadn't pushed a baby out of her hoo-ha.

"I've got some news," he said.

"You're joining AARP?" She picked at the corner of her letter. She didn't want this man back, did she? No, not the man. She wanted a marriage and a large family. He never really wanted to share a marriage with her, and his cheating had proved it. He ended the large family dream back when her eggs still dropped on a regular basis. She thought she didn't care about the latter—how wrong she was—and was too blind to realize she was the only player on the marriage team.

"Stop being so bitter. I have something to tell you. This is going to come as a shock, because no one was more surprised than me. I can't believe I'm about to say this out loud—"

"Could you get to the point?" Why was he calling her with his news? Did he really care what she thought any longer? What was he going to announce? Early retirement?

"Annie and I are getting married," he blurted in one swift breath.

The phone slipped from her hands. She grabbed at it like a hot potato. "What?"

"I want to buy your half of the house. Before you say a word, just listen. I'll pay more than the market value for it. You know as well as I do we'll never get full price for it if we sell, but if you'll sell your half to me, you'll get more than you expected."

She gripped the phone tighter.

"What do you say, Grace? It's a good deal. Better than you'll get any other way."

"Why do you want the house so badly?" She gripped the kitchen chair, trying to steady herself. She couldn't bear the idea of that woman living in her house. The house she had decorated with careful planning, from the colors on the walls to the pillows on the couch. The cabinets she kept cleaned and organized. The lamppost she had installed by the front walk because it was too dark for guests at night. All belonging to that woman? Over her dead body.

"I want to do this for you. I buy the house, you make the most money on your share, and you're rid of me. It's what you want. To be rid of me."

She wanted him out of her life—no point in denying that little truth. "We have a child together. I don't think we'll ever be completely rid of each other, as you say." She flopped down in the chair, creating a wind that sent the mysterious letter floating to the floor.

"Will you accept my offer?"

"I need time to think about it." The money would be nice. They hadn't had any bites on the house, and Larry couldn't afford the mortgage here and his rent forever.

"We could have the sale completed in thirty days."

"Thirty days? I don't have another place yet. I can't find a place that quickly." She had barely begun looking. Research needed to be done first. She wanted to create a neighborhood prospectus. The new house would most likely be where she'd finish out her later years. She couldn't buy a house that had the perfect number of rooms on a pretty yard without careful consideration.

He heaved a sigh. "Listen, Grace, I know this is coming as a shock. I'm a little shocked too, but we want the house."

"Larry, I can't make a split-second decision like that."

"Yeah, I know."

She wanted to reach through the phone and strangle him. "Don't make me out to be the bad guy in this one. It's not fair. I need some time."

Chloe shuffled into the kitchen in her slippers, yanked open the freezer door, and pulled out the cookies-and-cream ice cream. "Is that Dad?"

Grace covered the phone. *How can you tell?* she mouthed. It couldn't be the rise and tightening of her voice. Oh no. Not that.

"Did he tell you Annie is pregnant?"

"Your girlfriend is pregnant?" she yelled into the phone.

"What? How did you—?"

"Shut up, Larry. Just shut up. Chloe told me. That's why you want this house so badly, you jerk."

She stifled a groan and dropped her head between her knees to keep the room from tipping on its side. Larry, with his thinning hairline and paunchy belly, was getting married again and having a baby, having another child she'd wanted so badly her insides had ached for years. He had never wanted more children.

"I have my child," he had said, flipping through the newspaper as if they had been discussing the weather. "I don't want any more."

"I knew you might be upset. I don't blame you."

"Don't tell me you know how I feel."

"You're right. I don't. Annie loves the house. It has everything we're looking for, including good schools. She wants to be settled in before the baby comes."

Annie loved the house? When had she seen it? They wanted their new child to go to the schools Chloe had attended. Grace thought she might be sick. "And if I say no?"

"You'd be spiting no one but yourself. This is the only way to guarantee more than a fair sale price. If you want to sell it to strangers, then we will. I'm going to get married either way."

Grace went to the faucet and filled the glass with cold water. She gulped it down, hoping to stop the sweats. She stepped on the letter, and the paper creased under her foot. Her damp fingers stuck to the paper as she swiped it from the floor.

Larry was getting on with his life. Had been even while they were still married. In a few short months, Chloe would be off at college getting on with hers. Where would that leave Grace?

She stared at the phone number at the bottom of the letterhead. "You've got a deal." She ended the call and threw the phone down on the table.

She could go to Tennessee and check out this house. She could call the law firm in the morning for more details. If she liked what she heard, she would make a plan to go. What harm would it do to just see the house? She didn't have other options anyway. She hated when Larry was right. She stood to make the most money with his offer. She'd be an idiot not to take him up on it, and he was banking on that.

The idea of that woman living in her house still made her skin itch. "It's just a house, Grace. Stop being ridiculous." But it was her house. The house where she raised Chloe. The house she wanted grandchildren to visit. Was the house she shared with Larry ever really a home? Well, maybe, for about five minutes.

She could use a few days away. If this house in Tennessee really was hers, she could sell it and have extra money to buy something nicer than she originally thought. Maybe something with a porch she could sit on in the mornings with a cup of tea.

Buying a new house in town would be a fresh start. Didn't she deserve one too? A way to show Larry she didn't need him.

But did she really want to run into them at the grocery store? Or the library? Or any number of places the new Mrs. Starr would show up with her rounded belly and then later with her child in tow. It would be bad enough to deal with them at Chloe's college graduation in four years or when she married and had children of her own. She shook her head at the thought of Larry's new child possibly being close in age to a child of Chloe's. The man was pathetic.

She didn't want to move away. She loved Silverside with its tree-lined streets and parks. She could smell the ocean from her front lawn. Her life was there. How could she live somewhere else? No town would speak to her the way Silverside did.

She'd sell her half to Larry and hope for the best. In the meantime, she'd go to Tennessee and learn more about this mysterious house. She needed to start living again. Even though her insides shook with the idea of jumping on a plane to some area unknown without the safety net of a plan, she knew she had to. For once, Grace Starr would take a risk. Hopefully, taking a chance didn't backfire.

A word about the author...

From an early age, Stacey Wilk told tales as a way to escape. At six she wrote short stories in composition notebooks, at twelve she wrote a novel on a typewriter, and in high school biology she wrote rock-star romances in her binder instead of paying attention.

But it wasn't until many years later, inspired by her children and a looming birthday, that she finally took her storytelling seriously. And published her first novel in 2013. Since then, she's gone on to publish fourteen more so women everywhere could fall in love and find an escape of their own.

She isn't done telling stories. Not by a long shot. If you want to read her emotional and honest books about family, romance, and second chances, visit her at:
http://www.staceywilk.com

To see what she writes next, follow her Facebook group for her amazing readers, Stacey's Novel Family:
https://bit.ly/2FK8Lae

Or join her newsletter:
https://bit.ly/2A0jEFk

Thank you for purchasing
this publication of The Wild Rose Press, Inc.

For questions or more information
contact us at
info@thewildrosepress.com.

The Wild Rose Press, Inc.
www.thewildrosepress.com